# Ten Journeys
# Through the Unknown

## Heather Beck

ISBN: 1-894936-58-2  9781894936583
Saga Books
Sagabooks.net

# CONTENTS:

1. Gnome Genome

2. Kingdom of Sugar

3. Eyes of Red

4. A Weird Twist of Fate

5. Werewolf Hunting

6. Home Grown Flowers

7. The Secret Oracle of an Egyptian King

8. Cold Territory

9. Curses Never Die

10. Long Live the Bonsai

# Gnome Genome

# Gnome Genome

Seventeen-year-old Meghan Bradford opened the sliding door that led to the backyard and walked onto the warm patio. It was a hot July morning and Meghan planned to spend it relaxing on a hammock.

"The hammock," Meghan sighed, "is the only thing I like about this place."

Meghan and her family had just moved from the prairies of Saskatchewan to the big city of Toronto. The Bradford's were used to the beautiful scenery of an open landscape. Now that they lived in a three story townhouse, all they had to look at was their neighbor's backyard.

"It's all her fault," Meghan said aloud, while thinking about her mother. "If the bank hadn't promoted her to their headquarters I would be swimming in my pool right now."

Meghan approached the hammock and threw herself on it. Everything seemed to happen in slow motion as she felt her body tumble over and fall to the ground. Meghan's head hit the ground with a sickening thud. For a moment, all she could see were red and yellow stars on a black background. However, her eyesight soon returned to normal, bringing a horrible headache with it.

"Are you alright?" Meghan heard somebody shout. She rubbed the side of her head with her right hand then looked up. She saw a boy, who was around her age, leaning over the adjacent metal fence. "Are you alright?" he repeated.

"I...I'm fine," Meghan replied, trying to catch her breath after having the wind knocked out of her.

"Are you sure?" the boy inquired once again. "I saw you fall off the hammock; it looked pretty bad."

"I'm fine," Meghan snapped. He must think I'm a complete klutz, she thought in embarrassment.

"I'm glad you're okay," the boy smiled. "My name is Justin Grove. I saw your family moving in last week. How do you like your new house?"

"It's okay," Meghan lied, finally getting up from the ground. I must have hit my leg pretty bad, she realized as pain shot through her left leg. "It's different here," Meghan added, ignoring the pain.

"Where did you come from?" Justin inquired, not noticing Meghan's discomfort.

"Saskatchewan," she replied.

"Saskatchewan? Whoa," Justin muttered. "Toronto must be very different for you!"

"Tell me about it," Meghan replied with a laugh.

"So, will you be going to Eastern Heights High School in the fall?"

"Yes. It will be my last year of high school." Meghan smiled, while thinking about the freedom she would have after graduating from high school. Unknown to her parents, she planned to delay going to college to travel instead.

"Next year is my last also," Justin replied casually.

"That's nice," Meghan replied, not knowing what else to say. She felt as if the conversation would soon be coming to an abrupt end. To avoid an awkward silence, Meghan gave Justin a polite smile then headed into her house. She made a beeline to the refrigerator to put ice on her throbbing head. I'll never sit on another hammock as long as I live, Meghan thought, while entertaining a new phobia of swinging ropes.

* * *

"Hello neighbor! I see that you're staying clear of that hammock."

Meghan looked up from the chair, in which she was sitting, to see Justin leaning over the fence.

"Wouldn't you?" she asked with a smile.

"Probably," Justin replied laughing. "Do you have any plans for today?" he asked quickly.

Meghan raised the novel in her hands and directed her eyes towards it. "Other than catching up with the latest Janice Moore book? No."

"Would you help me with something then?" Justin inquired. Meghan shot him a curious look but nodded anyway. "You see," he began to explain; "the neighbor's cat came into my yard, climbed a tree, and has now become stuck up there."

"Why did the cat run up the tree in the first place?" Meghan wondered out loud.

"My dog chased him up there," Justin confessed.

"Why don't you just get a ladder and climb up there?"

7

"I'm afraid of heights."

Meghan made a display of rolling her eyes. "You're weird," she teased. Justin looked at her with pleading eyes.

"You don't understand," he moaned. "The owner of the cat, Mrs. Hull, really has it in for me. She thinks my dog is a hazard to public safety. Mrs. Hull would go berserk if she found out that her precious cat was stuck in my tree."

"Alright, I'm coming," Meghan said as she stood up and placed her book on the chair.

Justin opened the metal gate that led to his yard. "Thanks," he said as Meghan walked through his backyard.

Meghan helped Justin get a ladder from his garage and carry it to the tree. She looked up into the tall tree to see a frightened black cat clinging onto a branch.

"Poor thing; she looks really scared," Meghan commented as she began to climb the ladder.

"When you get the cat, make sure you hold her tight," Justin called up to Meghan. "Don't let her get away."

Meghan reached the top of the ladder then began to climb the branches on the tree. The maple tree's harsh bark scraped Meghan's hands. She winced in response. Meghan looked into the terrified green eyes of the cat, trying to forget about her own discomfort. "It's alright, kitty," Meghan said soothingly as she reached up to grab the cat. "Ouch!" Meghan wailed after the cat had lunged forward and scratched her. She watched in anger as the cat hurried swiftly down the tree with hardly any difficulty. "I thought you said that thing couldn't get down by itself," Meghan yelled at Justin, not knowing if she was angrier at the cat or Justin.

Meghan pressed her hurt hand against her white t-shirt as she began climbing down the ladder. "Hold the ladder tighter," she called down as the ladder shook slightly. Meghan's heart started to race as the ladder bumped violently against the tree with every step she took. She turned her head slowly to see that Justin was no longer holding onto the ladder. "Justin," she cried in rising panic, realizing that she was still seven feet off the ground. I can't believe he just left me here, Meghan thought furiously.

Meghan used both hands to steady herself as she carefully made her way down the ladder. The hand, which the cat had scratched, was very painful and bleeding a lot. As she slid her hands down the metal ladder, the scratched hand scraped against a sharp corner. Meghan's hand instinctively shot backwards. She screamed as she felt herself falling off the ladder. Meghan lay on the ground and let out a quiet moan. However, she was filled with even more terror as the ladder began to fall towards her. Meghan crossed her arms protectively over her face and waited to be crushed.

When nothing happened a few seconds later she opened her eyes and saw Justin holding the ladder. She watched him fling it in the other direction then hurry to her side.

"Are you okay?" he asked in a worried tone.

"No," Meghan snapped as she got up slowly. Her back, as well as her doubly cut hand, throbbed painfully. "Why did you leave me on the ladder like that?" she demanded.

"I am so sorry," Justin said sincerely. "Mrs. Hull's cat began to chase me after she had climbed down the tree. I had to get away from her."

Meghan was flabbergasted at Justin's excuse. "The cat wouldn't have hurt you," she hissed, "because it left all its claws in me!" Meghan shoved her bleeding finger towards Justin's face. He backed away in disgust.

"I'll…I'll get you a bandage," he offered.

"Don't bother," Meghan snapped as she walked back through the metal gate.

* * *

Later in the afternoon Meghan was still thinking about the incident at Justin's house. She was not only mad at Justin's behavior but also disappointed. She had thought Justin seemed like a nice guy who had potential to become a great friend. But now that she knew better, she never wanted to lay eyes on him again. The ringing of the doorbell interrupted Meghan's thoughts.

"I'm painting my nails, you'll have to get the door," Mrs. Bradford called to Meghan from the bedroom next door. Meghan complained under her breath but got up anyway. When she opened the door the vision of the person, whom she had just been thinking of, appeared.

"What are you doing here?" she snapped.

"I came to apologize and present you with a peace offering." Justin smiled sweetly while Meghan glared angrily.

"So, where's the peace offering?" Meghan asked, breaking the silence that had followed her glare.

"Oh," Justin exclaimed, as if remembering something. "It's in my backyard. It's too heavy for me to lift. Can you come and get it?"

"You want me to pick up the peace offering?" Meghan asked in astonishment. "You're unbelievable!"

"Please Meghan; I really want you to have it."

"What makes you think I can lift it?"

"You look stronger than me," Justin said with a wink.

"Thanks, I think," Meghan said with a confused laugh. "Okay, I'll go get it. What is it anyway?" Meghan asked as she closed the door behind her and headed to Justin's house.

"You'll find out," he said mysteriously. "But before you do, I have something to confess."

"What is it now?" Meghan asked, annoyed at yet another disturbance in their friendship.

"I lied when I said I was afraid of heights. I am actually afraid of cats. That is why I ran away when the cat came down the tree."

"Why didn't you just tell me that in the first place?" Meghan asked, rolling her eyes.

"It sounds better to be afraid of heights than a furry little cat," Justin confessed.

"It's okay," Meghan said. "But I am never ever going to climb a ladder for you again. I don't care if it's you up there," Meghan said, pointing to the tall maple tree. "You'll just have to stay there!" Justin laughed and Meghan soon joined in.

"Here it is," Justin said as they stopped in the corner of his backyard.

"Excuse me?" Meghan asked, not sure if she had heard Justin correctly.

"It's behind the leaves," Justin explained, sensing Meghan's confusion.

Meghan bent down and pushed the long dark leaves away from the fence. Against the fence, in the very corner, was a large potted plant. "That's the peace offering?" Meghan asked in confusion.

Justin nodded. "You like it, don't you?"

Meghan looked at the potted plant. The pot was a deep shade of red and had a high curve at the top to keep the soil from spilling over. The plant was like no other Meghan had ever seen. Although the soil was a healthy shade of dark brown, the trunk of the plant was a sickly color of yellow. Each branch contained several thin green needles. The needles looked as if they belonged to a pine tree. "It's definitely a different gift," Meghan finally answered Justin. "What type of tree is it?"

"A pine tree," Justin answered in an uncomfortable tone of voice. "So, are you going to take it to your backyard?" he asked in a hurry.

Meghan looked at Justin suspiciously. "Why are you so keen to get rid of such a pretty potted plant? Does it have a disease that will kill all the other plants in my backyard?"

"No!" Justin exclaimed, trying to look and sound hurt. "I really like this plant but I want you to have it."

"If you like it so much why do you keep it behind another plant?"

"I didn't want anyone to steal it. You ask a lot of questions," Justin replied with a nervous laugh.

Meghan was still not fully satisfied with Justin's answer but she took it as the truth anyway. She bent down and pried her fingers under the red pot. "It is heavy," Meghan commented as she grunted out loud.

"Don't break it," Justin advised nervously.

"I won't," Meghan said in annoyance. "Ouch!" she said suddenly, letting the plant fall a few inches to the ground. The potted plant fell to the ground with a thump, but it did not break.

"Did it jab you?" Justin asked, still using the same nervous tone.

"Yes," Meghan replied, holding tightly onto her finger.

"I jabbed myself on one of the needles before," he said solemnly.

"Well, thanks for the heads up," she replied, picking up the plant again. "I should stay away from you. I always get hurt when we're together."

"I'm really sorry," Justin said in a sorrowful tone. "I am very, very sorry."

Meghan walked through the metal gate that Justin held open for her. She cast him a weird glance. "It's okay," she said, prolonging the word okay. "It doesn't hurt anymore."

"I know," Justin replied.

"Uh huh," Meghan said, after Justin had become suddenly silent. "Um, thanks for the plant," she said as she placed it against the wall on the side of the house. Meghan had just turned her back to Justin for a second but when she turned around again the gate was locked and he was nowhere to be seen. He really is weird, Meghan thought as she headed into her house.

* * *

Meghan woke up in the middle of the night with a pain in her hand. At first, she thought the pain was from the cat scratch or the cut from the ladder. She began to panic, thinking she had contracted either rabies or blood poisoning. Meghan soon realized, however, that it was the other hand which was giving her pain. It's from the pine needle, Meghan realized.

In the dark, she hurried through her bedroom and the hallway until she came to the bathroom. She flickered on the light then looked at her finger and gasped. Her index finger was red and swollen. It was double the size of what it used to be. At the tip of her finger, where she had been jabbed, was a small dark green circle.

"Mom! Dad!" Meghan cried as she ran into her parent's bedroom.

"What's wrong?" Mr. Bradford asked, sitting upright in bed.

"I jabbed myself on a pine tree and now my finger is swollen and has a dark green mark!" Meghan was beginning to panic. Her face flushed red and her head bobbed in fear. She placed a hand on her chest to see if her heart was still beating properly.

"A pine tree?" Mrs. Bradford asked, finally sitting up in bed. "How could you? We don't have any pine trees in our yard."

"It was a potted pine tree," Meghan answered. "I got it from the boy next door."

"I didn't know you had made a new friend! Is he nice?" Mr. Bradford inquired.

"He's just swell," Meghan said cheekily, forgetting about her panic. "Can we please concentrate on my infected finger?" she added, remembering her panic once again.

"You'll be fine," Mrs. Bradford said soothingly. "Why don't you have your father take a look at it?"

Mr. Bradford grumbled something about Meghan being a hypochondriac but he got up anyway. He followed her to the bathroom where she showed him her finger.

"That is weird," Mr. Bradford admitted, upon studying her finger. "Was the plant sprayed with any chemicals?"

"I don't know," Meghan confessed.

"Do you feel alright apart from your sore finger? Do you have a fever?"

"I'm okay," Meghan replied. "I just feel panicky about my finger."

"That's natural, for you anyway," Mr. Bradford said with an affectionate kiss on his daughter's head. "I'm sure you're fine. I'll take another look at your finger in the morning. If the swelling hasn't gone down we can go see a doctor."

Meghan nodded, already feeling calmer. "Thanks," she said, heading back to her room.

"Goodnight," her father replied.

\* \* \*

Meghan woke up the next morning to find that her finger was no longer swollen or painful. She did, however, still have the unusual green mark.

"How's the finger?" Mr. Bradford asked as Meghan entered the kitchen.

"Its fine, but I still have the green mark."

Mr. Bradford looked at the finger that she offered. "I really don't know what that is," Mr. Bradford said, after a minute of examination.

"Well, I'm sure it'll go away just like the swelling and pain did," Meghan reasoned as she pulled her hand away. She was no longer concerned about her finger. She was too busy looking forward to spending the day in the backyard. "I'm going to eat outside," Meghan explained as she took her bowl of cereal and headed towards the sliding door.

"Meghan?" Mr. Bradford called her back.

"Yes?"

"Your mother and I will be leaving for her new associate's wedding in about an hour. Will you be alright by yourself?"

"Of course," Meghan said, rolling her eyes.

Minutes later, Meghan was soaking up the morning rays while chomping on some cold sugary cereal. Meghan spent most of the morning outside. She felt lonely without her parents or friends. In the quietness, Meghan's thoughts returned to her home and friends in Saskatchewan. Her thoughts were suddenly interrupted by the sound of the neighbor's door opening. Meghan looked up, hoping to see Justin. Instead, she saw someone who was presumably Justin's mother.

"Hello neighbor," Mrs. Grove said, upon seeing Meghan looking at her.

Like mother, like son, Meghan thought to herself with a secret smile. "Hi," she replied, getting up to shake Mrs. Grove's hand. After a few moments of general chitchat, Meghan decided to inquire about Justin. "Is Justin home today?" she asked, hoping to find someone to hang out with.

"Justin," Mrs. Grove said wistfully, tears filling her eyes.

"Is everything okay?" Meghan asked, shocked at Mrs. Grove's emotional reaction.

"Oh, everything is fine now but it wasn't two weeks ago." Mrs. Grove stopped talking to dab a tissue at the corner of her eyes.

"What happened?" Meghan inquired, hoping that Mrs. Grove would continue to talk.

"He disappeared for a week."

"Excuse me?" Meghan choked. "He disappeared? What do you mean by that?"

"He just vanished. Then one day he showed up. He offered no explanation to his whereabouts. I was in such a frantic state; I still am actually. Did he say anything to you about where he went?"

"No. I didn't even know he had been missing. He said nothing about it."

"Of course, you hadn't moved into your new house at that point. I was just hoping that he had talked to you." Meghan shook her head and spread her arms and fingers towards Mrs. Grove, indicating that she knew nothing. Suddenly, Mrs. Grove grabbed Meghan's hand and stared at it in shock. "No," she gasped.

"What?" Meghan demanded, trying to pull her hand away from Mrs. Grove.

"You have the mark also," Mrs. Grove said in a cold voice.

deck in her backyard. Meghan's eyes searched the area, but she could not find the source of the red light.

"It looks as if it's coming from my house," Meghan realized with a shudder. She was too afraid to leave her room. Instead, she leaned over the open window as far as she dared to and looked down at the house. What she saw made her gasp. The red light was coming from the potted pine tree. Meghan quickly pulled herself upward and stared at the Grove's house.

"What kind of plant did you give me?" she asked in a squeaky voice. Meghan gulped hard then leaned over the window once again. The red light was still coming from the potted plant but now it was blinking. Instinctively, Meghan looked at her index finger. In the pale moonlight she could see that the green mark on her finger had got bigger. Meghan shut the window tightly then fastened the lock on her bedroom door. She then proceeded to her bed and shook in fear.

"Stop it, Meghan," she suddenly told herself. "Stop being afraid all the time." She forced herself to stop shaking then went to the window and opened it again. She looked at the potted pine tree and saw that all its needles were now flashing. Meghan backed away from the window and tried to calm her racing heart. "What should I do? What should I do?" she asked herself through deep breaths of air. She wished her parents would hurry back from the wedding. "I have to find out what's going on," Meghan said out loud, while thinking of the cliché about a cat and its curiosity.

Meghan quickly put on a pair of jeans then rummaged through her closet. After finding her baseball bat Meghan unlocked her bedroom door and headed down the stairs. The hallway was very dark. All the bedroom doors were closed so that moonlight was unable to lighten up the hallway. Meghan tried to remember the placement of the tables and staircase as she continued to maneuver throughout the house. Her memory failed her as she took a step forward and felt nothing but air underneath her foot. Meghan made a desperate attempt to grab for the banister, but she did not have enough time. She felt her body in freefall before she landed at the bottom of the staircase. The baseball bat flew from her hands and tumbled down after her.

"Ouch," Meghan moaned in pain. She lay at the bottom of the staircase for a moment, afraid to move her body just in case anything was broken. Although her side ached; she had not broken any bones. She tested her arms and legs then pressed on her ribs. "You're okay," she told herself, trying to clam her nerves.

Ding Dong.

Meghan's whole body tensed up at the sound of the doorbell. She knew her parents had a key and that they would never ring the doorbell as to wake her up and give her a fright. Meghan looked at the door, wondering who was behind it.

Ding Dong. Ding Dong.

Meghan's heart began to beat faster.

Ding Dong. Ding Dong. Ding Dong.

The blood in Meghan's veins ran cold as she listened to the persistence ringing of the doorbell. She had no idea who was behind the door. The Bradford's did not know anyone in Toronto, except for some of Mrs. Bradford's associates, who would all be at the wedding right now. Meghan also knew that Grove's. The weird and unpredictable Grove's, Meghan thought. Her thoughts were interrupted by a new sound which came from the door.

Meghan slowly got up and went towards the door. She had no intention of opening it; she just wanted to test her theory on the origin of the new noise. Shakily, Meghan placed her hand gently upon the door handle. Her heart missed a beat as she felt it move under her fingers.

It's trying to break in, Meghan thought in a panic, not knowing what "it" was. Her breath came in shallow rasps as she stood on her tiptoes and peered through the peek hole in the door. Two flashing red lights greeted her.

"No!" Meghan screamed in fear as well as frustration. She began to pound on the door with both fists. "Leave me alone," she cried. "Whoever you are, leave me alone!"

In reply to her shouts of protest, the person behind the door began to pound back. The pounding continued, getting fiercer as the seconds ticked by. The door began to rattle and Meghan heard the noise of the lock being broken.

Meghan spun around and ran quickly down the basement stairs. The old wooden stairs creaked and rattled under the sudden weight of Meghan. She had just reached the bottom of the stairs when she heard a loud crash from upstairs. Whatever was behind the door was now in the house.

Meghan had run down to the basement because there was a large window in which she could escape. Her only concern now was getting out of the house before the thing got to her.

The window was easy to see against the pale moonlight. Meghan unlocked the window and pulled it open. She knew she did not have time to be quiet as she pulled the small black handle on the screen and ripped it open. Meghan jumped through the open window and pulled herself onto the damp grass. She was almost completely on the wet grass when a pair of cold hands grabbed her ankles.

Meghan shook and kicked her feet until the person let go. Unable to resist the temptation of knowing who had broken into her house, she looked behind her. "Justin!" she cried.

Justin's glowing red eyes stared into Meghan's as if he were trying to hypnotize her. Meghan backed away from Justin in shock and began to run. She had only taken a few steps when she found herself amongst an array of red lights. The red lights, which came from the potted plant, pulsated and grew larger. The lights grew into long beams and encompassed Meghan.

Breaking out of the spell that the brilliant lights cast upon her, Meghan attempted to run once more. As Meghan bumped into the beams, she realized that she could not break through them. If I can't get pass the light beams, maybe Justin can't get through them, Meghan thought. She peered through the light beams in search of Justin. He had disappeared as quickly as he had appeared.

Meghan had just started to relax when she felt someone tap her on her shoulder. Meghan turned around slowly; not wanting to see what she thought was behind her.

"Your turn," Justin said, almost sadly.

"Go away," Meghan shouted in terror. "Just go away."

"You're the one who will be going away," Justin replied in the same sad voice. "I'm sorry, but it was the only way I could save myself. I wish you the best of luck so that you may return in a week. I will watch and wait for you," he promised. Meghan watched with wide eyes as Justin walked backwards, until he had vanished behind the light beams.

"Wait! Tell me what you mean," Meghan demanded as she pushed against the light beams. The light beams resisted her efforts and grew larger and brighter in response. She was forced to close her eyes as they began to ache in the brightness. Meghan let out a defeated whimper as she saw the light beams closing in on her. Meghan said a prayer as she felt the light beams sweep over her body.

* * *

Meghan's eyes fluttered open. She lay on her back, shivering from the late night dew that covered the grass. Darkness surrounded Meghan, but with the passing of a cloud the moonlight allowed her to see large pine needles above her head.

"Huh?" Meghan exclaimed out loud, sitting up in haste. She strained her neck and stared up at the large pine needles which hovered over her head. No, they are not hovering, Meghan realized. As she looked to her side, she noticed familiar looking yellow branches and a trunk.

Meghan slowly got to her feet and walked towards the trunk. She ran her hand over the sickly looking bark. It was not rough and sturdy, like she thought it would be. Instead, it was mushy and smelled like decaying eggs. Meghan wiped her hands on the grass in disgust. A pungent smell came from her hands. However, it did not smell the same as the bark. Meghan raised her hands to her face and gagged in response. She had not noticed earlier but the dew also had a horrible smell to it.

"What is this place?" Meghan muttered out loud. She took a few steps forward then she began run. She had to get to the end of the garden or, in her wildest fear, the edge of the pot.

Meghan's feet left the slippery grass and entered onto the dark rich soil. She could not ignore the alarm bell, which was going off in her head, any longer. I'm in the potted plant, Meghan thought in a panic. How could this happen? I must be dreaming.

Meghan was so involved with her thoughts that she did not realize she had neared the edge of the red pot. I have to be dreaming, she thought, just before her right foot went over the edge. A shrill scream escaped from her mouth as she realized that she was going to fall to her death.

The dark image of the deck came hurdling towards her face. She knew she would be splattered on the ground in a matter of seconds. Meghan suddenly felt herself being pulled up. She experienced whiplash as a large net caught her and sent her flying backwards. She shook from the near death experience as she was lifted up.

Meghan soon reached the top but what she saw frightened her just as much as the deadly fall. As Meghan was pulled back over the

19

edge she came face to face with four little, evil looking men. She let out a scream and struggled to free herself from the net.

"She's a silly one," said one of the little men.

Hearing the man's voice made Meghan silent. He spoke in a high squeaky voice that would either make you laugh or wince and cover your ears. Meghan stared at the four men from behind the netting. They were shorter than her and had unusually large heads. Their eyes were so large and black that Meghan was unable to tell where the pupil ended and where the iris began. Maybe they don't even have pupils, Meghan thought in a shudder. The men were chubby and dressed in a robe like outfit which was spilt in half by the color red and green. Although they wore the traditional colors of Christmas, they looked anything but jolly. Their jet black hair made them look very evil.

"You're right," another man replied. "First she jumps out of the pot then she struggles to escape from the net which saved her life." The four men laughed hysterically; their laugh sounded like a dozen rats being stepped upon at once.

"Who are you?" Meghan cried, unable to control her frustration and confusion any longer.

"We're gnomes," one of the gnomes, who hadn't spoken yet, replied, "and soon you'll be one too!"

Meghan stared at the gnomes with a blank expression then laughed. What a weird dream, she thought. I'll play along and see what happens next. "Will you please let me out?" she asked kindly.

The gnomes looked at each other in surprise. "She's not screaming or crying like the others," one of the gnomes observed.

"We'll let you go if you promise not to jump over the pot again," another gnome bargained.

"I promise I won't jump again," Meghan answered truthfully.

The gnomes looked at each other and nodded in unison. They worked together until Meghan was free. Her neck felt sore from the whiplash but she blamed it on the way her physical body must be sleeping.

"My name is Meghan," she said, offering her hand to each gnome.

"I'm Nonie," the first gnome said. Nonie's hand was short, stumpy, and very difficult to shake. Meghan shook the three remaining gnome's hands, learning their names along the way. "Konie, Monie, Donie, and Nonie," Meghan replied out loud. "What unusual names!"

"Would you like to know why you're here?" Nonie asked while looking very confused over Meghan's calm presence.

"Sure," Meghan replied with an amused smile, still believing that she was dreaming.

"I'll start at the beginning then," Nonie said. "You are in the Garden Gnome's Pot. It's where Konie, Monie, Donie, and I have called home our whole lives. A few months ago the Garden Gnome's Pot was sprayed with a chemical. The chemical killed many of the gnomes and the delicate environment of the pot. After we were sprayed with the chemical the appearance of our pine tree deteriorated. The owner of the pot jabbed himself on a pine needle when he was lifting the pot. The blood from his finger supplied our tree with energy and it began to grow again. The next thing we knew our owner had shrunken to our size and had joined us within the pot. After conducting careful scientific research, the other gnomes and I realized that when he jabbed himself blood was transferred. Our owner not only gave us blood but we gave him our blood as well. He was injected by a gnome genome. This explained his new size and location in the pot. We soon figured out that we could only survive through human DNA. As the days passed our owner began to grow back into his normal size. When we saw this happening we tested out hypothesis and figured out that by injecting him with our genome our environment thrived and he became small once again. However, we didn't think it was fair for us to keep the owner of the pot with us forever. We wanted to give him a chance to escape. After careful consideration, Konie, Monie, Donie, and I decided that we would let our DNA disintegrate in his body if he passed three games."

"And if he didn't pass?" Meghan asked in curiosity.

Nonie chuckled evilly. "Our owner passed all the games so we never put any more of our genome into him," Nonie explained, not answering Meghan's question. "However, before he left we put a spell on him. The spell insured that he would find us new blood. The spell worked and soon a nice young man named Justin Grove came and played with us. He also passed the games. Once again, we let him go under the spell to bring use new blood." Nonie stopped talking and took a deep breath. He looked at Meghan, waiting for her reaction.

"Whoa," Meghan said with a smile. "I have some imagination! Who knew I was capable of having such a detailed dream?" she chuckled to herself. "This is definitely the most interesting dream I've had in a while."

"It's not a dream. It's real. We're real. And you're really here."

"Uh huh," Meghan said with a mocking smile, while reaching out to pinch the gnome's face. "Aren't you a weird little thing?" Meghan said, as if she were talking to a baby. The gnome's skin felt soft and blubbery between her fingers.

All of a sudden, Nonie hissed then bit Meghan. His long black teeth scraped her skin, making her bleed. Meghan looked down at her hand in shock. "That hurt," she said in a cold realization. "This...this is real. It's really happening."

"Shall we start the games?" Nonie said with a little smile. There was something about Nonie's smile that didn't seem completely innocent.

"Okay," Meghan whispered. "I'll play."

"A wise decision," Nonie said, nodding in approval. "I hope all your decisions are as wise because if they're not you'll be staying here for an awfully long time."

"I'm not going to lose," Meghan said forcefully, realizing the severity of the situation. "What's the first game?"

The gnomes led Meghan back to the tree. Konie scurried away and arrived back a minute later with several pine needles. The pine needles were different colors consisting of green, yellow, purple, and blue. They were bundled together with a piece of rope. Meghan watched as Konie untied the pine needles and let them fall to the ground. She noticed that one of the pine needles was black.

"The game is called Pick up the Pine Needles," Konie explained. "The purpose of the game is to pick up the pine needles in a careful manner. You may only keep the pine needles which do not move any of the other pine needles. Each pine needle has a point system. The blue pine needle is worth 20 points, the purple 15, the yellow 10, and the green 5."

"What about the black?" Meghan asked, interrupting the gnome.

"Whoever moves the black pine needle must forfeit the needle in which they intended to pick up and must take the black one instead. If the black pine needle is kept to the end, the player whose turn it is must pick it up. Whoever possesses the black pine needle will lose 100 points. The winner of the game is the person, or gnome," Konie added with a giggle, "who has the most points."

"Wait a minute," Meghan interjected. "My chances of winning are only one in four."

"We realize that," Konie said. "That is why only one of us will play against you. You may take your pick, Meghan."

Meghan looked at the gnomes and examined their fingers. She wanted to play against the gnome who had the least dainty fingers. Meghan thought Monie's hands looked a bit bigger than the others.

"I'll play against Monie," she said confidently.

Monie looked at the other gnomes. They all sighed in disappointment.

"Another wise choice," Nonie said.

"Let's begin," Monie said. "You may go first."

Meghan walked around the pile of small colorful pine needles. She began to reach for an accessible purple needle.

"Wait!" Monie shouted suddenly. "In the excitement we forgot to pick the High Spectator."

"The what?" Meghan asked in confusion, a bit upset at the interruption.

"The High Spectator," Monie explained. "That is the gnome who watches the game from above. He'll be able to get a better view of what is happening."

"I'll go," Donie volunteered, scrambling up the tree and placing himself on a branch. Meghan jumped back as a large yellow liquid drop fell from the branch that Donie was sitting on. The gnomes looked at each other in concern.

"Hold on just a minute," Meghan said, while staring at the yellow gooey mess. "How can I trust you to call the plays truthfully?"

"We have an oath," Monie replied. "Human beings may think gnomes to be devious, but that it not the case. We always keep our promises and play fair."

"Let the game begin!" Donie called from above.

Meghan took a deep breath and reached for the purple pine needle. She winced as the purple needle bumped slightly into a yellow one. She continued on, hoping that Donie had not noticed.

"Foul!" Donie's squeaky voice rang out happily. Meghan's chest tightened in fear. She could not believe that the game had got off to such a bad start.

Monie took his turn and successfully retrieved the yellow needle which Meghan had bumped.

"Monie: ten. Meghan: zero," Donie called out loud.

Meghan examined the pile of needles and chose to go after another purple one that lay near the edge. Ever so carefully, Meghan pushed the purple needle against the green grass and slid it out. "Yes!" she cried, after retrieving it successfully. "Meghan: fifteen. Monie: ten," she called up proudly to Donie, who pouted his large pink lips.

"The game isn't over yet," Konie spoke from the sidelines.

Monie stepped closer to the pile of pine needles and examined them for a few minutes.

"Hurry up," Meghan said impatiently. Monie cast Meghan an angry glance then bent down to pull a blue needle. "It moved!" Meghan shouted triumphantly. Monie grunted, but let go of the blue needle. Meghan went directly to the blue needle, which Monie had left, and got it successfully. "That's thirty points for me," Meghan said happily. "How much do you have?" she mocked Monie. Monie cast another glare at Meghan then reached for a green needle. He retrieved it successfully then poked Meghan in the face with it.

"Ouch," she cried, rubbing her hurt check. "Did you just take more DNA from me?"

The gnomes all laughed. "Of course not," Monie said between high pitch giggles. "The pieces in Pick up the Pine Needles are fake. Don't you know anything?"

"When it comes to this weird place? No," Meghan admitted.

"On with the game," Donie shouted from the tree branch. "And do hurry up; I don't know how much longer this branch can hold me for."

Meghan looked up to see the branch dripping more yellow liquid. She almost felt sorry for the gnomes and their decaying pot in which they lived. She forced back all sympathetic emotions and reached for a blue needle. She slid her fingers gently over the needle until it began to slip from the pile of needles. Meghan let out a sigh of relief as she successfully retrieved the blue needle without disturbing any other needles. She now had fifty points.

The game continued on for another half an hour. Meghan was doing well at one hundred and sixty five points. She was using the strategy of going only for the blue and purple needles. The problem with the strategy was that there were less blue and purple needles than yellow and green. Since there were less, the blue and purple needles were more likely to be under other needles, thus making them harder to retrieve. Monie was also doing well at one hundred and forty five points. His strategy was to go for the easier to retrieve, but of less worth, yellow and green needles.

As the game neared the end, only four pine needles remained-two greens, a yellow and the dreaded black. Meghan's heart was racing. It was her turn, but she did not know what type of move to make. All the needles were overlapping. The needle that would most likely be a success was the yellow one. If she picked it, Monie would be forced to attempt for the green one. From watching his ability throughout the game, Meghan did not think he was capable of retrieving it successfully. If he did not get the green pine needle, Meghan would take it. Then Monie would easily get the last green one and she would be stuck with the black needle, thus losing one hundred points.

Not really sure if her plan was a smart one or not, Meghan went for the yellow needle and purposely made it touch the green one.

"Foul!" Donie called out.

Monie looked at Meghan suspiciously but went for the yellow needle anyway. He got it successfully.

"Meghan has one hundred and sixty five points. Monie has one hundred and fifty five points," Donie shouted down from the tree.

Meghan went for the green needle, bringing it out then taping it against the other green needle.

"Foul!" Donie shouted once again. Meghan smiled. She made sure that the green needle was easily accessible for Monie. Monie went for the needle and got it.

"Meghan: one hundred and sixty five. Monie: one hundred and sixty," Donie called.

Meghan took a deep breath and tried to sooth her nerves. This was one needle she really wanted to have. The end of the green needle was touching the black one. Trying to control her hands that were shaking slightly, she lowered them and gently slid her fingers along the green needle. She pulled it slowly until it was far away from the black

25

needle. Meghan held the green needle in her hand and sighed. She could not believe she had just played a game in which her freedom depended so heavily upon.

Monie took the black needle and grunted.

"Final score," Donie called. "Meghan: one hundred and seventy. Monie: fifty five." Donie climbed down the tree quickly and congratulated Meghan. "Good work; you played well. However, you chose to play against Monie, our worst game player. Now that you have played with him, you can't pick him again. I must warn you that our games get harder as they go on."

"What game is next?" Meghan asked, trying not to show the fear that Donie had just installed in her.

"No more games for today," Nonie said grumpily. "Tonight we eat and rest. We play tomorrow."

"Sounds fine to me," Meghan muttered, relaxing just a little.

\* \* \*

Meghan woke up the next morning, wondering where she was. It did not take long for the events of yesterday to come flooding back to her. At first she thought it was a dream, but the scratchy blanket, which was made from intertwined pine needles, made Meghan realize that this was really happening. She flung off the blanket and walked towards the gnomes. They slept upright and looked like they were made from plastic. They looked like the type of gnomes one would find in a garden, but Meghan knew better.

She touched Nonie, surprised at the heat which was generated from the plastic looking body. As she reached to touch Nonie's face, Nonie grabbed her hand. Meghan jumped backwards and let out a scream. Nonie laughed. His laughter awoke the other gnomes. Meghan watched as they stretched then headed to the base of the tree.

"Hey, where are you going?" Meghan yelled, running after the gnomes.

"To get breakfast," Donie replied.

"But last night we nibbled on pine needles," Meghan protested.

"Yes," Konie replied. "But that was dinner. For breakfast we have sap."

"Sap?" Meghan repeated, pursing her lips at the thought of licking anything that came from the decaying tree. She watched as Nonie brushed aside some pine needles and revealed a tap at the base of the tree.

He took five bowls, which were made from intertwining pine needles, and turned on the tap. At first, crystal clear sap poured from the tap but soon yellowish goo took its place.

Nonie sighed. He had only filled two bowls but he turned off the tap. "This always happens," Nonie explained. He handed one bowl to Meghan and the other to Donie. "As you probably figured out, we'll die if we do not get the genome of other living creatures."

"Why don't you gather the genome from animals?" Meghan asked, while sucking the sap. It tasted surprisingly good.

"It would be too hard to get an animal to jab itself on our needles. Obviously, it is easier for us to communicate with humans. Besides, our potted plant can only survive on the human DNA structure."

"This is too weird," Meghan muttered as she watched Nonie turn on the tap again.

"Maybe," Nonie replied, "but it's all we know."

"It's time for another game," Nonie announced, after everyone had finished their morning sap.

"Is this necessary?" Meghan began to plead, not wanting to risk her freedom once again.

"It's your only option," Nonie said sadly. "I'm sorry. I really don't want to take you away from your family and friends, but if we want to survive it has to be this way."

Meghan suddenly thought about her family. She wondered if gnome time was the same as human time. Meghan shook her head sadly, thinking about her worried parents searching for her when the whole time she was, ironically, in the potted plant that leaned against the wall of their house. These thoughts made her sadness turn into anger. "Why did you make Justin target me?" she demanded hotly, remembering Justin's look of remorse when giving her the plant.

"We did no such thing!" Konie replied in a hurt tone. "A human who wins all three games is let go then must get another human to touch a pine needle. However, we do not tell the human who to choose. That is the human's own responsibility."

"Thanks Justin," Meghan muttered angrily under her breath. "So, what's the next game?"

"Build a Tower," Monie replied.

"Excuse me?" Meghan asked with a racing heart. Meghan knew that she did not have the skills to build a tower.

"Build a Tower," Monie repeated. "Each player is given 100 pine needles to start with. Then they have to use the needles to build a tower. The rules of this game are few and simple. You may build the tower in anyway you think best. The player who builds the highest tower in the shortest amount of time wins. If one of the player's tower falls that player is automatically disqualified. Oh and another thing," Monie added. "There's no time limit. The game continues until one player's tower falls."

"What size will the pine needles be?" Meghan inquired.

"The large size," Monie replied, "the size that is on the tree."

"You will climb the tree as you build," Konie added, upon seeing Meghan's confusion.

"Well," Meghan began. "What are we waiting for? Let's get started!"

Once all the pine needles were collected, the game began with Monie whistling between his two index fingers.

Before the game had started Meghan had examined the pine needles carefully and created a plan. When the game started Meghan was thankful for her planning. She drove four pine needles into the ground, leaving just a few millimeters in between each pine needle. Meghan then placed a single needle on the ground and measured the length. With this measurement, she drove in four more pine needles. She then began placing the needles on top of the side structures, making sure that each needle was snuggly between two needles. Meghan continued to build, making her tower as sturdy as possible. She was now climbing up the soft yellow tree, while trying to drag a dozen loose pine needles with her. Meghan was working on an almost empty stomach. Sweat was beginning to form on her forehead; she glanced at Konie, whom she had picked as her competitor. He was building fast, but not quite as fast as Meghan was.

Meghan turned her head from Konie's direction and concentrated on building her own tower. Her back ached and her legs were tired, but she kept on going. She had just started her seventeenth layer when she heard a loud crash and screams.

Meghan looked down from her tree branch to see Konie lying on top of his now dissembled tower. She scrambled down the tree and gathered beside the other gnomes. "What happened?" Meghan asked.

"The branch he was sitting on broke," Monie explained.

"Is he alright?" Meghan asked.

Monie nodded in relief. "He has a bad sprain, but he'll be fine. Right, Konie?" Monie asked with a comforting smile.

"Yes," Konie replied quietly. "It hurts, but I'll be okay."

Meghan watched as Nonie helped Monie make a leg brace for Konie out of pine needles.

"Congratulations," Donie said suddenly to Meghan. "You've won your second game."

Meghan tried to hide her smile but was unsuccessful in doing so. "Thanks," she replied as modestly as she could.

\* \* \*

That night Meghan tossed and turned under her woven pine needle blanket. Images of her mother and father kept running through her mind. She thought about how worried they must be. Meghan was also worried about the tall tales Mrs. Grove would be telling her parents. "Your son gave me the green mark, not the other way around," Meghan muttered, while thinking about Mrs. Grove.

"Can't sleep?" Nonie asked, seemingly appearing out of nowhere.

"No," Meghan sighed as she sat up. She always got mixed emotions around the gnomes. On the one hand, Meghan felt sorry for them. However, they were also the reason that she was stuck here in the first place. Well, Justin gets some of the blame also, Meghan thought in loathing.

"How do you feel?" Nonie asked, sitting down beside her.

Feeling uncomfortable, Meghan moved away slightly. "Do you even care?" she shot back.

"Yes," Nonie said quietly. "I like humans. There isn't a day that goes by without the feeling of guilt accompanying it."

"Oh, boo hoo," Meghan mocked. "Do you actually expect me to feel sorry for you?" Silence followed Meghan's question. "Well, I don't," she lied. "How did this weird place come into existence anyway?" Meghan asked quickly, trying to cover up her red face, produced by her lie.

"How does anything come into existence? I don't have the answer to that question. I can only have faith that my world was created by the will of a higher power."

29

Meghan shot Nonie a half smile. "We're not that different. It's too bad that we have to be on opposite sides."

"Yes it is," Nonie agreed. "Get some sleep," he advised, getting up.

Meghan watched the gnome walk away. Things keep on getting weirder, Meghan thought, before her eyelids gave into the temptation of sleep.

* * *

Meghan woke up to a sweet smell the next morning. Her eyelids fluttered open to see Monie waving a bowl of sap in front of her face. When Monie realized that he had wakened Meghan, he laughed in a high pitch tone.

That's one sound I don't want to wake up to everyday, Meghan thought, referring to Monie's laugh. "Thanks," she said, taking the bowl of sap from Monie. She drank it without enjoying its sweetness; she was too anxious about today's game to enjoy anything.

"It's time to play," Nonie announced, after Meghan and the other gnomes had finished their bowls of sap.

Meghan was surprised to find herself feeling hurt by Nonie's announcement. Shaking off the emotion, Meghan stepped forward. "Yes," she replied in a strong voice, "let's begin." She was determined not to let Nonie sense her fear.

"Today's game is called Flag Hunt. The objective of the game is to find the green flag which Monie has hidden in the tree. The only rule is there are no rules. The players may use any force they deem necessary to win. Whoever reaches the flag first wins."

"Alright," Meghan said absorbing the information Nonie had just given her. "Let's get this game started. I'll play against Donie."

Nonie spoke up before Donie had a chance to say anything. "I'm flattered that you consider me worthy enough competition to avoid. However, the rules of our land clearly state that one of the gnomes, who plays against the human, must include me."

"You didn't tell me that," Meghan said, looking suspiciously at Nonie. "How was I supposed to know?"

"Well, you know now," Nonie said defensively. "Let's play."

Meghan approached the tree with Nonie. She looked into the tree, searching for the flag.

Nonie snorted in amusement. "I can guarantee that you won't find the flag by simply looking up at the tree. It will be well hidden."

"I bet you already know where it is. Monie probably told you where he hid it." Meghan secretly hoped her words would hurt Nonie. By the expression on his face, she was sure that they had.

"Go!" Monie yelled suddenly. Monie's call had startled Meghan and left her a few moves behind Nonie. She quickly regained her bearings and scrambled up the tree, in pursuit of the hidden flag. Meghan decided that it would be in her best interest to follow Nonie, just in case Monie had told him the location of the flag.

Meghan climbed the tree with difficulty. The branches felt damp; they made a sucking noise whenever she placed or removed her hand. Strategically, Meghan made her way over to the cluster of pine needles which Nonie was furiously searching through. She positioned herself on a branch under Nonie and began searching also. She was just about to pull herself to a nearby cluster when Nonie stuck his leg out and kicked Meghan in the ribs.

"Ouch," Meghan moaned at the sudden pain. She let go of the branch and reached to comfort her throbbing stomach. When she felt herself slip from the branch, she grabbed the end of the branch in which Nonie was sitting on. She watched in horror as Nonie lifted his fist in the air and prepared to hit Meghan's hand. She quickly moved her hand and scurried to the trunk of the tree. She was afraid that the flag was indeed hidden there. At least that would explain Nonie's uncharacteristic behavior. When Meghan saw Nonie leaving that side of the tree, she quickly dismissed the thought. Instead, she began to climb higher in the tree.

Meghan searched through the clusters of pine needles that littered the branches. She felt as if she had been searching for hours, yet there were still many unchecked branches. Meghan began to fear that Nonie would find the flag and that she would be doomed to spend the rest of her life inside a potted plant. Meghan looked above her head to see the tree getting thinner. I'm near the top, she realized, shivering at the thought of being so high off the ground. Meghan continued to look up at the tree. She was devoid of any hope as she thought about her family and friends. When a strong wind blew, Meghan noticed something fluttering at the top of the tree. She raised her body and narrowed her eyes, trying to get a better look at the object. She gasped when she realized that it was the green flag. Meghan's gasp alerted Nonie, who was less than four meters away from her. She looked at him, praying that he had not seen what she just had. The twinkle in Nonie's eyes and the crinkling of his skin around them, indicated they he had also seen the flag. With a swift jump, Nonie began to race towards the top of the tree.

Oh no you don't, Meghan thought with determination as she sped after Nonie. Her legs ached and her breath came in shallow puffs, but she did not care. Meghan climbed swiftly up the tree. She had soon passed Nonie and was just about to reach for the flag when Nonie bit her. Meghan felt Nonie's teeth penetrate through her skin, but she kept on stretching. She stretched until she had the flag firmly in her hands.

"Not again," Nonie muttered in disappointment as he saw the flag in Meghan's hands. "You won fair and square," he commented. "Now it's time for you to go home."

A smile appeared on Meghan's face but it disappeared as quickly as it had come as she saw Nonie reach out and push her off the branch in which she was standing.

\* \* \*

Meghan's eyes fluttered open. She saw a dark sky above her head. She sat up, fearing that she was still in the potted plant. However, what she saw made her smile. She was lying on the deck; beside her was the potted plant. She was no longer in the plant nor was she the size of a gnome. She kneeled close to the potted plant and searched for the gnomes. She could not see them but she dared not to touch the needles in a more thorough search for them. "Meghan, you made it back! I'm so glad that you're okay."

Meghan was so deep in thought that the external noise frightened her. In response, Meghan jumped forward and reached her hand out to steady herself. In doing so, her opened hand pressed against the red pot. Her index finger touched a pine needle. She felt the pine needle slowly pierce her skin. Meghan stared at the hurt finger in terror then turned around to see who had made her jab her finger once again. Her stomach churned when she saw a guilty looking Justin standing in the light of the moon.

"I wish I'd never met you," she said through clenched teeth.

\* \* \*

# Kingdom of Sugar

# Kingdom of Sugar

Clayton Baxter did not make a sound. He dared not to even breathe. Clayton pressed his ear against the door and listened. He heard nothing but silence. Ever so carefully, Clayton placed a key into the keyhole then gently pushed the door open.

Clayton's tense body relaxed when he saw that the room was dark and empty. Smiling to himself for getting away with such a devious plan, Clayton quietly jogged to his bedroom. He opened his bedroom door then muffled a scream as a pair of hands fumbled over his mouth.

"How could you?" asked an upset voice. The hands released their grasp over Clayton's mouth then turned on the light switch. The sudden bright light felt odd to Clayton. "How could you?" the upset voice asked again. Clayton spun around to see his mother. He tried to hide the brown paper bag, which he was holding behind his back, but he was not fast enough. Mrs. Baxter grabbed the brown paper bag and ripped it open. "Oh," she moaned in disappointment, when she saw the contents lying on the floor.

Clayton turned his head away from the mess in shame. "I'm sorry," he hardly managed to say. Mrs. Baxter bent down and picked up the candy wrappers that had fallen from the brown paper bag. Clayton could not watch his mother throw the handful of candy wrappers into the garbage can; he was too disgusted at himself.

"We need to have a serious talk," Mrs. Baxter said, motioning for her son to sit down in a nearby chair. Clayton obediently sat down. "You promised me that you would cut back on the candy. However, it seems to me that you've been eating more than ever. It looks like you've eaten a pound of candy in just one night!"

Clayton lowered his head in shame. "Yes I have," he admitted. "I bought the candy just an hour ago and have already eaten it all," Clayton moaned. "I'm a monster!"

Mrs. Baxter patted her sobbing son's back. "You are not a monster," she reassured him. "You just have an extra sweet tooth."

"But I *am* a monster! I've broken my promise to you," he cried, while looking at his mother with tearful eyes. Mrs. Baxter patted his head soothingly. "I also have a stomach ache," Clayton added with a hiccup.

"We can talk about this in the morning," Mrs. Baxter said, while looking at the clock that read 10:10 PM. "We will come up with a sugar reduced diet and I'll make sure you stick to it." Mrs. Baxter smiled sympathetically at her son. "Remember to brush your teeth well before going to bed," she added, before leaving his room.

Clayton changed into his pajamas, brushed his teeth, turned off the light switch, and then climbed into bed. He felt extremely hot so he kicked off his bed covers. Clayton tossed and turned, trying to get comfortable. However, no matter how hard he tried, he just could not relax. Clayton felt warm blood rushing furiously throughout his veins. He felt his face flush warmly. Clayton turned onto his side and moaned. He prayed for his stomach to stop churning as he fell into a restless sleep.

* * *

The loud thumping upon his head woke Clayton up. At first he thought he was only dreaming, but when something hit him on the head and it hurt; Clayton knew that he was awake. Clayton screamed when he realized that he was no longer in his bedroom. Still in his pajamas, Clayton jumped up to get a better look at his surroundings. However, in doing so, he tripped and fell on the object that had hit him on the head. Clayton was lying next to a large green gum drop. The gum drop was a light shade of green and was molded into a teardrop shape. It had white sugar all over it. When light hit the gum drop it sparkled brilliantly. Although he was confused, Clayton was somewhat happy with finding such a large candy. He was about to reach out and grab the green gum drop when suddenly a red gum drop hit him on the head. "Ouch," he moaned, while rubbing his head. Suddenly, a yellow gumdrop hit his head. Clayton let out a scream of terror as he looked up to see hundreds of gum drops falling from the sky.

Clayton mimicked a turtle that was retreating into its shell as he curled up in a small ball and put his hands over his head to protect himself. He cringed every time he felt the large gumdrops hitting him on his back. As the gumdrops continued to rain on Clayton, he realized that he needed to find shelter if he were to survive. Clayton came out of his turtle position then began to run. Keeping his head low and covered by his hands, Clayton ran until he spotted a house. When he reached the house, that looked as if it was made out of gingerbread, Clayton pounded on the door with one hand.

"Shoot," he cursed aloud, when no one answered the door. Although Clayton wanted protection from the falling gum drops, he was frightened as to what may have opened the door. How in the world did I get here? And where is here? Clayton questioned as he pressed himself against the side of the house.

The thick frosting that had been dried in place over the edge of the roof provided Clayton with some protection. He waited until the raining of gum drops became less then eventually stopped. Clayton looked in awe as the fallen gum drops melted into beautiful puddles of yellow, green, purple, red and blue. Clayton left the protection that the side of the gingerbread house yielded and then gazed upon the house in its entirety. The gingerbread house stood only six feet tall and was twenty feet wide. The walls were dark brown and were held together by a thick white frosting; the same frosting that decorated the edges of the roof and hung down like icicles. The white frosting was also used to outline the door and the windows.

When Clayton heard a dripping noise he turned his attention to the drain pipe that was made out of a long candy cane. Running down the candy cane drainpipe was the melted gumdrops. Clayton watched in fascination as the melted gum drops gathered in a multi-colored puddle at the edge of the house. Clayton kneeled down beside the puddle and stared at it in amazement. "It's beautiful," he said aloud, while contemplating licking up the sugary goodness. As his hand reached for the puddle, all Clayton could think about was tasting the melted gum drops.

"Hold it right there!" screamed a small voice.

Clayton turned around slowly then froze in terror. There, standing in the opened doorway of the gingerbread house, was a small gingerbread boy. Clayton gaped in horror at the gingerbread boy adorned with sparkly blue sugar. The gingerbread boy had silver balls for eyes and a smile made from licorice. He stood small at three feet and had dark gingerbread skin. The most magnificent aspect of the gingerbread boy was its human characteristics. It was shaped like a boy and could move its whole body easily. Clayton squirmed when he saw the gingerbread boy's sliver ball eyes being covered with a thin layer of gingerbread as it blinked.

"What are you? Where am I?" Clayton asked suddenly, no longer feeling tempted to eat anything that came from this strange place.

"You are in the Kingdom of Sugar. Don't you know anything?" the gingerbread boy asked, while rolling his silver ball eyes.

"How did I get here?" Clayton asked, feeling a growing lump inside his throat.

"I can't tell you how you got here, but I can tell you why!" the gingerbread boy said with a bit too much enthusiasm as he moved closer to Clayton.

Feeling threatened by the gingerbread boy, Clayton stepped backwards. "Alright, tell me why I'm here," he demanded, trying to sound brave.

"You've been chosen to come here because of your dedication to all things sugar," the gingerbread boy said smirking. "We want to repay you for your loyalty."

Clayton moved back again as the gingerbread boy advanced towards him at a faster pace. Who was he referring to when he said "we"? Clayton asked himself silently.

"Sugar tastes great, doesn't it?" The gingerbread boy asked, moving even closer to Clayton. "But I know something that tastes even better than sugar!"

"What?" Clayton asked, while gulping in fear. He had a feeling that he did not want to know the answer.

"Humans!" the gingerbread boy yelled, before leaping for Clayton. Clayton quickly jumped out of the gingerbread boy's way. He watched in amazement as the gingerbread boy fell on the ground and into a gum drop puddle. Clayton stared in horror as the gingerbread boy tried to pull himself from the gumdrop puddle.

"The puddle must be drying up and turning sticky once again," Clayton reasoned aloud.

"Help me!" the gingerbread boy pleaded.

"No chance!" Clayton yelled as he turned around and started running from the gingerbread boy.

"I wasn't really going to eat you. I was just kidding!" Clayton heard the gingerbread boy call to him.

Just kidding? I don't think so, Clayton thought. He gulped hard as he ran through the strange land. Clayton knew that he was in real danger. Somehow, he had entered a land full of sugary treats that liked to eat humans. "This is no joke," Clayton said over the sound of his thumping heart.

37

\* \* \*

Clayton ran and ran. He ran until he could run no more. Completely out of breath, Clayton collapsed on the ground. For the first time since arriving in the Kingdom of Sugar, Clayton took a long look at his surroundings. The blue sky and white clouds looked as if they were made out of cotton candy. The sun looked like a large orange lollipop. The bark on the trees looked like cracked gingerbread, while the leaves looked like green cotton candy. Even the ground was made from gingerbread and green cotton candy. Clayton had never seen so much candy before, but for some reason he was not tempted by it. After resting for a little while, Clayton rose to his feet and began walking.

Not wanting to go back and face the gingerbread boy, Clayton headed down the long turning gingerbread path. The edge of the path was adorned with the silver balls that were used as the gingerbread boy's eyes. Clayton shuddered and tried not to look down. He imagined that the silver balls belonged to the gingerbread people, who were watching him right now, and were going to jump out of the ground and attack him at any moment. The scary thoughts made Clayton walk faster. He wondered how he would ever escape from this strange land that was inhabited by candy that liked to eat humans.

As Clayton held his head high, unwilling to look at the creepy silver balls, he saw a dark purple mountain rise high in the sky. White creamy foam sat at the tip of the mountain. When Clayton had reached the mountain's base, he stared up in awe at it.

A brown sign made out of gingerbread caught Clayton's attention. He read the candy cane writing out loud, "Jelly Mountain. Proceed at your own risk."

Clayton backed away from the mountain in fear. He did not like the way that the jelly mountain quivered and he certainly did not like the way that the white creamy foam was slowly sliding downwards.

Clayton shivered before turning to his left side and walking along the shaking purple jelly mountain. He was upset to see that once he turned the corner of the large mountain another jelly mountain was there. Clayton sighed in frustration when he realized that there were miles of Jelly Mountains that rose high into the sky.

Clayton decided that he would have more luck if he went back down the gingerbread path. Clayton did not know what he was looking for exactly; he just knew that he had to keep moving if he wanted to get out of the Kingdom of Sugar alive.

Clayton had not gone far when he heard a familiar shout. Clayton gasped in horror when he saw a gingerbread man and woman, along with the gingerbread boy who was covered in dried gum drop liquid, running towards him. The very sight of the three angry gingerbread people would have made Clayton laugh if he were not so scared.

Not knowing what else to do, Clayton ran back towards the Jelly Mountains. He gulped when he re-read the caution sign. Clayton tried to ignore the feeling of intense fear that was coursing through his body as he jumped onto the mountain.

It was his hands and feet that sank into the Jelly Mountain first, followed by the rest of his body. Clayton took a last breath of air as he prepared to be engulfed by the jelly. He closed his eyes and waited to die.

Clayton's eyes flew open when he felt his body hit against something hard. He stared down at his hands and noticed that they pressed against something hard. Clayton had only fallen into the Jelly Mountain by a foot before the hard inner layer of the mountain stopped him. He let out a loud sigh. He was so happy to be safe.

However, that feeling of security did not last long when he heard the angry shouts of the gingerbread people. Clayton looked behind to see the gingerbread people only a few feet away from the Jelly Mountain. Seeing no other alternative, Clayton began to climb the mountain. It was hard work dragging his body from the jelly; however, with a burst of strength, he managed to pull himself out of the sticky mess. Making sure that only his hands and feet touched the jelly, Clayton made his way slowly up the mountain. Clayton looked around once more and was pleased to see that the gingerbread people were not following him up the mountain.

"You'll never make it over these mountains," Clayton heard the gingerbread boy shout angrily. "And even if by chance you do make it over the mountains, you'll never survive the evil candy bears."

"You would have a better chance if you faced us, boy!" the gingerbread man snickered. "The evil candy bears have a bigger appetite then us!"

Clayton knew that the gingerbread people were shouting more terrifying warnings at him but, thankfully, he could not hear the rest of their words over the loud winds that blew up high on the mountaintop. Clayton scrambled up the rest of the purple Jelly Mountain. Why would they think I couldn't climb this mountain? Clayton asked himself, with a little smile on his face as he reached for the white foam.

Clayton suddenly realized why the gingerbread people had warned him about climbing the mountain. Clayton's hands, feet, and then his whole body began to sink into the white foamy mountain top. However, there was no hard core in the mountain to stop Clayton from falling deep inside. Clayton felt a surprisingly large amount of pressure from the white foam that covered his whole body. He hadn't had the chance to take in a breath of air before the white foam had engulfed him. Clayton's chest tightened and his lungs ached for oxygen. Without thinking logically, Clayton gulped for air. Instead of getting air, he got a mouth full of vanilla ice cream. Clayton was surprised to taste the sweetness in his mouth as he swallowed it then began swimming in the ice cream.

Clayton flung his arms back and forth, hoping to move towards the top of the mountain. He began to advance but not by much. His muscles were getting really sore and his chest felt like it was going to explode. Clayton was sure that he was going to die. He did not know how far he had sunk into the mountain, but he knew that he would never see the brightness that the orange lollipop sun yielded again. This is the last chance that I have to survive, Clayton told himself as he took one final burst of energy to propel himself forward. Clayton's legs kicked and his arms punched through the ice cream until he reached the surface and burst through it.

Clayton took a huge, and very much appreciated, breath of fresh air. Panic struck his heart as Clayton began to sink back into the vanilla ice cream mountain. Not allowing himself to become stuck in the situation that he was in moments ago, Clayton kicked his legs and flapped his arms until he was tumbling down the other side of the mountain. Clayton formed himself into a ball so he would not sink too far into the ice cream topped mountain. When he reached the purple part of the Jelly Mountain, Clayton planned to loosen his body; however, he was going so fast that his body tightened into an even smaller ball. He continued rolling down the mountain, while feeling the jelly gathering all over him. Finally, Clayton reached the bottom of the mountain with a loud thud. He just sat there in shock, throbbing all over.

Then he started laughing hysterically. Clayton did not know why he was laughing. Perhaps, he laughed because he had come face to face with death and lived. Or perhaps, it was because he had proven the gingerbread people wrong. Clayton suddenly stopped laughing when he remembered what else the gingerbread people had said. He remembered them distinctly saying that he would not survive even if he did get over the Jelly Mountain safely. He remembered the gingerbread man saying that they had a lesser appetite than that of the evil candy bears. Who are the evil candy bears? Clayton wondered. Trying to shake the terrifying thought from his head, Clayton got up and began walking once again.

\* \* \*

Clayton's stomach growled in hunger. He noticed a small blue pond off to the side of the gingerbread path. As he approached the pond then leaned down he noticed that the pond was not filled with water.

"That shouldn't be a surprise," Clayton said out loud, referring to the not-so-normal pond. Clayton felt a bit better when he heard the sound of his own voice. He looked carefully into the pond. It was a dark blue and had chunks of ice floating throughout it. Confident that he knew what the pond contained, Clayton bent down and tasted the expected blueberry flavor of the slushy. Clayton felt joy overcome him as he stuck his face into the blue slushy pond and drank.

As he lifted his face out of the pond, he saw something that he had not noticed before. It looked like a pond, only much larger than the one Clayton was kneeling over, and it looked as if it was frozen. As Clayton advanced towards the pond he realized that it was indeed frozen. He also noticed that the pond was white and that it had thin lines of red and green running throughout it.

"It looks like a gigantic candy cane ice rink!" Clayton exclaimed aloud, when he had reached the frozen pond's edge. He stared in awe at the beauty and vastness of the candy-cane ice rink.

Clayton saw the thin stick figures first and then he heard the noise that they made as they glided towards him. Although Clayton had seen strange things since arriving in the Kingdom of Sugar, these figures took the prize for the weirdest. Clayton counted six candy-cane people. They were all about seven feet in height and were white with thin lines of red and green running around them. The figures had two arms that matched their body and large black eyes. Clayton shook his head as he realized that he was probably in danger. He turned around and prepared to run.

"Don't go," said a voice that sounded as if it were talking through a pipe. Clayton turned around quickly and realized that the candy-cane people had a small slit for a mouth. "Don't go," the candy-cane person said again. Clayton watched in amazement as the other five candy-cane people nodded their heads, indicating that they did not want him to leave.

"Are you guys good?" Clayton asked shakily. Clayton watched in fear as two candy-cane people hopped off the ice and went behind him. He felt himself panicking as the candy-cane people formed a circle around him. Clayton held his breath as one of the candy-cane people drew its face close to his.

"Of course!" the candy-cane person exclaimed, obviously pleased with himself for giving Clayton a scare.

Clayton let out a deep breath of air then smiled. "So, you can tell me how to get home, right?"

One of the candy-cane people looked Clayton up and down. "I knew that you weren't from here!" it exclaimed. "We have a lot of different inhabitants in the Kingdom of Sugar but nothing that looks like you."

"Thanks... I think," Clayton said, not really sure if he should take that comment as a compliment or not. "Can you help me get home?" Clayton asked, remembering why he was talking to the candy-cane people in the first place.

"Do you want to play with us on our ice rink?" one of the candy-cane people asked.

Clayton felt his face go red in anger. Why aren't they answering my question? He wondered.

"Oh yes," another candy-cane person replied enthusiastically. "Our new friend can be the goalie while the rest of us split up into teams of three." All the other candy-cane people nodded happily in agreement.

"But I want to go home," Clayton whined. He did not care if he sounded like a baby; he really wanted to go home and get away from all the weird creatures that resided in the Kingdom of Sugar.

"So you don't want to play with us?" one candy-cane person asked sadly.

Not wanting to upset the candy-cane people, Clayton put on, what he hoped was a sad, pitiful face and sadly added, "I just want to go home."

"We will help you if we can," a candy-cane person said kindly. "Where is this place that you call home?"

"Earth," Clayton answered, wondering if he was still on Earth.

"Did you say Earth?" a candy-cane person asked in shock.

"Yes," Clayton said, suddenly getting the dreadful feeling that he had said the wrong thing.

"Are you a human?" one of the candy-cane people whispered, as if not wanting anyone else to hear what he was asking.

"Yes," Clayton repeated. As soon as the word had escaped his mouth, Clayton regretted what he had said. The candy-cane people licked their non-existent lips hungrily. How could I forget that the inhabitants of the Kingdom of Sugar eat humans? Clayton scolded himself. "Well, thanks for inviting me to play with you, but I really should be going," he said as he started to back away.

"Just hold on a minute," a candy-cane person said slyly.

"I really have to go," Clayton said, with rising panic in his chest.

"Just stay for one more minute," the sly candy-cane person said again.

"No!" Clayton yelled, turning around and running as fast as he could towards the familiar gingerbread path. As soon as he had returned to the gingerbread path, Clayton stopped for a quick breath and looked behind him. His whole body shook as he saw that the candy-cane people were still running after him. Luckily they could not move fast since they had no legs.

"So much for being good candy-canes," Clayton said spitefully as he began to run again. I have never had so much exercise in my life! Clayton thought as he looked behind himself once again. For some reason the candy-cane, people looked a lot smaller. I must be running a lot faster than them, Clayton reasoned. As he continued to run Clayton kept looking behind himself. The candy-cane people looked close; however, they also looked very small. Clayton's lungs ached and his legs began to develop cramps. He knew that he was slowing down.

Soon, Clayton was too tired to run anymore. He slowed down to a jog then finally to a fast walking pace. I'll never make it, Clayton though sadly as he looked behind one last time. What he saw made him laugh.  There, running only a few feet behind Clayton, were the seven foot candy-cane people who had somehow shrunken down to five inches tall.

"What happened to you guys?" Clayton asked in a baby voice. He saw the candy-cane people jumping up and down in anger.  Clayton was sure that they were speaking but they were so small that he could no longer make out what they were saying.  "I can't hear you," Clayton said in a loud voice, hoping to annoy and deafen the candy-cane people at the same time.  He laughed again as he picked up one of the candy-cane people and flung it off the gingerbread path.  He did the same with the remaining five.

Clayton walked back down the path just a little bit, trying to find the cause of the shrinking of the candy-cane people.  He soon realized what had happened when he saw the chips of candy cane scattered over the harsh gingerbread.  "They must have been grated down by the gingerbread path," Clayton reasoned out loud.  The smile, which had played on his face for the last few minutes, disappeared as Clayton thought about how the candy-cane people had destroyed their lives by giving into their greed.  "They just couldn't control their cravings for humans," Clayton thought sadly, while thinking of his own craving that had ruined his life.

* * *

Once he had finished resting after the candy-cane people incident, Clayton began walking down the gingerbread path once again.  "I am getting really sick of you," Clayton said to the gingerbread path.

After half an hour of walking, Clayton came to the edge of a dark, dense forest.  He gulped in fear.  The forest looked very scary.  He was sure that there would be equally scary creatures residing in the forest. However, the gingerbread path went into the forest, thus Clayton was going to go into the forest as well.

Clayton felt courage swell in his chest as he entered the dense forest.  The thickness of the dark green cotton candy leaves easily blocked out the brightness of the orange lollipop sun.  Despite the fear of being in such a strange place, Clayton found himself in awe over the dense forest.  The trunks of the gingerbread trees were massive.  They must be at least six feet wide, Clayton thought.  The silver balls that lined the gingerbread path were more abundant and shiny than the other silver balls that Clayton had seen earlier.

As a soft breeze swept through the forest, Clayton blinked in surprise over what he saw. Every time a breeze blew throughout the forest, the cotton candy leaves would shake then release green sparkly sugar everywhere. The scene was so beautiful that Clayton stopped walking and just stared at the glittering sugar as it fell to the ground. A noise behind Clayton made him snap back to reality. He quickly glanced behind to see what had made the noise. At first Clayton saw nothing, but when he looked down he gasped in horror. There, only two feet away from him, was a black snake.

Clayton turned and ran in fear. He glanced back to see if the snake was following him. When Clayton realized that the snake had not even moved, he stopped running and cautiously walked back to the snake. Clayton's heart raced as he neared the snake once again. He had hated snakes for as long as he could remember. Clayton stood a few feet back from the snake as he eyed it suspiciously. Then suddenly, he burst out laughing.

Clayton's whole body relaxed as he realized that his "snake" was nothing more than a black string of licorice. It must have fallen from a tree when the wind blew, Clayton realized, reaching for the black string of licorice. "It's heavier than I thought it would be," Clayton said out loud. He saw no harm in taking a tiny bite of the licorice as he brought it closer to his face. Clayton could already taste the sugary goodness as he closed his eyes and parted his lips and prepared to take a bite of the licorice. Clayton's eyes flew open as he heard a hissing sound in front of his face. He screamed in horror as he saw two yellow eyes and a red tongue hissing violently. Clayton dropped the licorice snake then prepared to run. Unfortunately, he had dropped the licorice snake too close to his feet. The snake had no problem wrapping itself tightly around Clayton's ankles. Clayton tried to run but instead he fell to the ground in a heap.

The hissing sound grew deafening as the licorice snake tightened its grip on Clayton. Clayton felt his feet and legs tingle in pain as the snake continued to squeeze him. He's going to squeeze me to death then eat me, Clayton realized in horror. As his legs went numb, Clayton knew that he had to act now if we wanted to survive. Struggling to get up, Clayton finally managed to sit upright by pulling on a nearby branch. With a cry that was full of pain and rage, Clayton lunged himself forward and sank his teeth deep into the snake. Clayton heard angry hisses as the licorice snake uncoiled itself from around his ankles then slithered away quickly.

Clayton rubbed his throbbing ankles and waited for the blood to return to them. Slowly, the feeling returned to Clayton's legs and feet. Not knowing what else to do, he shakily got on his feet then began to walk deeper into the forest.

* * *

Clayton's feet ached and his stomach growled. He had been walking for two hours since the snake attack. "Where am I walking to?" Clayton heard himself ask out loud. He had no idea where he was going or how to get out of the Kingdom of Sugar. He only knew one thing for sure and that was that he never wanted to see another candy as long as he lived.

"I wonder how long I will survive out here," Clayton said, being only a little bit comforted by the sound of his own voice. He wondered how long he had been in the Kingdom of Sugar. It seemed like days. Clayton wondered if the orange lollipop sun had set already.

Feeling completely exhausted and devoid of hope, Clayton stopped walking and sat on the hard gingerbread ground. Not really caring if anyone had ever walked on it before, Clayton began digging then eating the gingerbread. Clayton really didn't want to eat anything that contained sugar, far less anything that came from this weird land; however, Clayton knew that if he didn't eat he would not have the energy to even keep his eyes open.

Clayton picked a few silver balls to eat then leaned against a thick tree to rest. He felt his head nodding forward and his eyes getting heavier. Giving into temptation, Clayton lay back on the ground. He had just got comfortable when he heard a weird noise. Clayton was so tired that he just ignored the noise. However, the noise kept on growing louder and closer. It sounded like a child who was sloppily chewing on the stickiest candy ever invented. Clayton opened his eyes in concern then let out a horrified scream.

Right before his eyes was an eight-foot yellow candy bear. The candy bear was a transparent yellow and only had indentations as features. Clayton could see right through it. He gulped when he realized that there were green, blue, purple, and orange candy bears behind the yellow one. Although Clayton was terrified to see a herd of candy bears, it was the one feature that Clayton hadn't seen on the candy bears until they opened their mouths, which made him open his own mouth in another horrified scream. Every candy bear had two rows of razor sharp teeth.

"They always scream," the yellow candy bear in front of Clayton remarked as he leapt towards him. Clayton's cries for help were muffled as the candy bear hit into him. Clayton felt a coldness that chilled him right down to his bones as he was engulfed into the candy bear's body.

I've been eaten, Clayton thought in horror. He began kicking and thrashing in protest. Clayton was in shock when he passed right through the yellow candy bear's body. I wasn't eaten. I just moved through his body, Clayton realized in surprise as he looked at his arms and legs that were covered in sticky candy bear residue. Clayton turned around to see the expression of rage on the yellow candy bear's face. Clayton ducked out of the way just in time as the yellow candy bear grabbed for him angrily.

"After him!" the yellow candy bear yelled to the others.

Clayton ran full force towards the candy bears as the candy bears did the same thing towards him. Clayton heard a sickening splash as he ran through a candy bear's body. He heard the candy bear moan in pain. Clayton ran through a purple, green, and then orange candy bear. He looked ahead of himself and was relieved to see no more candy bears.

As Clayton ran towards the candy bear free path, he could hear the angry threats and protests from the candy bears that were just feet behind him. Clayton looked behind himself to see the herd of candy bears who were bearing their long sharp teeth. Clayton continued to run until a sudden cramp struck him in his right side. As he grabbed his side and fell to the ground in pain, the candy bears surrounded him, wearing evil expressions on their faces. Clayton stared in horror as the candy bears formed as tight circle around him then started to attack. All Clayton could hear was a ringing in his ears.

\* \* \*

The ringing grew louder until it became distinguishable as an alarm clock. Clayton groaned as he turned on his side to hit the sleep button on the alarm clock. As soon as he had touched the alarm clock and had shut off the ringing, Clayton suddenly sat straight up in bed. Fully awake now, Clayton remembered his horrifying experience in the Kingdom of Sugar. He shivered with fear. It was just a dream, he told

47

himself as he headed to the kitchen for breakfast. But it seemed so real, Clayton thought, before stepping into the kitchen.

"Clayton!" Mrs. Baxter shouted angrily when she saw Clayton.

"What's wrong?" Clayton asked in concern.

"How could you?" Mrs. Baxter asked in disappointment. "After having that talk with you last night I was so sure you'd cut back on sugar."

In confusion, Clayton looked into the small mirror that hung over the counter top. He gasped when he saw smears of gingerbread across his mouth and face. "The Kingdom of Sugar," Clayton whispered in horror.

Mrs. Baxter sighed. "Clayton, you have to stop eating so much sugary treats. You've become obsessed! Promise me once and for all that you will seriously cut back on the candy and that you will never go to the Kingdom of Sugar again."

She thinks the Kingdom of Sugar is a candy store, Clayton realized. "I promise," he said solemnly. "Believe me, the Kingdom of Sugar is one place I never want to return to!"

As Clayton headed to the bathroom to wash his face, Mrs. Baxter smiled at him in relief. She was happy to see her son so determined to cut back on candy. Mrs. Baxter's eyebrows knitted in confusion as she spotted something on the floor. When she bent down and picked it up, she sighed in disappointment. In her hand she held a small yellow candy bear. "I guess Clayton will need a lot of help to cut back on the candy," Mrs. Baxter said out loud.

"I'll take care of him," a tiny sinister voice said. Mrs. Baxter looked down at the yellow candy bear in her hand and screamed.

\* \* \*

# Eyes of Red

# Eyes of Red

"Have you sent out all the invitations?" Count Darkness hissed, while sucking on his package of blood.

"I have," Mrs. Darkness responded, while slurping on her own package of blood. "All sixty two invitations have been sent out to the members of the Association of Vampires. They were told to meet us at the abandoned animal shelter in Fall Valley." Mrs. Darkness threw her empty blood package into a nearby trash can. She flicked her long black hair over her shoulders. Mrs. Darkness, like her husband, was a vampire. Both Mrs. Darkness and her husband were the leaders of the Association of Vampires, a group that gathered every year for a week in late October. Count Darkness and Mrs. Darkness were tall, thin and very pale. They dressed in tight black clothing and wore a lavish black and red cape. However, the most prominent feature that they possessed was their fiery red eyes.

"Good," Count Darkness said, letting a trickle of blood run down his mouth as he smiled. "I can't wait to see all my children of the dark!"

\* \* \*

"I'm going to dress up as a cat for Halloween," Lisa told her friend Francine, as they walked down the halls of their school.

Francine looked at Lisa as if she were from another planet. "You've got to be kidding," she snorted rudely.

"Kidding about what?" Lisa asked in confusion.

Francine sighed. "How old do you think you are, Lisa?"

Lisa twirled her long brown hair around her index finger. "What do you mean?" she asked, still confused.

"Aren't you a little old for trick or treating? We *are* in college now."

"I wasn't planning on going trick or treating," Lisa defended herself. "But I *was* looking forward to getting dressed up and handing out candy to children."

"You're not handing out candy this Halloween," Francine said mysteriously. Lisa raised her eyebrows in curiosity. "You're coming to our first college party tomorrow."

"I don't think that's a good idea," Lisa said, raising her hands in protest.

"Why not?" Francine asked, with her hands on her waist.

"I don't really like big crowds," Lisa stated. "I'm also not into dancing. It would be a waste of time."

"No it wouldn't," Francine protested. "Besides, you're going whether you like it or not!" Francine pushed Lisa towards the classroom door as the other students began to file in.

"There's no way I'm going to that Halloween party," Lisa told herself in determination.

\* \* \*

A bright moon lit up the dark blue sky. As the airplane descended towards the ground white sky lights cast beams of brightness outside the airport. Count Darkness pulled the plastic cover down harshly over the airplane window.

"Even though the lighting is false, I still don't like it," Count Darkness complained loudly.

Mrs. Darkness hushed her husband. "You'll make people suspicious," she said, glancing around the small, almost empty airplane. She could only see fifteen other people. "I guess Fall Valley isn't a very busy place," she added to her husband.

"That's the reason why we're coming here," Count Darkness replied quietly. "We need a place to gather where we won't draw attention to ourselves. This is a peaceful congregation, remember?" He raised his pointy black eyebrows high at his wife.

"I'm not the one who drained that poor teenager almost a year ago," Mrs. Darkness reminded Count Darkness. "I'm not the one who broke the oath. I fully understand the importance of our oath to drink only packaged blood." Mrs. Darkness crossed her arms and stared coolly at her husband.

"I realize my mistake and I won't do it again."

"You better not," Mrs. Darkness warned sternly.

"I promise," Count Darkness said, while smiling at his wife. Mrs. Darkness quickly put her hand over his mouth. Count Darkness did not realize that he had just shown his fangs.

The airplane descended into the night's cool air then hit the ground with a bump. The passengers, along with Count Darkness and Mrs. Darkness, exited the airplane then headed to the terminal to get their luggage.

51

"Isn't it dark enough without sunglasses?" a cheeky employee taunted. He was referring to the thick, dark sunglasses that Count Darkness and Mrs. Darkness were wearing. Mrs. Darkness just shook her head and smiled at him with a closed mouth. "Whatever," the cheeky employee remarked before walking away.

Count Darkness and Mrs. Darkness waited as the conveyer belts went around and around. However, their luggage never came.

"Where are they?" Count Darkness whispered to his wife, referring to their luggage that contained many packages of blood.

"I don't know," Mrs. Darkness answered in a panic. She made sure she was covering her mouth as she spoke. "They're not going to be coming on this conveyer belt, that's for sure. We've already been waiting for over an hour. Maybe we should ask an employee for help."

"How do you suppose we do that?" Count Darkness snapped. "If we talk to anyone they'll see our fangs. They would put us on the next airplane."

"An airplane to where?" Mrs. Darkness asked in confusion.

"I don't know. To the city that paid the highest price for two main attractions of a freak show, I suppose."

"Calm down," Mrs. Darkness warned. "We'll check out all the conveyer belts."

Count Darkness and Mrs. Darkness spent the next two hours watching all the conveyer belts slide by. But still, their luggage was nowhere to be found.

"It's not here," Mrs. Darkness said in distress. "We have to leave now. The sun will start to rise soon and I'm getting hungry; really hungry." Count Darkness watched his wife look around at the people in the airport.

"Control yourself," he whispered forcefully when he saw her licking her lips. "Keep you fangs in check and let's get out of here."

Count Darkness and Mrs. Darkness quickly fled the airport and headed to the abandoned animal shelter that they would call home for the next week.

* * *

Witches laughed and werewolves howled. Lisa felt like crying. There she was, listening to the scary sounds that came from the college's sound system, and watching Francine dance with two good looking boys at once.

I should have stayed home. I'm making myself look like an even bigger loser, Lisa mentally abused herself.

"Hi there," a deep voice said from behind Lisa.

"Hi," Lisa replied, being startled out of her self-defeating thoughts.

"I'm Jeff," he said, offering Lisa his hand.

"I'm Lisa," she said, shaking his hand. Lisa looked at Jeff and blushed. He's really cute, Lisa thought excitedly. Lisa glanced at Francine and was pleased to see her casting jealous stares towards her and Jeff. Jeff stood tall at five foot ten. He looked slender but lean. Lisa loved the short brown spikes that his hair was modeled into, but it was Jeff's eyes that were the main attraction. His eyes were an unusual color of blue. However, if you looked closely enough you could see a purple tint in them. He must be wearing contacts, Lisa concluded.

"So, do you go to school at Fall Valley College?" Lisa asked, hoping to start a conversation with Jeff.

"No I don't. I was just driving by and decided to check this place out."

An awkward silence followed. The level of awkwardness rose even higher as Lisa caught Jeff looking at her neck.

"Do you want to move over to that lounge and talk? It's so noisy here."

"Sure," Lisa said, relaxing a little bit. She followed Jeff to the lounge and sat down to start the two hour conversation that they were about the have.

* * *

"We've drank all the blood packages that were brought by the other vampires," Count Darkness said, pounding his fists on an empty animal cage.

"It's not their fault," Mrs. Darkness replied sensibly. "We did say that we'd supply the blood."

"It's a good thing we also told them to supply their own blood for the first night!" Count Darkness added, rising slowly from the rusty old animal cage that he had been sitting on. "Tell all the vampires to meet in the main room in an hour. I'll have just enough time to make the announcement before we must sleep."

Mrs. Darkness looked at the serious expression on her husband's face. "No!" she cried.

"We wouldn't arrive home in time and I'm already thirsty. We have to do it," Count Darkness told his wife, as if reading her mind.

Mrs. Darkness nodded her head sadly. "I'll get everyone together," she said, leaving the small kennel room where she and her husband were temporally residing in.

"My fellow vampires," Count Darkness began, when all the vampires had gathered in the main room of the abandoned animal shelter. "You are all aware that the luggage, which contained our blood packages, has been lost at the airport. I thank you all for sharing the blood that you had. But now that it's gone our situation is dire. I know that we all took the oath to never feed on a human again, but it's either them or us. We must feed tomorrow night!"

\* \* \*

"So, what's his name?" Francine slyly asked Lisa the next day.

"Whose name?" Lisa played dumb. She tried to force back the smile that was itching to play upon her lips.

"Don't be silly," Francine scolded. "You know who I'm taking about."

"No, I don't," Lisa said innocently.

"The guy from the party last night," Francine said. "You would have talked to him until the rising of the sun if he hadn't left after his cell phone rang."

"You must have been watching us pretty close to know why he had to leave," Lisa said smiling. Her heart soared when Francine could not think of a comeback. "His name's Jeff," Lisa continued. "And he's really polite and interesting."

"Does he live around here? I don't think I've ever seen him before."

"No. He's from a neighboring town. I'll be seeing him again though. He gave me his cell phone number." Lisa had to control herself from jumping up and down with joy when she saw Francine's face turn a ghastly shade of envious green.

\* \* \*

As dusk gave away to complete darkness and the yellow moon shined brightly in the night's sky, sixty two vampires descended from the ceiling panels in which they had been hanging upside-down from. Count Darkness raised his arms to call the vampire's attention.

54

"Take no more than necessary then bring them back here where they can change fully and become part of our association." Count Darkness hovered above the ground and was about to lift the wooden sheet that covered a window. He solemnly added before leaving, "Control the urge to over indulge." With that said, Count Darkness flew out the window and was followed by fifty nine other vampires. Two vampires remained behind.

"I'll bring you back an already bitten human so you can just suck the blood from it," one of the vampires offered to the other. The vampire with no fangs nodded to show his appreciation. "Don't worry," the generous vampire said. "You'll fangs will grow in soon. It's almost been a year since you were bitten." The vampire without fangs nodded again in understanding. He watched as his friend flew out the window to find a victim for both of them.

\* \* \*

The fresh air felt great against Count Darkness' face. He, along with the other vampires, had spent two nights in the heavily secured building. Wooden sheets covered all the windows and the doors were shut tight with bolts. Count Darkness was sick of staying in the abandoned animal shelter. He wanted to be able to make an attack. He saw the perfect opportunity. A young man was coming out of an apartment building. Count Darkness watched from behind a nearby tree as the man walked around the side of the building. Count Darkness emerged from behind the tree and silently followed the man to his car. Count Darkness hovered above the ground as to not make any noise, and then he attacked.

Count Darkness grabbed the man from behind and held on tight as he sank his fangs through the man's jacket and into his flesh. Count Darkness sucked in delight. The man's blood was so warm and fresh- much better than the packaged kind he got from hospitals.

Count Darkness had to force his fangs from the man before he drained him completely. With the collapsed man in his arms, Count Darkness flew high into the night sky. He smiled to himself, thinking about how the young man didn't have time to scream. I've still got it, Count Darkness thought happily to himself.

\* \* \*

"Lisa, have you seen or heard from Shawn today?" Francine asked, running up to Lisa.

55

"No I haven't. Why?" Lisa questioned.

"He was supposed to pick me up in his car last night but he never showed up!" Francine shrieked in panic.

"He probably forgot that you two had a date," Lisa replied, rolling her eyes at Francine's overreaction.

"No. He would never forget. Besides, I was talking to him on his cell phone when he was walking down the stairs of his apartment. He was coming to pick me up but he never showed up!" Francine was yelling now and people were beginning to stare.

"Calm down," Lisa began to say.

"Calm down? Calm down?" Francine shrieked even louder. "After he left his apartment building he didn't answer any of the phone calls that I made an hour later. Now, he hasn't shown up for class. That's not like him, Lisa. Shawn always comes to class!"

"Have you tried calling his house?" Lisa asked, now also concerned.

"Yes. His parents said that he didn't come home last night. They have called all his friends but they haven't seen him either. Lisa, I am so worried!"

Lisa hugged Francine and tried to calm her down. Lisa was now very concerned, but not just about Shawn. She was concerned about the poor attendance in every one of her classes. Lisa shook the scary thoughts from her head as she said goodbye to an upset Francine and exited the school to start the twenty-five minute walk to her house.

When she was almost home Mrs. Hopkins, Lisa's next-door neighbor, came running towards her.

"What in the world is wrong?" Lisa cried as she saw Mrs. Hopkins' tear stained face.

"It's my husband. He's gone!"

"Calm down," Lisa heard herself say for the second time that day. "What do you mean he's gone?"

"He..." Mrs. Hopkins choked on her words, "he went out grocery shopping last night but never came home. I've been searching the streets for him all day long. I've even called the police but no one has found him yet!" Mrs. Hopkins hugged Lisa and began to cry harder.

"It will be alright," Lisa promised. She tried to sound cheerful but deep down inside she knew that things were not alright.

\* \* \*

Too many people had disappeared in the town of Fall Valley. Lisa was getting more than just a little bit suspicious. She decided that it was time to do some investigating.

Lisa crept out of her house at 9:45 PM that night. She locked the door behind her then ran down the driveway. Beginning her ten-minute walk to downtown Fall Valley, Lisa hurried past the poorly lit streets. She did not know what she was looking for; just anything out of the ordinary. Lisa did not have to wait long. Within minutes of entering the downtown area, Lisa spotted a tall dark figure that was wearing a long dark cape and creeping in the darkness. She ducked behind the row of cars parked on the street and watched the figure as it followed a middle-aged woman who emerged from a nearby restaurant. Lisa followed the suspicious figure as it followed the woman. Lisa felt her chest tighten as she realized that the figure was getting closer to the woman.

He's going to attack her, Lisa realized in fear. Should I warn the woman? Lisa asked herself just seconds before the dark figure jumped out from the darkness and into the light of a street lamp. Lisa muffled a scream from behind her hands as she saw the figure grab the woman and bite her neck.

Lisa felt dizzy as she sprang up quickly and ran as fast as she could towards her house. As she ran, hundreds of questions ran through her head. Who was that person? Where did it come from? Was it really sucking that woman's blood? Was it a vampire? Shouldn't I have stayed and helped that poor woman?

Not caring whether she woke up her parents of not, Lisa hurriedly unlocked the door to her house and banged it shut behind her. Running up to her room, Lisa felt her cheeks burn from something more than just extreme exercise. She was flushed with fear.

\* \* \*

"Francine!" Lisa yelled to her friend the following day. After a sleepless night, Lisa knew she needed to tell someone about what had happened.

"What is it?" Francine snapped at Lisa. She took some books from her locker and placed them in her backpack.

"Have you heard from Shawn?" Lisa asked, ignoring Francine's vicious tone of voice.

"No," Francine wailed emotionally, while turning away from her locker. "It's so horrible!"

"Francine, what has happened to him?" Lisa asked, swallowing hard.

"The police have been searching for him but all they have found is..." Francine choked back a sob. "All they have found is part of the collar from his jacket," Francine choked again. "It had his blood on it. It had Shawn's blood on it!"

Lisa felt her face flush warmly once again. "I think I know what happened to Shawn," Lisa said slowly.

Francine's eyes went wide. "Oh Lisa, tell me!"

"He's been bitten by a vampire!" Lisa exclaimed, after moving closer to Francine.

Francine stepped back from Lisa and looked at her as if she were crazy. "A vampire?" she asked slowly.

"Yes," Lisa nodded solemnly.

"A vampire?" Francine repeated again, in a shocked tone. Suddenly, Francine reached out and slapped Lisa.

"Ouch," Lisa cried, placing her hand gently on her face. "Why would you do that?" Lisa asked in bewilderment.

"I can't believe you!" Francine yelled. Several students had stopped walking down the hall and turned to stare at Francine and Lisa. Francine noticed the attention that she was causing so she stepped closer to Lisa and hissed, "Shawn could be dead. How could you think now is the time to be telling jokes?"

"It's not a joke. I'm telling you the truth!" Lisa screamed in annoyance.

Francine shot Lisa a look of complete disgust. "Do me a favor, Lisa. Just stay away from me." With that said, Francine fled down the hall and to class.

Lisa stood all alone in the crowded school hallway. "If Francine won't believe me, surely my parents will," Lisa said quietly.

* * *

"That's nice," Lisa's mother said, after being informed that a vampire had been attacking people in Fall Valley.

"Nice?" Lisa cried in confusion. "It's not nice it's...it's deadly!"

"Deadly you say?" Lisa's mother questioned, while flipping through the day's mail.

"Yes!" Lisa yelled.

"Are you feeling okay?" her mother inquired.

"Yes," Lisa said again, but in a much calmer tone this time. She knew that her mother did not believe her. In a rage of anger, Lisa grabbed her jacket and ran out the door. She needed some fresh air and a quiet place to think. She thought about calling Jeff and telling him about what had been going on. Lisa knew that he would believe her. But then again, Lisa did not want Jeff to think that she was a complete idiot. She had only known him for three days after all. "Three days," Lisa said out loud. It seemed like such a short period, but in that time she had got to know Jeff so well. They had talked on the phone many times and for many hours. They had also talked about meeting up sometime soon. Lisa knew that she had fallen hard for him.

Lisa looked up as the moon rose into the dark sky. She shivered as she realized that her thoughts about Jeff had led her far from home. She had just turned around when she saw a familiar figure clothed in black.

The figure looked shorter than the one Lisa had seen the night before. However, the two figures shared one trait in common; they both lurked in the dark.

Lisa sank into the protection of her own darkness as she watched the mysterious figure stalk down the dark side of the street.

Fear pumped through Lisa's veins as she followed the figure. "Oh no," she quietly gasped as she saw the figure sneak towards a house. Lisa stopped walking and watched as the figure peeked through a low window on the house. Lisa was relieved to see the figure quickly abandon the house and begin walking fast down the street.

Lisa started to walk also but she had to struggle to keep up with the figure who was walking at an unusually fast pace. Lisa found herself running just to keep the figure in view as it headed down an empty road. Lisa recognized the street as the location of the abandoned animal shelter. She has got her three cats from there and had often volunteered there. However, that was a long time ago; the animal shelter had been abandoned for five years now.

To Lisa's surprise, the figure headed towards the abandoned animal shelter. Then to Lisa's complete shock, the figure flew high into the air and entered through a window. Stunned, Lisa stared at the window then fell backwards on the ground.

"What in the world?" Lisa exclaimed as she climbed back on her feet. "They must be vampires," she concluded confidently. "And somehow I must find a way into that building right away!"

I can't believe I'm doing this, Lisa shrieked internally. They'll suck me dry. Lisa carried a long steel ladder, which she had found at the side of the animal shelter, as quietly as she possibly could. Luck had definitely been on her side when she found the ladder. Lisa cringed as the ladder banged against the building's wall. She closed her eyes and waited for a vampire, or two, to emerge from the building then sink their fangs into her neck.

When nothing happened three minutes later, she opened her eyes and started climbing up the ladder. When she had reached the top of the ladder she peered in and almost screamed.

There, right before her eyes, were tons of vampires. All the vampires were tall and wore black and red capes. Their skin looked very pale. Since the candles inside the building and the moon outside were the only source of light, Lisa could not see the finer details of the vampires.

Although seeing the vampires was a frightening sight, seeing the humans locked up in animal cages was even more frightening. Lisa quickly climbed down the ladder then put it back against the side of the wall. She ran home as fast as she could. Lisa shuddered as she thought about all those humans that were in cages. She let out a sob as she remembered seeing Francine's friend, Shawn locked in one of those awful cages.

"No matter what, I'll kill those vampires tomorrow night." Lisa felt courage and willpower course throughout her body.

\* \* \*

"That will be twelve dollars and seventy four cents please," the cashier at Lisa's local grocery store said, while giving her a curious look.

It was Saturday, the day after she had seen the herd of vampires. Lisa had got up early to buy all the garlic the grocery store had. She received more curious stares as she carried the carton of garlic to her house. She was grateful that her parents were not home but were visiting friends this weekend.

As soon as Lisa got home she began peeling the garlic then crushing it into liquid with a blender. After she had blended a jarful of garlic, she poured it into a large spray bottle. She repeated this process until she had four spray bottles filled with garlic juice. Next, she borrowed wooden sticks from her father's workshop in the basement and sawed them into pointy spears. Now that she had got all the necessities, all there was left to do was put "operation: kill the vampires" into action.

* * *

Hidden in the safety of the bushes, Lisa waited for the vampires to emerge from the abandoned animal shelter. The sun had set and the moon was just starting to rise in the sky. Suddenly, Lisa saw one dark shadow fly from the window. She watched in amazement as sixty more vampires flew from the same window and disappeared into the night sky. Lisa gulped as she realized that the vampires were looking for more blood.

She waited a few minutes to make sure that the coast was clear then she quickly and quietly ran to get the ladder and set it up. She climbed in silence then peered in the window. Lisa saw a sole vampire, walking back and forth, while guarding the sleeping humans in the cages. Lisa had to suppress a scream as she saw more than four dozen humans in separate cages. The number of bitten humans had grown from last night.

Why hasn't anyone been able to find you guys? She silently asked the prisoners. Lisa waited until the lonely vampire had exited the room then she sprang into action.

Carefully, she lifted her leg over the windowsill and placed it on the wooden plank that was located just below the window. Slowly, Lisa lifted her other leg over the windowsill and onto the plank. With the expertise of a tightrope walker, Lisa managed to walk along the long wooden planks until it reached a plank that was lower than the one she was on. Lisa made her way around the square building, getting lower with every plank she walked on. She did this until there were no more planks to walk on. Looking down at the ground, she calculated that the distance was no more than five feet. Grabbing for one of the garlic spray bottles, Lisa jumped to the floor and landed on both feet. However, her jump had caused a loud thud.

Lisa's heart pounded wildly as the vampire emerged from a nearby room and walked slowly towards her. Although the vampire held a white candle, Lisa could not see its face because of the large black hood it wore.

61

"Stay back," she warned in a shaky voice. "This bottle is filled with garlic," she further threatened.

The vampire continued to walk slowly towards Lisa. It was tall, just like the other vampires.

"I'll spray," Lisa yelled, raising the bottle higher. She could not believe that she was so close to a real vampire. However, her amazement soon turned to dread as the vampire continued to advance towards her. It's going to bite me, she thought in fear. "Get back," she yelled loudly. Her shout of protest woke the human prisoners, who had been sleeping just moments before. Lisa heard shouts of joy from the prisoners, but she did not give them any attention. She was too affixed on the vampire, just three feet away from her, who was pulling off its hood. Lisa felt the blood in her veins freeze as the vampire's hood fell to his shoulders.

"Jeff?" she asked in a tone that was just above a whisper.

"Lisa," Jeff whispered in an upset tone.

Lisa allowed her hand that held the garlic spray to fall to her side. "This can't be happening," Lisa said in shock. "Tell me that you're not a vampire, Jeff," she begged.

"I...I wish I could, Lisa. But I am. I am a vampire."

Lisa felt her neck stiffen in fear and her heart ache in sadness. "But...but how?" she stammered.

"I was bitten by a vampire almost a year ago. It takes a year for a bitten human to become a full vampire. The transformation is almost complete. I'll be a full vampire in two weeks."

"No. That can't be," Lisa protested.

"You think this is a shock for you? Imagine how I felt when it happened. I couldn't believe what I had become." Jeff sighed sadly. "In two weeks my fangs will grow in and I'll never be able to talk to a human again. I went to that Halloween party because it was my way of saying goodbye to a normal life. I didn't plan on meeting someone as special as you there. I didn't mean to create this unbelievably great friendship."

Lisa felt like running towards Jeff and embracing him, but instead she backed away.

"Don't be afraid. I would never hurt you," Jeff said, seeing her concern.

"How can I trust you? I haven't even known you for a week!" Lisa exclaimed, totally overcome with emotion and shock.

"Is that all?" Jeff asked in surprise. "It feels like I've known you for months."

Lisa felt that familiar feeling of fondness for Jeff returning, but once again she resisted it. Instead, she walked over to the animal cage that contained Shawn. "He went to my school," Lisa cried. "How could you bite a boy that's your own age?" Shawn's eyes met Lisa's in a plea for help. Lisa had to turn away. She could not stand seeing him so upset and frightened.

"I've never bitten anyone!" Jeff cried. "I couldn't even if I wanted to- which I don't! I don't have my fangs yet. I swear, Lisa, I will never bite a human being."

"How many vampires are there?" Lisa asked shakily, wondering if there were more vampires that she hadn't seen.

"There are only sixty two vampires in the world," Jeff replied.

"Have they always lived here? Why haven't there been vampire attacks before now?"

"The vampires live all over the world. Some live together, others live alone. We are all part of the Association of Vampires. We meet in different towns every year. The leaders of the Association of Vampires, Count Darkness and Mrs. Darkness, decided to hold the annual meeting here because I live close by." Jeff stopped to take a breath of air. "We are good vampires, Lisa. We usually drink packaged blood, which comes from hospitals. My fellow vampires have only been biting people because our packaged blood supply was lost."

Lisa felt her stomach churn. "Do you drink blood?"

Jeff nodded. Lisa felt like gagging. Forcing the nausea way, she said in a serious tone, "Jeff, your fellow vampires are attacking people in my town. I can't let this happen. I have to stop them."

"No," Jeff begged. "Our meeting ends tomorrow night. We will all be gone by then."

Lisa looked at the rows of cages filled with frightened, recently bitten humans. "I can't," Lisa said regretfully, raising the garlic spray bottle in her hand. Lisa's heart raced as she prepared to press down the release button. Then Lisa almost dropped the bottle in fright as loud bangs from outside echoed throughout the building.

"In here," Jeff urged, shoving Lisa into Count Darkness' and Mrs. Darkness' room then closing the door shut. Jeff's heart raced as the vampires entered the building just seconds later.

"Why are the humans awake?" Count Darkness questioned, after landing right in front of Jeff.

"I don't know. They just started to stir," Jeff said, praying that the prisoners wouldn't tell Count Darkness that there was a human in the kennel room. Even though Lisa had tried to kill him, he couldn't bear to think about harm coming to her.

"Just make sure the locks on the cages are secure and give them something to eat and drink," Count Darkness commanded. Jeff gave Count Darkness a curious look. "No, not blood. Give them human food and water. They haven't even started to transform into a vampire yet. It will be four months before they stop eating human food and begin drinking blood. Surely you remember that stage in you transformation."

"Actually, I don't. Things still seem blurry," Jeff snapped. Jeff hated Count Darkness. He was still infuriated over the fact that he had taken his life away. However, Jeff's hatred for him soon turned into a feeling of fright as he saw Count Darkness head towards his room. "How was the hunting tonight?" Jeff asked, trying to keep Count Darkness from going into his room.

"Fine," Count Darkness replied suspicious. Then suddenly his eyes clouded over in realization. "Ah, I know what you're doing," Count Darkness hissed.

"You...you do?" Jeff stuttered.

"Yes," Count Darkness smiled, revealing blood stained fangs. "You are trying to find out if I brought any blood back for you." Count Darkness laughed. "Another vampire has your supply," he informed him, before marching to his room and opening the door.

Jeff closed his eyes and waited to hear the dreadful sound of Lisa's scream. Jeff opened his eyes when he did not hear Lisa scream or Count Darkness gasp. He was shocked to see that Lisa was no longer in Count Darkness' room.

Lisa held back a sneeze as she crawled through the dusty vents. She was relieved to see the room that Jeff had pushed her into. Years ago, Lisa used to spend hours in the kennel room, looking for cats to adopt. She knew this room and the rest of the building from top to bottom. She also knew that the only way to survive and defeat the vampires would be through the large grey vents that ran throughout the whole building.

"Don't just stand there. Go feed the humans," Count Darkness commanded.

"I...I have to go to the grocery store to get more food," Jeff lied.

Count Darkness sighed. "The sun will be up soon. You must hurry because we lock the windows before the sun comes up- whether you're in the building or not."

Jeff gulped in fear then flew out the window and into the late night sky. He had no intention on going to the twenty four hour grocery store. He was looking for Lisa. Jeff had no clue how she managed to escape, but he knew that he had to find her before she killed them all.

Lisa looked through the vent's small square window. She had just seen Jeff fly out the window. He's probably looking for me, Lisa realized. Feeling like the devil himself, Lisa smiled. She smiled because she could now kill all the vampires, excluding Jeff.

Lisa quietly crawled through the vents, hoping that she was not making any noise. She carefully maneuvered herself until she reached the fan that was located in the main room where the vampires were.

She quickly grabbed the three bottles of garlic from her backpack and poured the liquid right in front of the vent's fan. The odor was already overpowering. Lisa crept from the fan and retraced her steps back to the kennel room. She looked down the small square vent to see Count Darkness there. She sighed internally. She would have to wait for him to leave. However, Lisa did not have to wait long as she heard a vampire scream to Count Darkness. She heard unhappy hisses and screams of terror.

Quietly and quickly, Lisa removed the small square door from the vent and jumped down. She peeked out the opened door of Count Darkness's room. She was relieved to see all the vampires gathered at the opposite side of the room. The garlic smell was present in the room, but it was not overpowering.

Taking a risk, Lisa ran from Count Darkness's room and to the stairwell that led down to the basement. Lisa's heart almost stopped beating as she heard a vampire yell, "intruder!" Lisa looked behind her to see a herd of vampires, who were all covering their noses and mouths, running towards her. Without thinking twice, Lisa turned and ran down the stairs to the basement. Her feet pounded on the dusty, dark cement

65

floor. Her hand reached out to turn the power switch on to activate the vent's fan. However, an icy cold hand grabbed her before she could pull the switch.

The hand pulled her around. Lisa screamed. An inch from her face was a bloodthirsty vampire. The vampire's skin was a ghastly shade of pale green. His eyes were bright red and blood dripped from his long white fangs, indicating that he had just enjoyed a live meal.

"No," Lisa screamed, before kicking the vampire in the shins. The vampire loosened his grip on Lisa and cried out in pain. Taking advantage of the situation, Lisa pulled away from the vampire and turned the vent's fan on.

Lisa grabbed the wooden spear from her jacket and forced it towards the twelve vampires that had followed her down the stairs. The vampires hissed in protest, but retreated when Lisa shoved the spear forward again. She did this repeatedly until the vampires were back in the main room.

As soon as she reached the main room she choked on the strong garlic smell. However, she smiled through the stench as she saw the vampires begin to wither. She stared in horror and in amazement as the vampire's skin began to drop from their faces and their bones turned to dust.

Wails of horror could be heard from the dying vampires. The wails began to die off as the vampires did. Soon, smoky black clothing and dust from the vampires surrounded Lisa. Despite the horrible setting, Lisa smiled. She had defeated the vampires and saved her town. Shouts of happiness came from the prisoners.

"Let us out," a prisoner shouted. Lisa bit her bottom lip in confusion. She did not want to let the prisoners out because she knew they'd turn into vampires. She quickly turned around and began breaking down the bolted door. "Come back," the prisoners shouted in terror, but Lisa did not stop. She had to find Jeff and tell him that he could not go back to the garlic infested animal shelter.

Jeff looked up at the sky in panic. The sun would start to rise in about half an hour. Despite the cold, Jeff felt beads of sweat drip down his forehead. He still hadn't found Lisa. He was sick in fear for himself and his fellow vampires. Although all he wanted to do was stay and look for Lisa, Jeff knew that he had to get back to the animal shelter. He didn't doubt Count Darkness' ability to lock him out. Jeff turned around and hurried back to the shelter.

"Jeff, Jeff!"

Jeff turned around when he heard someone calling his name. "Lisa?" he cried in surprise. "I was looking for you. We have to talk!"

"No, I have to talk and you have to listen," Lisa began. "I am so sorry but all the vampires have been killed." Jeff gasped in shock. "I poured garlic in front of the vent's fan and turned it on. The smell killed them instantly." Jeff began to back away from Lisa. "Don't run," she begged, when seeing his discomfort. "I saw you leave. I wouldn't have hurt you Jeff. I...I really care about you," she confessed. Lisa saw Jeff's face relax and almost form a smile. "You can't go back to the animal shelter. Come home with me. I can hide you for the day- just until you can return home."

"Alright," was all Jeff said.

As they began to walk to Lisa's house, Lisa handed Jeff a container filled with blood. "I found this," she confused. "I thought you might be hungry." Jeff gratefully took the blood and drank it in a fury. Still grossed out by the fact that her friend was a vampire, Lisa looked the other way.

\* \* \*

When the sun had set the following night, Lisa prepared to say her goodbye to Jeff. Jeff emerged from the closet in Lisa's room where he had been hiding during the day.

"I guess you'll be heading home now," Lisa said unhappily.

Jeff nodded. He was still upset at Lisa for killing his friends. He knew that he would miss the vampire that had fed him for the last few days.

"Don't be mad at me," Lisa pleaded. "You would have done the same thing if you were in my shoes."

Jeff stood quietly for a minute, thinking about what Lisa had just said. "I suppose you're right," he confessed. "After all, you did spare me."

"Of course I spared you," Lisa said, moving closer to Jeff. She was not afraid of Jeff at all anymore. The fact that he didn't have fangs yet also helped ease Lisa's mind.

67

Jeff moved closer to Lisa. "I would have spared you also," he confessed. He reached out to Lisa and pulled her closer. He brought his face close to Lisa's.

"Wait!" Lisa suddenly cried out loud.

"What's wrong?" Jeff asked in surprise.

"The prisoners! They are still locked up. I left them like that because I needed to find you. I was also afraid that they would turn into vampires." Jeff just laughed. "What is so funny?" Lisa demanded. "We have a really big problem here!"

"No we don't," Jeff reassured her. "They were exposed to garlic within the first three weeks of being bitten. The transformation has not started yet. In fact, it has been stopped completely because of the garlic. They are normal human beings again." Jeff sighed. "I just wish I had known about the garlic antidote. After I was bitten, I ran away. Count Darkness found me two months later. But by that time it was already too late." Jeff shook his head as if trying to erase the thought. "Well, no point in worrying about the past. Where were we?" Jeff asked, coming closer to Lisa again.

Lisa smiled just before Jeff's soft lips touched hers. "I really like you," Jeff said smiling.

"I really like you too," Lisa began to say. However, she never had a chance to finish her sentence as she saw Jeff hunch over in pain then shrivel until he was nothing but dust. "Oh my gosh!" Lisa cried in cold realization. "How could I forget about having garlic-bread for dinner?"

* * *

# A Weird Twist of Fate

# A Weird Twist of Fate

Knock, knock, knock.

"I'm getting dressed," nineteen-year-old Judith called to the person who was knocking upon her bedroom door.

"Alright, Miss Forge," Judith's housekeeper, Marion, said from behind the door. "Please hurry. The guests have started to arrive and your mother and father would like you to come to the dinning room immediately."

"I'll be there in a minute," Judith said through a sigh. Judith hated the fancy dinner parties that her parents always dragged her too. For the first time since Judith was just a small girl, Mr. and Mrs. Forge were hosting a fancy dinner party at their house. Throughout the years Judith's parents had spent endless hours telling her that she must dress and behave properly at dinner parties. Although Judith hated every minute of it, she always acted like the proper young lady that her parents wanted her to be. Unfortunately, that was not the person Judith wanted to be. Judith was gothic and that choice of lifestyle clashed with her parents. Mr. and Mrs. Forge had old-fashioned values, were very posh, and thrived at formal occasions. Even though Judith wanted to wear her black dress to dinner parties and decorate her face with black makeup, she had always worn the light pink dress that her mother insisted on.

Judith's heart raced as she looked into the full length mirror and saw a witch staring back at her. Judith looked the epitome of a witch as she stared at her reflection in the mirror. She was wearing a tight fitting long black dress that had red lace around the waist. The ensemble was completed with the black lipstick, eye shadow, and heavy eyeliner that covered her pale face. Her long straight black hair fell over her shoulders as she turned away from the mirror and headed out of her bedroom. She was anxious to get her big entrance over with. Judith knew that her parent's would not be impressed whatsoever. In fact, they would probably ground her for life. Normally Judith would not violate her parent's wish for her to appear as a "normal" teenage girl. However, Judith could not hide who she really was anymore. She wanted her parents and their friends to see her as she really was. Judith wanted her parents to accept and respect the real young lady that she had become. Judith was sure that her parents would act according to her wishes when they saw how important it was to her.

Judith could hear adults talking and wine glasses being clinked as they greeted each other. Judith took a deep breath then entered the beautifully decorated dinning room. At first no one seemed to notice her. They were all too busy bragging to each other about how well their careers were going or how wonderful their children were. Judith began to have doubts about her debut when she saw her parents talking to Mr. and Mrs. Patterson. The Patterson's were highly respected in the community because of the extensive work that they did for charities. They also established the Helping Hands for Children charity that assisted children and their parents who were on welfare or were unemployed.

Judith was about to turn around, run back to her bedroom, and change into the traditional light pink dress, but her eyes met Mrs. Patterson's before she had the chance to run away. Judith watched in fear as Mrs. Patterson's eyes went wide in surprise.

"Who is that?" Judith heard Mrs. Patterson ask Mrs. Forge.

"I guess this wasn't such a good idea after all," Judith muttered as her mother turned around and stared at her daughter in shock. Judith tried to back away from her mother, who was marching forcefully towards her, but bumped into a wall instead.

Nothing was said as Mrs. Forge grabbed her daughter's arm tightly and led her into the next room. Mrs. Forge closed the door between the two rooms before she began to yell. "Judith Hyacinth Forge!" Her mother exclaimed. "What do you think you're doing?"

"I...I just wanted to show everyone my true colors," Judith stuttered.

"Black is not a color, it's a tint," Mrs. Forge seethed. "How dare you show up to my party like this. You know the rules but you deliberately disobeyed them. I don't know what else to say except that you've disappointed your father and I deeply. I don't even want to think about the opinion Mr. and Mrs. Patterson must have of our family now."

Judith felt her blood boil in anger. "Don't you care about how I think and feel? I'm sick of having to go to all these fancy dinner parties while pretending to be someone that I'm not." Judith blinked furiously as she tried to keep her emotions under control. "Look at me, mother," Judith said sadly. "This is who I truly am."

Mrs. Forge remained silent while bearing a face that lacked emotion. Then suddenly her face tightened in anger. "Go to your room and stay there for the rest of the night. I cannot bear to look at you for a second longer while you are wearing that silly Halloween costume." Sadness swept over Judith's entire body as Mrs. Forge exited the room, shutting Judith out in the process. She did not try to hide the tears that poured from her eyes as she pressed her ear against the door and listened to her mother's and Mrs. Patterson's conversation.

"That wasn't Judith, was it?" Judith heard Mrs. Patterson ask in surprise.

"Yes it was," Mrs. Forge said with fake enthusiasm. "Judith is playing a witch in the community play. Our Judith is really interested in drama. She wanted to give all our guests a preview, but I told her that she simply could not. I wouldn't want the play's coordinator to be upset about their finest talent exhibiting her gift before opening night."

Judith's mouth dropped open. I can't believe that my own mother is denying the true me, Judith thought hysterically.

"Drama? Oh, you must be so proud of Judith," Mrs. Patterson said in relief.

"I am," Mrs. Forge replied with false pride.

Judith could not stand to hear any more lies. Hot tears saturated her face as she ran to her bedroom and flung herself onto her bed.

\* \* \*

The warmth from the sun that shone through the window woke Judith up the following morning. She sat up slowly, wondering why her eyes felt so funny. Judith got the answer to her question when she looked down and saw that she was wearing a tight black dress. She sighed heavily as the events of last night returned to her mind. Judith got up from her bed and stretched. She realized that she had fallen asleep crying and had not changed into her pajamas nor had she brushed her teeth. However, Judith knew that she had more important things to worry about. A gentle knocking upon the door startled Judith out of her thoughts. I hope that's mother, bearing an apology, Judith thought.

"Come in," Judith called out loud. Her heart sank as Marion walked into her room. I should have known better than to expect an apology from my mother, Judith scolded herself. I bet she wants an apology from me. Well, that's certainly not going to happen. I have a right to be who I want to be.

"Are you feeling alright?" Marion asked in concern.

"I suppose so," Judith replied, not knowing what else to say.

"Aren't you going to get washed?" Marion asked, while looking at the black smudged makeup that covered Judith's face as well as her white pillow, which she had slept on.

"I just woke up," Judith explained.

Marion nodded in understanding. "Breakfast was served quite some time ago, but I can make something for you to eat," Marion offered.

Judith shook her head. "It's alright. I think I'll go over to Samantha's house then grab something to eat at a coffee shop." Judith stopped talking when she saw Marion shifting uncomfortably. "What is it?" Judith asked, knowing that her mother most likely caused the housekeeper's discomfort. Judith always hated how demanding her mother was to Marion and the other previous live-in housekeepers. She thinks she is so much better than everyone else just because she has money, Judith thought scornfully about her mother.

"Mrs. Forge said that she wanted you to clean out the attic and compile any items that can be given to the Helping Hands for Children charity," Marion explained.

Judith could not believe her ears. Judith knew that her mother was only making her do this to save face with the Patterson's.

"And once you're done," Marion continued with a red face, "your mother would like you to drop the items off at Mr. and Mrs. Patterson's house personally."

"I wonder why," Judith asked rhetorically as she seethed out loud.

* * *

After a purposely prolonged breakfast, Judith trudged towards the attic. She did not want to think about all the dust that would cling to her black top and jeans once she was inside the attic.

Judith had lived in the same four story house her whole life. The house had been in the family for generations. Judith knew the story of how her great, times thirteen, grandfather had built the house with his bare hands very well because of her parents continuous bragging about it. Judith's distant ancestors had cleared the once heavily forested area and had used the trees they had cut down to build the house. At first, it was just a small one-story house, but over the years many additions were made to it, thus making it into the magnificent house that it is today. As her parents had reminded her countless times, the house was valued at over one million dollars.

73

Judith entered the storage room where the door to the attic was located. She slowly maneuvered herself through the piles of antique furniture and odds and ends that were no longer being used. Judith pulled on a thick brown rope to release the stairs that led to the attic. Slowly and carefully, Judith made her way up the rickety old stairs. A smile played upon Judith's lips as she thought how bad her mother would feel if anything happened to her while she was cleaning out the attic.

As Judith proceeded to climb the stairs she was met with the complete darkness of the attic. She felt an inch of dust as her hands clutched to the attic's floor. She moaned in disgust as she stepped into the attic. The air was so hot and dense that she could not breathe. Every time she moved her feet, more dust would fly up into the air. Judith reached for the small flashlight, which she had put into her pocket, and then shone the beam in front of her. She let out a small gasp as she realized that she was not alone in the attic.

Three tall women were standing at the other end of the attic. "What are you doing up here?" Judith yelled, trying to frighten the intruders away. Her heart raced as she waited for a reply. "How did you get up here?" Judith demanded, when she received no reply for her first question. The three women stood still and refused to talk. Judith swallowed hard as she approached the women. She clutched her flashlight then shone it on a woman's face. Judith screamed in horror when she saw that the lady had no face.

Judith turned around and ran as fast as she could. She knew that she had to get out of the attic and get help. Who will ever believe that there are three faceless women in our attic? Judith thought in a panic as she ran down the stairs that led to the storage room. Judith fled from the storage room and ran to get Marion. As Judith searched the house for Marion, her heart began to slow down. She began to think clearer and more logically. She also began to remember that her great, times nine, grandmother was a dressmaker who used mannequins to display the dresses that she made. Images of herself and her mother playing with the mannequins filled her head. Judith laughed at herself for being so frightened by some oversized dolls.

When Judith had gone back into the attic she made a beeline for the mannequins. She shone the flashlight on the doll's faces then laughed with relief as she squeezed the lifeless, cold arm. Judith smiled

74

to herself as she began to clean out the boxes that were filled with old clothing; she loved it when she got a good fright.

* * *

Judith went back up to the attic the next day. Although she had spent the whole day of yesterday cleaning and sorting through the items in the attic, there was still a lot more work to be done. Judith would not admit it to her parents, but she was actually having fun looking through all the old clothing that belonged to her ancestors. Of course, she didn't have the chance to talk to her parents since the incident two nights ago. Both of her parents seemed to be avoiding her. Judith sighed, realizing that it was more peaceful to stay away from her parents than to start a feud. She was very upset that her parents would not listen to her opinion.

Judith tried to push the unhappy thoughts from her head as she made her way to the back of the attic. She carefully lifted an old dusty cloth from the top of an object. Judith's eyes went wide when she saw an old-fashioned wooden trunk underneath the cloth. The wooden trunk was made from a very dark wood. Upon closer investigation, Judith realized that the trunk was once painted black.

Unable to suppress her curiosity any longer, she pried her fingers under the lid of the trunk. Judith groaned under the heavy weight of the trunk's lid, but the required effort was well worth it when she saw what was inside. Tucked neatly away was a pile of black dresses. Judith gently unfolded a dress and studied it carefully. The dress was a faded color of black and had sharp cut fringes at the edge of the long sleeved arms. Lace that resembled a spider's web ran along the low neck line. Judith ran her fingers over the cold fabric while wondering who had owned such a beautiful gothic dress.

Judith put the dress aside and began searching through the rest of the trunk. She looked in awe as she unfolded one beautiful black dress after another. When Judith picked up the last black dress and unfolded it, she heard a loud thud on the floor beside her. Then she began to cough furiously.

Judith felt her eyes itch and her throat burn. Her mouth was dry and itchy. Judith waved one hand in front of her face, while she covered her mouth with the other hand. Whatever fell from the dress disturbed the dust, Judith thought as she continued to cough. The dust began to settle as Judith opened her eyes to see a black leather book lying at her feet. Judith let out a few more coughs as she bent down to pick up the

75

book. Just like everything else in the attic, the leather-covered book was very cold to touch. Judith opened the book then began to read out loud. "This journal is the property of Miss. Judith Hyacinth Forge." She stopped reading as her blood went ice cold. Judith never knew that she was named after one of her ancestors. She swallowed hard as she thought about the likelihood of finding a journal that belonged to someone with the exact same name as you. Judith knew that the chances were slim to none. In curiosity, fear, and excitement, Judith turned the next page.

"June 28th, 1605. I received this journal as a birthday present from my dear older sister, Iris. I am so excited about turning nineteen today because it signifies the path to adulthood that I am about to take. The most exciting thing about being an adult is being able to be who I really am. I want to show the world the real me. Iris and I are very much alike, but she is afraid to admit who she really is. She is the sensible one and has spent endless hours lecturing me on why we must keep our true identity a secret. Iris believes that if we tell mother and father, as well as their friends, that we are witches they will disown and perhaps kill us. But I don't believe that. I know that my mother and father will accept me as I am."

Judith stopped reading and tried to process what she had just learned. She remembered seeing the name Iris Forge on the family tree diagram that hung in her father's study, but there were no records of a Judith Hyacinth Forge, other than herself of course. Judith realized that Iris Forge was her great, times nine, grandmother who was the dressmaker who used the mannequins.

A shiver went down Judith's spine as she realized that Iris never had a sister. Hoping that the answers would be written in the journal, Judith began to read aloud again.

"As a birthday present to myself I made a beautiful dress out of black fabric. Oh, the bother I endured to obtain fabric in the color of black. Such fabric is considered satanic. I strongly disagree. Although I practice magic and consider myself a witch, I certainly do not participate in any evil deeds. I use my magic for good and perhaps some lighthearted humor. I wish people could see that witches are not bad people. Let me correct myself; people *will* see that witches are not bad people. And I will be the one to prove it!"

Judith closed the journal shut. Her head was racing with so many thoughts that she needed a minute to gather them all into logical sentences. She wondered what had happened to exclude Judith from the family tree diagram. She also wondered if the connection between her and her ancestor's name was just a coincidence. What Judith wondered the most, however, was how her ancestors had become witches in the first place. Judith had always been interested in fictional witches, but she never believed in them. Taking a deep breath, Judith opened up the journal and began to read. She had a strong feeling that at least one of her questions would be answered in the journal.

"June 29$^{th}$, 1605. I'm going to do it, journal. I'm going to use my magic powers in front of my mother and father, and all their guests, at the dinner party that my parents are hosting. And I'm not going to tell my sensible sister about my plan because I know that she would never allow me to do such a thing. I am going to wear the first black dress that I secretly made with my sister. I know that I have other black dresses to choose from and that my first black dress is old and tattered, but that does not matter. That dress symbolizes my beginning path to witchery. It was the first real thing that I was proud of. Tonight is the night that I, Judith Hyacinth Forge, will forever change prejudice against witches."

Judith stopped reading as she turned the page and saw that it was blank. She flipped through the rest of the pages and sighed heavily when she realized that they too were blank. "I'll never know for sure why her family rejected her, but I can take a guess. I bet Judith went ahead with her plan and used her magic in front of her parents and guests. They must have been so shocked and horrified that they disowned her. It's almost like what happened to me the other night. Ancestor Judith and I both wanted to show everyone our true selves, but they shunned us; I guess grandmother Judith's parents went a bit further than mine did," Judith sighed in realization.

Judith folded the black dresses and put them back in the trunk. She wrapped the journal in one of the dresses and placed the two items in the trunk also. Judith wanted to keep the journal safe. She was sure that no one else had seen it. Judith was sad, however, that she would never find out what had happened in the end.

\* \* \*

It took three full days of work to clean the attic and box the items that would be given to the charity. Judith kept the trunk that contained the journal and the dresses well hidden at the back of the attic. She planned to try a dress on one day. With Marion's help, Judith was able to get the boxes to the Patterson's. Mr. Patterson had been delighted to see such a donation. Judith's face went red when he commented on the big heart that she must have to donate so many items. However, her face went even redder when he wished her luck on the community play in which she was starring.

After her trip to the Patterson's Judith felt so tired and embarrassed that she collapsed on her bed. Judith had been resting for half an hour when her telephone rang. "Hello?" she answered.

"Hey Judith! How are you doing?" Judith did not need to ask who was calling. It was Samantha, her only friend at school. She was also the only other gothic person at Judith's school. But unlike Judith, Samantha was much more open about her beliefs.

"Hi Samantha! I haven't talked to you since the last day of school. I am okay, I guess. How are you?"

"I'm okay, I guess," Samantha said, unintentionally repeating Judith. Judith smiled. She knew that Samantha and herself were very much alike. "My mom took my book of spells away from me when I threatened to turn my brother into a toad," Samantha continued. "So, you can imagine how bored I am. Do you want to hang out or something?"

"Sure, I can be over in twenty minutes," Judith answered.

"Um, actually," Samantha stuttered, "I don't think that is such a good idea. My mom is pretty mad at me. She says that she wants me out of the house for a few hours. Is it okay if I come over to your place? That way we can practice the spells in your magic book."

"I guess so," Judith replied uncertainly. Judith knew that her parents did not like Samantha very much. They believed that Samantha had influenced Judith to become gothic.

"Great! I'll see you in twenty minutes, okay?"

After Judith had got off the telephone to her friend, she waited outside for her to arrive. Twenty minutes later, Judith saw a girl, who was wearing a black lace top, a short black skirt and red fishnet tights, coming down the street.

"Hi Samantha!" Judith called out to her friend. Samantha waved back to Judith then stopped walking to let a car pull up Judith's driveway. Judith felt her heart sink as she saw her mother come out of the car with a disgusted look on her face.

"Hello, Mrs. Forge," Samantha greeted pleasantly.

"Samantha," Mrs. Forge greeted with an unfriendly smile. "That's quite an outfit you're wearing."

"Thank you," Samantha replied, not really sure if Mrs. Forge's comment should be taken as a compliment or an insult.

"Would you mind answering one question for me?" Mrs. Forge suddenly asked Samantha.

"What is it?" Samantha asked in confusion.

"What do your parents think about your eccentric clothing?"

"Mother!" Judith yelled loudly in shock.

"It's okay. I actually get asked that question a lot," Samantha said, trying to hide her embarrassment. "My parents don't really like my choice of clothing but have accepted it and have accepted me."

"Your parents must be very understanding. I know that I could never accept a child that dressed in such a foolish manner."

Judith felt hot tears sting her eyes.

"I...I think I better go home," Samantha said awkwardly.

"Yes, I think that would be a good idea," Mrs. Forge replied.

Judith watched in shock as Samantha walked quickly away. "I can't believe how you just insulted Samantha!" Judith cried.

"I did not insult her," Mrs. Forge said, while flinging her hands in the air as if to dismiss the thought. "In fact, I might have smartened her up."

"She doesn't need smartened up. She's the smartest girl in my math, science, and history class!" Judith cried.

"Don't make such a fuss," Mrs. Forge scolded her daughter. "I did you a favor by getting rid of that weird girl. You need to make friends with proper young ladies. I can introduce you to..."

"I don't care about you and your ideal of the prefect young lady. I'm just like Samantha. When you insulted her you insulted me also. Why do you have to judge those who don't mimic your beliefs?" With that said, Judith raced into the house and up to the attic.

Judith did not know why, but as soon as she had entered the attic she ran to the trunk and pulled out the black dress. She hurried to place the dress over her head and pull it down over her body. Judith instantly felt better when she thought about her ancestor Judith. She felt as if her ancestor was on her side. Judith knew that her ancestor had gone through the same problems with her parents as she had. She was positive that ancestor Judith had felt the exact same way she did.

Judith looked at the black dress which she was wearing and smiled with pride. She felt an overwhelming connection with ancestor Judith. Judith stared at the black dress as she twirled around. She felt hypnotized by the deep black color and the smooth surface of the fabric. Suddenly Judith's surroundings started to spin. They spun so fast that everything became a blur. "What is happening?" Judith cried out, just before everything went black.

Judith's head throbbed in pain as she began to open her eyes. It took a few minutes, but her head stopped throbbing and she eventually regained her vision. "What am I doing on the floor?" Judith asked out loud, as she realized that she was lying on the attic's floor. As Judith got to her feet she realized that the attic looked different. The three mannequins were dressed in lavish flower print dresses. Tools, which a dressmaker would use, were sprawled out on the floor as if someone had recently been working on them. Judith also noticed that there were old-fashioned looking trunks all around the attic. She shivered as she realized that the attic had definitely changed. Judith backed up towards the attic's exit then began to run.

As Judith ran out of the storage room and throughout the other rooms, her heart raced. All the rooms were different. She knew that she was in the right house; she just did not know why it had changed. "I have to see my room," Judith said out loud suddenly. She was not sure why, but Judith knew that she had to get to her room.

She was about to burst into her room but stopped short when she heard voices coming from inside the room. Judith quietly approached the room and peered through the crack of the slightly opened door. She almost screamed when she saw herself talking to someone.

"Judith, we have to keep this a secret," the person talking to the Judith look-a-like said.

"How can we possible keep such an incredible discovery a secret, Iris?" the Judith look-a-like replied. "We have just invented a spell that works!"

"I realize that," Iris sighed. "But do you realize what that makes us?"

"We are powerful witches that can successfully cast any spell that we wish," the Judith look-a-like cried enthusiastically. "Shhh..." Iris warned. "No one can find out that we're witches. They would kill us if they knew."

Judith let out a small gasp as she turned away from the door. Somehow, she had traveled back in time to when her great, times nine, grandmother was a teenager. Beats of sweat began to form on Judith's hairline. She felt her throat tighten and she found it difficult to breath. Her whole body tingled in fear. All Judith could think about was getting home to the year 2005.

Judith had just turned her back away from her bedroom when a hand grabbed her from behind. She was about to let out a scream when the same hand clasped over her mouth. Judith felt the person turn her around. Judith's eyes went wide as she came face to face with her grandmother Iris. Judith looked closely at Iris' face in wonderment. With bulging eyes, Judith watched Iris as she signaled for Judith to be quiet and to follow her. Judith did as she was told and followed her into a room that was used as a guestroom in the year 2005.

"I've been waiting for you to arrive," Iris said, before bolting the door shut. Judith gulped as Iris walked towards her with arms wide open. She's going to strangle me, Judith thought in horror. But to her surprise, Iris embraced her in a hug. "My dear sister," Iris muttered in Judith's ear.

"I'm not your sister. I am your very distant granddaughter. I know that I look like your sister, but I'm not."

"You are my sister," Iris forcefully replied. "You are my sister four hundred years from now."

"That can't be," Judith said in shock.

"Sit down," Iris instructed. "There are a lot of things that I need to tell you." Judith sat on Iris' bed and waited to hear the most incredible story of her life. "When my sister and I were taking a walk in the forest one day, we found a man in dire need of help. His leg was caught in a metal trap that had been set to catch foxes. My sister and I helped him out of the trap and back to his house in the woods. We came back every day to make sure that he was okay; we nursed him back to health. When we went for our usual visit to his house one day, he presented us with a gift. The gift was knowledge of witchery. He taught us basic magic skills, but he also taught us how to think for ourselves and how to

81

prepare our own spells. Soon my sister and I had become independent witches with powerful magic. My sister, Judith, wanted to tell everyone about her powers, but I knew better. I begged her not to tell anyone, but she did it anyway. Her foolishness killed her. She was killed by our neighbors. The same people who killed my sister planned to come after me because they thought, rightly enough, that I was a witch also. Before they could catch me I cast my most powerful spell ever. I cast a spell that made Judith not my sister but born four hundred years later. That way my sister never existed until hundreds of years later, so she could not be killed for being a witch. It also saved me from being killed. However, the spell did not work perfectly. I was consumed with magical guilt that plagued me day and night. The man in the forest cast the guilt spell upon me because I broke a cardinal rule of witchery. Luckily for me, the man in the forest had his spell cast back onto himself. He suffered from magical guilt for casting a mean spell on someone who had saved his life. To call a truce and stop the haywire crossing of spells, the man agreed to cast one final spell that would allow you, the future Judith, to come back and stop the original Judith from telling anyone that she is a witch. That way I would have never cast the spell in the first place."

Judith stared at Iris with her mouth wide open. "Are you serious?" she asked bluntly.

"I'm deadly serious," Iris replied with a stone cold expression on her face.

"How can the original Judith be here now if I am here also?"

"I haven't cast the spell yet," Iris explained.

"If you haven't cast the spell yet how can I be alive?"

"I'm sorry, but I can't answer those questions. You would have to understand the reasoning behind spells and the consequences of them to understand the events that are happening."

"Okay, okay," Judith said, throwing her hands up in the air. "I don't think I'm ready to understand magic so I'll just ask you what I should do to save ancestor Judith."

"By the rules of magic you are the only one who can save my sister by convincing her to keep quiet."

"But how do I get her to keep her mouth shut?"

"I can't answer that. You have to figure out a way by yourself."

Judith sighed. She had experienced so many weird things in the last hour that she no longer doubted anything. "I'm starting to hate magic," Judith commented out loud.

Judith only had four hours to figure out a plan that would stop ancestor Judith from revealing herself as a witch. Iris had hidden Judith in her bedroom and told her not to come out until she was ready to put her plan into action. Judith took a deep breath as she peered out from behind Iris' bedroom door then quietly walked down the hall to ancestor Judith's bedroom.

Judith took another deep breath as she tried to calm her racing heart. Then she ran into ancestor Judith's bedroom and yelled, "hold it right there!"

Judith blinked when she saw that no one was in the room. She had expected to see ancestor Judith. Judith walked over to her distant grandmother's desk when she saw the familiar black leather journal sitting there. She opened it up and began to read.

"June 29$^{th}$ 1605. I'm going to do it, journal. I'm going to use my magic powers in front of my mother and father, and all their guests, at the dinner party that my parents are hosting."

Judith closed the book with a thud. She did not need to read the rest; she remembered it all too well. Where is she? Judith questioned in a panic as she tiptoed to the door. She thought she heard people talking. Carefully, Judith slipped out from ancestor Judith's bedroom and crept towards the long staircase. Down below, Judith could see women dressed in maid outfits scurrying about and chattering in rushed urgency to each other. They must be getting the dinner party ready, Judith thought as she realized that she was running out of time. Judith hurried towards the attic as she realized that ancestor Judith was probably there, getting ready for the dinner party; getting ready to get herself killed.

Judith's heart began to race as she entered the storage room and saw that the stairs to the attic had been pulled down. Judith's hands clutched the thick brown rope that she had found in one of the closets in the house. As she climbed the stairs to the attic, she realized that they were not rickety like they were in the year 2005. Judith climbed in confidence until she spotted ancestor Judith trying on an old black dress.

As quietly as she could, Judith crept towards her. She tried to unravel the rope in her hands, but the rope fell to the floor with a light tap instead. Judith froze in terror as she watched ancestor Judith turn around and stare at her with wide eyes.

"Oh my..." ancestor Judith began to say, but Judith covered her mouth with her hands before ancestor Judith could finish her sentence. Judith hated herself for what she was about to do, but she knew that she had no other choice. She roughly pushed ancestor Judith towards one of the big trunks that littered the attic. Ancestor Judith crashed against the trunk with a sickening thud. Judith winced but continued to work fast. She quickly pulled out a long thin piece of black fabric that she had found in ancestor Judith's room then tied it around her mouth. Judith felt her heart ache as ancestor Judith moaned and weakly kicked her legs. Judith grabbed the rope that had fallen to the floor then tied it snugly around ancestor Judith and the trunk. When Judith was certain that ancestor Judith was tied securely, she ran from the attic and towards her bedroom. She knew that she did not have much time left.

"Judith dear, you look absolutely wonderful," the mother of ancestor Judith commented to her. Judith put on a fake smile.

"Thank you, mother," she said politely. Out of the corner of her eye, Judith saw Iris smiling gratefully at her. However, Judith thought she saw a tint of sadness in Iris' eyes.

After Judith had trapped ancestor Judith in the attic she had ran to her bedroom and changed into a pink and yellow flowery dress.

The dinner party seemed to last for hours. Despite all the unusual events that had happened to her today, Judith was bored out of her mind. She could have kissed the dark brown wooden floor when the guests began to leave.

"You may go to your room and get ready for bed," ancestor Judith's mother told her. Judith got up from the chesterfield upon which she was sitting and began to walk to her bedroom. "Oh, Judith," ancestor Judith's mother said. Judith turned around, afraid of what she might hear.

"Yes, mother?" she asked with a lump in her throat.

"Thank you for behaving so well tonight. You were certainly on your best behavior."

"Oh, it was no problem," Judith smiled. "No problem whatsoever."

"Thank you for all your help," Iris said to Judith, after they had entered the attic.

"I'm just glad that I could help save my great, times nine, grandmother. And I am sorry for having to constrain ancestor Judith like that," Judith said, casting her eyes in the direction of the tied up Judith.

"You did what you had to do to keep her from coming to the dinner party; that's all that matters."

Judith smile proudly, but the expression faded quickly as she thought about how she would get home. "How do I get home?" Judith voiced her concerns.

"I'll fix that," Iris said rather sadly. "I only need to cast one more spell." Judith watched in awe as Iris threw her arms widely in the air and began to chant. "Oh, man of the forest, the spell is complete. Undo the spells that were once incomplete. Make my actions, and yours likewise, never have happened and forever be disguised. Let there only be one Judith Hyacinth Forge; the one who existed in the year of 1605." Judith felt her stomach churn. She had a sickening feeling that she was about to get a bad deal from saving ancestor Judith. "Make it be," Iris said quietly as she lowered her arms sadly.

"No! Reverse the spell," Judith screamed, right before she disappeared forever.

* * *

85

# Werewolf Hunting

# Werewolf Hunting

"Welcome to Grizzly Bear Lodge. Do you have reservations?"

"I have reservations, but it sure isn't for this dump."

Bill McNeill, the owner of Grizzly Bear Lodge, glared at the two men who stood in front of his desk. Then he began to laugh. "It's good to see you both again," Bill commented to his best customers, Ethan and Mitchell Zimmerman. "How are you two doing?"

"We're doing just fine, Big Bear," Ethan replied.

Bill was often called Big Bear because he looked just like that. Bill stood tall at six foot two. He had thick curly dark brown hair and a heavy beard. "I hope that your rifles are loaded because the game is great around here. For some reason the deer have been getting closer and closer to the lodge. Of course, you can't fire your rifles unless you're three hundred feet away from the cabins," Bill reminded Ethan and Mitchell.

Bill owned one hundred and seventy five acres of land which he used as a deer hunting ground. He had also built big wooden cabins where his guests could stay overnight and for the off season.

"We most definitely do," Mitchell replied, as he handed Bill the registration cards for their rifles.

"Have a pleasant stay and come by tonight for a game of poker," Bill said as he handed Mitchell back the registration cards after he had checked them thoroughly.

"We'll stop by the main room in the lodge," Ethan promised. "However, we're going hunting first."

Bill waved goodbye to his customers as he watched them disappear through the opened wooden doors.

"It's so beautiful out here," Ethan commented as they walked in the woods. It was still early in the morning and the sun was just starting to rise. Dew covered the forest floor, making it very slippery to walk on. A soft breeze blew through the evergreen trees and chickadees chirped in the background.

"It's the perfect day for hunting," Mitchell commented.

"It sure is," Ethan replied.

"It's a lot nicer than being in the city," Mitchell began to say, but he was cut off as Ethan motioned for him to be quiet. They stood in silence for several minutes as Mitchell strained to hear what Ethan had heard. "What did you hear?" Mitchell whispered, no longer able to suppress his curiosity.

"I thought I heard a growl, but it's probably just the wind," Ethan answered.

"It probably was," Mitchell said, while giving his brother an unappreciative look. "Now can we please look for some real deer?"

Ethan and Mitchell walked deeper into the forest. The abundance of thick trees blocked out most of the sunlight, making it slightly difficult to see.

"There'll be a dozen deer in here," Ethan whispered quietly.

"That's great, but there's a problem," Mitchell whispered back.

"What's that?" Ethan inquired as he lifted his rifle higher as they turned a sharp corner in the woods.

"We won't be able to get a decent shot at the deer because it's so dark. Let's head back into the sunlight. At least we could see where we were going."

"Alright," Ethan agreed as he lowered his rifle. "Let's go back."

Ethan and Mitchell had just turned around when they heard rustling coming from behind a nearby bush. Mitchell looked at Ethan with wide eyes. Ethan put his index finger over his mouth, signaling for Mitchell to be quiet. Then he raised his rifle and crept towards the shaking bushes. Ethan's breath became shallow as he reached out to touch one of the shaking bushes. His finger tips had nearly touched the needles of the evergreen tree when a large animal jumped out from behind the bushes. Ethan did not even have a chance to scream for help as the animal tackled him to the ground. With its massive feet, the animal pinned Ethan by the shoulders then turned its head to bite his neck. Mitchell winced as he heard his brother moan in pain.

After biting Ethan, the animal raised its head to look straight at Mitchell. Their eyes met for an instant, and then Mitchell turned around and ran. Mitchell could hear the animal's heavy feet scraping the ground as it chased after him. It was not long until Mitchell could feel the animal's hot breath on his neck. Mitchell fell with his face to the ground as the animal pounced on him. Echoes of Mitchell's scream could be heard throughout the forest. Ethan and Mitchell never showed up to Bill's poker game that night.

* * *

Bill tossed and turned that night. No matter which way he turned, he felt a lump in his mattress. And no matter how many times he kicked his sheets off and then pulled them back on, he was always too hot or too cold. Bill sighed and opened his eyes. He had given up trying to sleep. Instead, he stared at the dark brown panels of lumber that held the ceiling together. He began counting the panels of lumber on the ceiling, hoping that it would be successful in putting him to sleep. Bill stopped counting as a large cloud blocked the light that was provided by the moon. Darkness overpowered the light which had been streaming through the window just moments ago. Bill sighed then turned around. He looked at the large window and watched shadows from nearby trees sway gently in the wind. Bill's eyes started to get heavy as they followed the movement of the trees. His left eye had just shut closed, and his right eye was just about to do the same, when he suddenly saw the shadow of something else other than a tree move outside the window. Bill sat straight up in his bed, now fully awake. He felt his blood go cold as he gazed out the window and saw a silhouette of a large animal.

Bill's hands shook fiercely as he slowly made his way out of bed. He walked backwards, keeping his eyes on the animal until he bumped against the door to the living room. Bill spun around and flung the door open. He ran to the fireplace and grabbed for the rifle that always hung above the mantel. Bill held the rifle high as he crept slowly back into his bedroom. He gasped out loud when he saw two red glowing eyes coming from behind the window. Bill's whole body shook and sweat formed around his forehead and beard. His throat made a loud sound as he gulped with a tight, dry throat.

They're like rubies, Bill thought as he stared into the glowing red eyes. Although his racing heart was telling him to hide, his eyes were telling him to proceed forward. Before he knew what he was doing, Bill was walking towards the window in a hypnotized state.

He had almost reached the window when the animal let out a horrifying howl. The howl was not one you'd expect to hear from an animal; it was a howl that was mixed with the blood curdling scream of a grown man.

Bill watched with a mixture of fear and amazement as the animal's silhouette lunged forward and scraped at the window. Bill yelled in pain as he heard long sharp nails slice through the window.

Acting in fear, Bill raised the rifle to his eyes and aimed it at the animal. His hands trembled as he pulled the trigger. He heard the bullet pierce through the window followed by the howl of the animal. Bill stepped closer to the window and saw the animal running into the woods. Bill let out a nervous sigh then fell back on his bed. He stayed in that position the whole night; sitting tensely with the rifle in his sweaty hands.

\* \* \*

When the sun rose the next morning, a puffy eyed Bill walked around the cabin to see his bedroom window. He looked at the scratched and bullet holed glass. Two sets of five claws had dug deep within the glass. As Bill's eyes drifted towards the ground he noticed massive wolf paw prints leading into the woods. He also noticed a small pool of blood that had dripped alongside the footprints. "I didn't hurt the wolf badly," Bill said out loud in realization. He took one last glance at the window and promised himself that he would replace the glass right after he had found and killed the wolf. "I can't let an insane wolf drive away my customers and kill all the deer," Bill kept repeating to himself as he followed the wolf tracks into the woods.

The wolf tracks sank deeper into the mud the further Bill followed them. He presumed that the wolf had calmed down and began to slow its pace. Bill also observed that the drippings of blood had stopped. With the rifle in a ready-for-anything pose, Bill continued to march alongside the wolf's footprints.

As Bill turned the corner he was faced with a very shady part of the woods. He gulped with a dry throat before entering the darkness. Bill's eyes adjusted to the change in light after a few minutes. He squinted at the ground, making sure that he was still following the wolf prints. He did not know if he was relieved or not when he saw the deep muddy wolf tracks.

The sudden noise of a chickadee's chirp made a tense Bill's head jerk up. In doing so, his eyes settled on some familiar pieces of clothing. Bill walked towards the clothing to get a closer look. Bill gasped as he saw two flannel shirts and two pairs of jeans lying on the ground. The flannel shirts looked as if they had popped open from the front; buttons from the shirts lay scattered near the clothing. The two pairs of jeans looked worse than the shirts. They looked as if they had been spilt open at the seams. Bill shivered as he realized that there were dots of blood all over the pieces of clothing. However, Bill shivered even harder as he realized that the shirts and jeans belonged to Ethan and Mitchell Zimmerman.

As Bill rubbed the edge of the flannel shirt in between his thumb and index finger, memories of the countless summers he had spent with the Zimmerman brother's filled his head. Suddenly, his fingers rubbed against something other than flannel. Bill looked closely at the fabric to see strands of long fur sticking to it. Bill had thought that the wolf had got Ethan and Mitchell when he had seen their ripped clothing, but now, with the new evidence staring him in the face, Bill had no doubt in his mind that the wolf had killed them.

Bill slowly blinked in an attempt to force back the tears that were threatening to spill down his face any minute now. He did not understand why Ethan and Mitchell's clothing was torn so neatly. He also could not fathom when the attack had taken place. He knew that Ethan and Mitchell never went hunting at night. "It must have happened early yesterday morning," Bill realized out loud. "But what kind of wolf hunts during the day?"

Bill's whole body tightened as he heard a noise come from behind him. It sounded like a quieter version of the wolf howl and man's scream that he had heard last night. With his back still to the growling animal, Bill slowly lifted his rifle higher and placed his index finger in front of the trigger. Sweat drenched Bill's entire body as he swung around fiercely and fired at the animal. Bill's eyes went wide in horror as he saw a flash of dark grey fur leap over a bush and disappear into the darkness of the forest. He had never seen an animal move so quickly. "That thing isn't just a regular wolf," Bill said in cold realization.

\* \* \*

News about the Zimmerman brother's disappearance had spread quickly around the lodge. Bill numbly handed back refund after refund to guests who were leaving early. Bill had a generous money back offer to unsatisfied guests; however, he never had to refund anybody's money until now.

Bill had notified the police, who had taken the torn clothing as evidence and had searched the area. However, the police had not found any dead bodies. They had abandoned the search saying that there was nothing more to search for. They did, however, promise to investigate the Zimmerman's house. This did not make Bill feel any better. It just made him believe even more that the wolf and the Zimmerman's disappearance involved eerie, perhaps even unexplainable, forces.

"Hello Bill," a friendly voice greeted, just after a frightened customer had hurried away from the front desk with his refund.

"Um, Ms. Clark," Bill stuttered, upon seeing his guest.

"Call me Manny; you always did before," she laughed. The smile on her face faded as she looked at Bill's face. "Are you keeping alright?" she asked in concern.

"I...I'm fine," he mumbled. Four nights of poor sleeping had taken its toll on Bill. For the last three nights, Bill had tensely laid in his bed as he listened to human-like howls. He would shut his eyes and pray for the sound to stop. He was too afraid to even look out of his window. Bill felt a dull ache throughout his entire body. It must be from all the stress, Bill reasoned to himself.

"You really don't look fine," Manny pressed. "Would you like to sit down?"

Bill just shook his head. "Can I see your rifle registration please?" he asked in a slurred tone. Manny held the card out to Bill, who fumbled with it, then dropped it.

"Bill, what is wrong?" Manny demanded with a stone cold face.

"Nothing!" Bill yelled as he clumsily picked up the rifle registration card and handed it back to Manny without looking at it. "Cabin sixteen," Bill grunted as he flung the room key at Manny. As he watched Manny walk towards her room, Bill heard that familiar howl, which was mixed with a human scream, in the distance.

"Mr. McNeill, you have to help me," a short blacked haired man cried as he came running through the main lodge doors.

"Help you with what, Mr. Anderson?" Bill asked with a heavy heart.

"It's my hunting partner, Taylor," Mr. Anderson said in a panic. "We were stalking deer in the woods when I had to go to the bathroom. I left Taylor alone for just a few minutes but when I got back he was gone. I called his name and searched around the woods for an hour but I couldn't find him. It's like he just disappeared. Oh, Mr. McNeill, you have to help me find my friend."

"I'm coming right now," Bill said as he headed to his house to get his rifle. I can't believe that this is happening again, Bill thought in horror.

Bill met Mr. Anderson in front of the main lodge. Mr. Anderson had gathered three other people, including Manny, to help with the search and rescue mission.

"We'll find Taylor," Manny reassured Mr. Anderson as they set out towards the woods.

"This is where I left Taylor," Mr. Anderson informed the group as they turned a corner and stepped into a shaded section of the woods. The group spilt up and began to examine every inch of the area.

"I think I see something," Manny commented suddenly. Everyone stopped their search and watched Manny as she walked over to a dark green bush and reached for the item. She pulled out a torn shirt and pair of torn pants.

"Those are Taylor's!" Mr. Anderson cried as he grabbed the ruined clothing from Manny's hands.

"This is where I found the Zimmerman's torn clothing," Bill said quietly.

Mr. Anderson looked up in fright. "What does this mean then?" Mr. Anderson yelled unexpectedly. "Are you trying to tell me that Taylor was attacked by the same animal that got the Zimmerman brothers? Are you telling me that Taylor is dead?" Mr. Anderson stepped closer to Bill, so that they were face to face. "What kind of place are you running?" Mr. Anderson asked as he glared at Bill then stepped back in disgust.

Manny and the two other men said nothing as they looked around frightened. "Let's just look for Taylor some more," Bill choked out as he began to move forward. He glanced backwards when he did not hear any footsteps behind him. "Aren't you coming?" he asked in confusion.

"I'm not going any deeper into these woods," one of the hunters said. "In fact, I'm getting out of here right now and heading home." The other man nodded in agreement. Even Manny looked down at the ground and nodded.

"There's nothing wrong with my woods!" Bill cried in frustration. "Go home if you want to, but I'm staying here and I'm going to search for Taylor, Ethan, and Mitchell, even if it takes all night."

"Come back to the lodge with us, Bill," Manny pleaded. "There's no point in all of us getting killed. We'll call the police and get them to handle it."

Bill shook his head sadly. "There's no point in calling the police. They couldn't find Ethan and Mitchell. I'm sure they wouldn't be able to find Taylor either. I know these woods better than anyone. I'm going to find all three of them. Are you with me or not?" Bill felt a wave of shock surge through his body as the others looked at the ground.

"I'm sorry, but it's just too dangerous," Manny muttered as she turned around and began to walk back towards the lodge with the others. Bill felt his heart fluttered with hope when Manny stopped walking and turned around. "Come back with us," she pleaded one last time. Bill shook his head. Manny's eyes clouded over before she hurried back to join the others. Bill watched the foursome walk away until they disappeared around the corner. Bill took a deep breath of air to calm himself down. Then he raised his rifle high in the air as he began his solo search for the three missing lodgers.

Although the sun had just started to set, darkness already surrounded the tired and hungry Bill. Bill had been searching for Taylor, Ethan, and Mitchell nonstop since he was left behind by Mr. Anderson, Manny, and the two other men. Bill was positive that he had searched the whole one hundred and seventy five acres that he owned. He was also positive that Taylor, Ethan, and Mitchell were no longer in his woods. He had found no other traces of them, other than the torn clothing. Bill felt like a failure and a coward as he headed back to the lodge.

Bill unintentionally kicked the small stones that were on the pathway as he walked quickly. When he felt a small stone bounce off the back of his heel for the first time, he disregarded it, thinking that he had accidentally kicked it up with his own heel. However, when he felt several other small stones hitting his heels, Bill began to run faster.

Small stones began to hit off the back of Bill's legs now. It felt like someone, or something, was throwing them at him. Bill increased his speed as he heard footsteps coming up fast behind him. The closer the footsteps seemed the higher up on Bill's body the small stones were being kicked up. Bill realized that a very large animal must be following him to disturb the path so much. When Bill felt small stones bounces off his lower back he stopped running, turned around and fired his rifle as quickly as possible. It took Bill a few seconds to realize that there was nothing behind him.

"What in the world?" Bill asked, regarding his situation. There was definitely something behind me, Bill thought as he ignored the stitch in his side and the weakness in his knees as he ran back to his house. When Bill arrived back at the lodge, he received a bigger fright than he had while in the woods; Mr. Anderson, Manny, and the two other men had never returned.

\* \* \*

"Do you realize that there are now seven people who have gone missing from your lodge?" the officer informed Bill over the telephone.

"Do I realize?" Bill stuttered in shock. "Of course I realize! I'm the one who reported the disappearances!"

"Calm down, Mr. McNeill. I just want you to realize that we have a serious problem on our hands. Clothing that belonged to Taylor Nielsen, Ethan Zimmerman and Mitchell Zimmerman has been found, but there is no evidence pertaining to the four latest missing people. Now, we believe that each and every one of them is still alive. My team of men have searched every inch of your surrounding property as well as any rivers or lakes. We have found nothing; that's a good sign."

"So where do we go from here?" Bill inquired.

"I am sorry to say that my commander has given me strict orders to close down the Grizzly Bear Lodge in twenty four hours if no further progress is made. Of course this order will be retracted if the wolf, which you claimed to have seen, is captured."

"And if I can't capture the wolf?"

"Then I'm afraid I would have to carry out my order and shut Grizzly Bear Lodge down indefinitely. If these people have been hurt, and it's not due to an animal, we will have to search for the person responsible."

Bill swallowed hard as he hung up the telephone. If he could not catch the wolf in twenty four hours his business would be shut down. Then the police would come in and look for the human killer. Bill knew that they would never find the human killer because he did not exist. Bill's seven guests were attacked by a wolf, not a person. Now all Bill had to do was catch the wolf and prove to the police that he was right.

\* \* \*

Grizzly Bear Lodge was almost completely deserted as Bill got ready to hunt for the animal that was more than just a wolf. With a fully loaded rifle and a pocket full of extra bullets, Bill jogged all the way to the section of the woods that was heavily shaded. Bill stopped dead in his tracks as his eyes fell upon a dark spot on the hard forest ground. When Bill had approached the mysterious spot and examined it closely, he realized that it was dried up blood.

Bill buried his head in his hands and began to sob. That blood stain had not been there before; therefore it must belong to one of the four latest victims. He felt his heart weaken in emotional pain as he thought about how out of control the situation was.

Suddenly Bill felt something drop on his head. His heart raced as he grabbed for the item that sat on his head and covered his face. He was not relieved to see that the fallen item was Mr. Anderson's torn shirt.

"Why is this happening?" Bill suddenly screamed fiercely as he threw the torn shirt on the ground. He looked up to see several more pairs of torn shirts and pants in the tree above. As Bill continued to stare up at the tree, he heard a familiar growl behind him. "Oh no," Bill said just above a whisper. He had left his rifle on the ground, next to the dried up blood puddle. Bill heard a loud crunch. It sounded as if something heavy had just stood upon his rifle and crushed it. I'm defenseless, Bill realized in terror as he turned around to meet his fate. Bill let out a scream as he came face to face with a horrifying looking wolf.

The wolf stood upright like a human. It was at least six foot tall and covered in dark grey fur. The fur was matted and stood up on its end in some places. The wolf's paws were massive; each paw had five razor sharp nails that were four inches long. Although all these features were terrifying, Bill found his eyes drawn to the wolf's face. The animal had a face that did not look as if it belonged to a wolf. It was very human like with a nose instead of a snout and human lips. However, the wolf's face was slightly covered in dark grey fur and housed two glowing red eyes.

Bill let out another scream when the wolf's eyes flashed a darker shade of red. It's half man, half wolf, he realized. It's a human-wolf. Bill turned around as fast as he could then he began to run.

Bill shot through the woods like a bullet. He heard the human-wolf a few feet behind him. When Bill had taken off so quickly, he had startled the human-wolf, which explained the reasonable gap between the two. However, Bill knew that the gap would not last for long. He had to protect himself and the best way to do this was through shelter.

97

I'll never make it back to the lodge, Bill reasoned. As a tall tree came into view, Bill got an idea. He made a beeline for the tree then jumped up to the lowest branch. He grunted and groaned as he pulled himself upwards. His stomach ached due to the strain, but he ignored the pain. Instead, he pushed himself harder. Bill's hands trembled as they reached for the branch closest to him. Although Bill was moving steadily up the tree, there were still two problems that he would soon have to deal with; the fact that the tree did not go on forever and that the human wolf was beginning to climb the tree.

Bill looked down in horror to see the human-wolf gaining on him fast. Bill panicked when he realized that he had reached the top of the tree. Bill was not thinking clearly as he inched his way to the end of the branch and stood up shakily. Then Bill jumped to the tree next to him. The sharp bark sliced his hands as he grabbed onto a thin branch. The branch swayed fiercely under Bill's weight. He grunted as he propelled himself forward and grabbed onto the tree's trunk with his legs. Bill clung onto the tree's trunk as he began to inch towards the thicker branches. Bill heard the human-wolf pounce from the other tree then he felt sharp claws dig into his left sneaker. Pain stabbed his foot, and then traveled through his body as the human-wolf hung onto Bill's foot.

"I can't hold on any longer," Bill cried out loud, as if he were talking to the human-wolf. Bill felt his arms being ripped from their sockets. His fingers burned as they rubbed against the harsh bark. Beads of sweat rolled down Bill's face as his fingers slipped from around the branch. Then he felt himself falling.

Six feet later, Bill landed with a hard thump on the ground. Pain shot through his entire body, but he was still alive. Bill's arms flung to his side to touch the ground, but instead of feeling the cold dirt, he felt a warm fuzzy animal. Bill almost passed out as he realized that he had landed on top of the human-wolf. Bill rolled off the human-wolf and stared at it in fear. He felt his heart slow down as he realized that the human-wolf was no longer breathing. The wolf's eyes were closed and its mouth was slightly opened. Bill cringed as he saw the dark red blood coming from the human-wolf's head and the stone that the human-wolf's head had hit. Bill fought back the urge to be sick. Instead, he ran through the woods until he was back at the lodge.

"I killed the wolf. Get your team of men over here right now," Bill yelled as soon as the police officer had answered the telephone.

* * *

"The human-wolf is this way," Bill yelled to the three police officers as he ran frantically ahead. Bill had not felt so relieved in days. He knew that the police officers would take the human-wolf body away and let Bill's business get back to normal. Maybe I'll even become famous for discovering a new species, Bill told himself excitedly. "It's just around the corner," Bill said to the police officers, his head turned backwards. "Here it is..." Bill voice trailed off as his eyes settled upon the empty ground. "It was here just an hour ago!" Bill cried. "I don't understand where it could have gone. I swear it was dead."

"I think the stress is becoming too much for you to handle. Let's get you home," one of the police officers said in concern.

"I'm fine, but that human-wolf won't be once I catch him again. And this time I'll kill him once and for all." Bill began to run deeper into the woods. He ignored the shouts of protests that came from the police officers as he tore quickly through the woods. Long thin branches covered Bill's pathway as if they were trying to reach out and grab him. The branches ripped Bill's clothing and his skin, but that did not stop him. Bill did not know where he was going; he only knew that he must find the human-wolf.

Bill did not have to look much longer when he heard that familiar growl from behind him. He grabbed for the nearest branch and tore it from the tree. Bill twirled around and thrust the pointy branch at the human-wolf. Terror shook Bill's body as he watched the human-wolf grab for the branch and break it in half. Bill tried to attack the human-wolf with the remaining stub of a branch that he held in his hand, but the human-wolf easily tore that in two as well. Bill tried not to look into the human-wolf's red glowing eyes as he slowly backed away. He jumped when he felt something hit his back. It took him only a few seconds to realize that he had backed himself into a tree.

"Oh no," Bill muttered quietly as the human-wolf lunged towards him. Knowing that he had nowhere to run, Bill closed his eyes and waited to die.

Bill's eyes flung open when he realized that he was still alive a moment later. The human-wolf's face was just inches away from Bill's; its red eyes glowed more fiercely than he had ever seen before.

"Come with me," it spoke in a harsh voice. Bill clutched tightly onto the tree, afraid that he would faint and fall to the ground. "Come with me," the human-wolf growled more fiercely.

Bill just stood and stared at the animal in shock, but quickly moved when the human-wolf snapped its jaws close to Bill's face. The burst of sour air that had come from the human-wolf's mouth still stung Bill's face as he walked behind the animal. Every so often the human-wolf would look behind itself just to make sure that Bill was still there. Bill was surprised that the human-wolf had not constrained him, but he was even more surprised that it had not killed him.

The human-wolf stopped walking when it came to a thick bush. "Follow me closely," the human-wolf instructed in the same harsh tone.

Bill did as he was told and got down on his hands and knees and crawled through the bush. Sharp pine needles and twigs ripped at Bill's already torn shirt and skin. He let out a sigh of relief as he entered into a dark cave. He watched in amazement as the human-wolf thrashed one of his long sharp nails against a stone. Sparks flew up as the human-wolf ignited a stick. Flames quickly bounced around the top of the stick.

"I never knew there was a cave in my woods," Bill said out loud as he looked around the cave in awe.

"Your woods?" the human-wolf hissed.

"Um, I never knew there was a cave here," Bill corrected himself, trying to keep the human-wolf happy. The human-wolf grunted, but Bill thought he heard a tint of laughter in the grunt. "I thought you were dead." As soon as the words had left Bill's mouth he regretted it.

"Nothing can kill me but a silver bullet; I'm a werewolf."

Bill did not doubt it. After seeing what he had already, he was prepared to believe anything. "How come I have never seen you until just recently?" Bill inquired.

"I would never show myself to a human unless it was absolutely necessary," the werewolf replied.

"Was it necessary to kill my friends?" Bill cried, unable to control his emotions and the urge to know.

The werewolf stopped walking and turned around to face Bill. Bill shuddered as he saw the anger in the werewolf's eyes. "I did not kill anyone," the werewolf insisted. "I will show you your friends."

"They're here? They're alive?"

The werewolf nodded and motioned for Bill to turn to the left. After taking the sharp turn to the left, Bill entered a brightly lit section of the cave. It took a few moments for his eyes to adjust, but soon they were filled with visions of seven werewolves. "No!" Bill choked out. The seven werewolves looked very familiar. He recognized them as Ethan and Mitchell Zimmerman, Taylor, Mr. Anderson, Manny, and the two men who had helped search for Taylor. "You didn't kill them but you did turn them into werewolves," Bill cried.

The werewolf let out an angry growl then leaped towards Bill. Bill tried to run but he tripped over a small stone. He looked on in horror as the werewolf lowered its face to his' and said, "I saved your friends. I brought them back to life." Bill stared at the werewolf in shock. He looked to his seven furry friends for help. They all nodded as if to say that the werewolf was telling the truth.

"Who killed them then?" Bill asked, still not sure if he could trust the werewolf.

"The deer," the werewolf said coldly.

"The deer?" Bill managed to choke out. "Why would the deer kill humans?"

"Why would humans kill deer?" the werewolf asked angrily.

"It's... It's a sport," Bill stuttered.

"Although I don't believe that the deer's actions are right, they are a lot nobler than yours," the werewolf commented. "They are taking revenge on those who have hurt and killed their ancestors."

"But how is that possible?"

"Animals are a lot smarter than humans realize," the werewolf warned. "There are hundred of species of animals that are rarely, or never, seen. I am one of them. My ancestors and I have lived in these woods for hundreds of years. When I saw the deer killing humans I tried to stop them, but they wouldn't listen to reason. I was out numbered by the deer and could only look on helplessly as they destroyed your friends. I knew that the only way your friends could live was if I bit them and turned them into werewolves. So when the deer left, I did just that. I am sorry that I had to do it, but at least I have new friends."

Bill looked at the seven new werewolves who cast a sad glance at him. "This was the only choice for us," a harsh voice that sounded like Manny's said. All the werewolves nodded in agreement.

"I came to your window that night to frighten you. When that didn't work I tore the clothing from your friends and placed it around the woods. I even tried frightening you by throwing small stones, but you still wouldn't go away. I must say that I was very unhappy about those people in uniforms that kept trampling through the woods. They were particularly hard to hide from."

"So, what now?" Bill asked in desperation. "Seven of my customers are werewolves, my lodge's reputation is ruined, and I have the police threatening to shut down my lodge to hold further investigations."

"I can't solve your problem with the police, but I think I can solve your killer deer problem..."

"How?" Bill jumped at the opportunity.

"Follow me," the werewolf instructed as he began to walk back the way that he had come. Bill hurried as he followed the werewolf out of the cave and back into the woods.

"Where are you going?" Bill asked in rising panic as he realized that they were heading to the clearing where deer were usually spotted.

The werewolf did not reply but increased his speed. Bill was running so hard just to keep up with the werewolf that he did not realize that it had stopped walking. Bill bumped into the werewolf's back and got a mouthful of fur in his mouth.

"Gross," he commented as he began wiping his mouth. Bill stopped worrying about the fur in his mouth when a large shadow fell upon him. Bill looked up slowly, and then gulped. Standing before him was a very angry looking deer. The deer, which Bill guessed was the alpha male, had dangerous looking antlers and a fierce gleam in his eyes.

"You have brought me a victim; I'm glad to see that you have joined our side," the deer said in a deep booming voice.

"I have brought him here so that you two could come to some sort of agreement. I know that you don't like killing humans and that you are only doing it to avenge the deaths of your ancestors and save your own hind. But there's a better way, a way that humans and animals can co-exist in peace and harmony."

Bill nodded furiously. "Yes, that sounds good. How can we accomplish that?"

"By drastically changing your behavior towards all animals, especially the deer," the werewolf told Bill. "Perhaps the deer will stop hunting humans, if humans stop hunting deer."

"The other deer and I could live by those standards," the deer said. "But you must stop all hunting in these woods and..." the deer added shyly, "you must put out salt licks for us every week."

Bill nodded. "I agree to those terms and promise to abide by them." Bill smiled as he shook the deer's hoof.

\* \* \*

Grizzly Bear Lodge was re-opened and ready for business three months after Bill had met the werewolf and alpha male deer. The lodge had been closed down for a month while the police searched the area. Of course, they had found nothing and had moved the search to the missing individual's hometown. After that, it had taken two months to redesign and advertise the new purpose for Grizzly Bear Lodge.

Bill smiled to himself as he read the promotional flyer for his lodge out loud. "Come to Grizzly Bear Lodge for the beautiful tranquility and scenery that is offered throughout the one hundred and seventy five acres of woods. At my lodge we celebrate the coexistence of animals and humans." Bill smiled even harder as he read his advertisement's tagline. "When you come to Grizzly Bear Lodge you never know what kind of animals you'll see!"

\* \* \*

# Home Grown Flowers

# Home Grown Flowers

"We've got quite an addition to our class," Mrs. Waybourne tried to say in a cheerful voice. However, sixteen year old Bridget Rye was positive that she heard confusion in her teacher's voice.

"It's weird that the school is putting all of them in our class. It's also weird that they are starting school so late." Lauren Weller, Bridget's best friend, said.

"This is Holly, Poppy, Jasmine, and Primrose Walker," Mrs. Waybourne introduced the sisters. "They have just transferred from...what school did you say you were from?"

"We didn't," Primrose, the smallest of the four sisters, said. Poppy, the tallest sister, shot Primrose a warning glance then smiled at Mrs. Waybourne.

"Where should we sit?" she asked, changing the topic.

"Um, we'll need more desks and chairs," Mrs. Waybourne stuttered, obviously surprised at Poppy's abruptness. "Bridget, Lauren, would you mind taking the Walkers to the janitors office? Tell him that we need four more desks and chairs."

"Yes Mrs. Waybourne," Lauren said as she obediently stood up. Bridget suppressed the urge to roll her eyes. Lauren was the most polite student in the class; she was always picked to do small chores for teachers because of this personality trait. Since Lauren and Bridget were always together, Bridget was called upon when the chore required two people. Bridget stood up with less enthusiasm than Lauren and walked towards the door. She stopped and turned around when she heard the class burst into laughter. Bridget felt her face flush with embarrassment. Are they laughing at me? Bridget thought in a panic. She turned around and was relieved to see that no one was paying attention to her.

"That is so gross!" A girl, who sat at the front of the class, shrieked.

"Poppy soiled her panties!" Another boy choked out. He was laughing so hard that there were tears flowing down his face.

"What are they talking about?" Poppy asked her sisters in confusion. Jasmine pointed directly to the mess on the floor. "I didn't!" Poppy protested in sudden understanding.

Bridget's eyes fell upon what the rest of the class was looking at. There, right where Poppy was standing was a pile of brown mush.

"What in the world?" Bridget exclaimed out loud in utter surprise and shock. "I'll show you the way to the bathroom," Bridget hurried to say. She had not meant to embarrass Poppy further with her comment but it appeared as if she had. Poppy's face was a dark shade of pink.

"I did not soil myself!" Poppy protested. "It is just mud!" Poppy's claim only made the already hysterical boy laugh harder. Bridget felt horrible for Poppy as the laughter became contagious. Most of the boys in the class were laughing while the girls looked on in disgust. Even Lauren looked as if she were about to be ill.

"That is enough class!" Mrs. Waybourne scolded. However, she also looked paler than usual.

"I think we should get the chairs and desks now," Lauren commented, trying to save Poppy's feelings.

"Tell the janitor that we need a mop and perhaps a change of pants for Poppy," Mrs. Waybourne instructed as Bridget, Lauren, and the Walkers began to leave the classroom.

"It really is mud," Holly said once they were in the hallway. "Show them your shoes," she instructed Poppy. Poppy obediently lifted her left foot then her right.

"They are covered in mud," Bridget realized.

"Of course they are," Holly said while rolling her eyes. "Look at Poppy's pants; they are clean. She just stepped in mud before coming to school."

Bridget did not like the way Holly was talking to her. Holly talked as if she knew everything. She's just angry because everyone was making fun of her sister, Bridget told herself, not wanting to think the worst of Holly.

"It really is mud," Lauren said in relief. Lauren was looking a lot more comfortable now.

"We've established that," Holly said.

"Let's just get the janitor," Jasmine said, walking straight towards the janitor's office.

"Hey! How do you know where the janitor's office is? Have you been there before?" Bridget asked in surprise, while trying to keep up with Jasmine.

"Actually, this is my first time being in the school. But I guess you could say I have an innate instinct that tells me where to go," Jasmine replied mysteriously. Bridget was confused over Jasmine comment but she was even more confused when she saw Holly give Jasmine a look of warning.

"Can we just get to the janitor's office?" Primrose whined. Bridget understood the look of surprise on Lauren's face. She had never heard an eleventh grader whine like a four year old.

"Stop whining," Holly scolded, as if Primrose's behavior was commonplace. "There is no rush to get there anyway. The janitor won't be there for another ten minutes; he is running late." As soon as the words came out of Holly's mouth she regretted it.

"How do you know that?" a flabbergasted Bridget asked.

"I just do," Holly replied quickly.

When the six girls finally reached the janitor's office, Bridget was shocked to find out that the janitor had not arrived yet. What's going on here? Bridget asked herself in bewilderment.

\* \* \*

Bridget was still thinking about the Walker sisters, especially Holly and Jasmine, later that day. There was something about them that did not seem normal.

"We should get to the gym before the bell rings or we'll have to wait in line for that single change room forever," Lauren said, putting her empty lunch container into her backpack.

Lauren's comment had brought Bridget back to reality. She had been so engrossed in her thoughts that she had forgotten that Lauren was beside her.

"Alright," Bridget replied. The two friends walked in silence the entire way to the gym's change room. I wonder if she is thinking about the Walker sisters also, Bridget contemplated about Lauren.

Bridget and Lauren quickly changed into their gym clothes then headed towards the gym's entrance.

"We have the whole gym to ourselves for at least ten minutes, Lauren commented, just before opening the doors. "Do you want to play some one-on-one basketball?"

Bridget never answered Lauren because she was too busy staring at the four girls who stood in the gym. They were all wearing the same t-shirts and shorts and had the same ghastly green shade of skin.

Bridget walked slowly towards Holly, Poppy, Jasmine, and Primrose. Lauren, who had seen the Walker sister's skin just seconds after Bridget had, walked slowly behind her friend.

"Hi," Bridget managed to say.

"Hi!" Primrose excitedly replied in a voice that sounded as if it belonged to a six year old.

"Your skin..." Bridget choked out.

"What about it?" Poppy asked in confusion.

"It's so green!" Lauren cried, while looking at the girl's arms and legs.

"You're so mean," Primrose said in a whimper. Bridget stared at Lauren in shock as tears began to roll down Primrose's face.

"Why are you crying?" Poppy asked Primrose, while wearing a blank expression on her face.

"She's crying because Bridget and Lauren are making fun of the color of our arms and legs. I told you we should have worn long sleeved tops and sweat pants," Holly said with a matter of fact tone.

"We're not making fun of you," Bridget honestly protested. "Please don't cry," she added to Primrose. "It's just that your skin doesn't look normal. Are you sick or something?"

"No, we are not sick," Jasmine replied bluntly. "We just went swimming in a polluted lake, that's all."

"You went swimming in a polluted lake?" Lauren cried out loud. "But that's so dangerous. You might be really sick!"

"We are not sick," Jasmine snapped back. "Now leave us alone."

Bridget and Lauren felt that familiar feeling of shock as they watched the four sisters walk away.

"Something is definitely not right here," Bridget muttered.

"You can say that again," Lauren replied shakily. "How do you explain swimming in a lake when there is still ice at the edges? The water would be way below zero."

"Their faces look healthy enough," Bridget quickly added. She remembered that the first thing she had noticed about the Walker's was their brightly colored faces.

Bridget and Lauren did not have a chance to discuss the sisters any longer as their classmates began to file into the gym. Bridget and Lauren heard laughter as well as gasps come from their classmates as

109

they saw the arms and legs of the Walker sisters. This only made Primrose cry even harder. After the gym teacher had calmed Primrose down he inquired about the colour of their skin. Holly said that it was caused by a science accident in their old school. The gym teacher said no more after Holly claimed that she and her sisters were in good health.

"One of them is lying," Bridget whispered to Lauren.

"Yes, but which one?"

"Probably both; I don't trust either of them."

\* \* \*

Bridget was so tired after her unusual day at school that all she wanted to do was go home and curl up in front of the television. However, she had signed up for the archery club which was starting today at 4:00 PM. Bridget did not have a lot of school spirit and usually didn't join after school activities. However, the decision did not belong to her. Her homeroom teacher, Mrs. Waybourne, had told Mrs. Rye that Bridget needed to be more involved in school activities. Her mother, who had high hopes of her daughter attending an Ivy League college, promised that Bridget would join a club. At first Bridget refused but after being lectured for hours, she finally gave in and agreed to join the archery club. Now that the time had come, Bridget wished that she had stood her ground and refused with more passion. Bridget sighed as she headed towards the gym for the second time that day. She sighed even louder when she saw who was already in the gym.

"Hello," Jasmine greeted upon seeing Bridget. However, the greeting was not friendly. Bridget did not like the sound of Jasmine's voice; it sounded cocky and superior. Bridget disliked the way that Jasmine was holding the bow and arrow even more. Jasmine held on tightly to the bow with her left hand but she was casually tossing the arrow up in the air and catching it with her right hand. Jasmine smiled smugly as Bridget watched in amazement. Jasmine precisely threw the arrow then caught it effortlessly.

"You better watch that you don't hurt yourself," Bridget advised.

"Oh, I won't hurt myself," she promised with a sly smile. Bridget backed up a few steps as Jasmine proceeded towards her with the arrow pointing forward.

I wish the others would hurry up and get here, Bridget though, realizing for the first time that she and Jasmine were alone in the sound proof gym.

"You look a little worried. Is everything okay?" Jasmine asked with false concern.

Bridget gulped hard as Jasmine brought the sharp silver tip of the arrow closer to her chest. "What...what are you doing?" Bridget stuttered. She watched in horror as Jasmine proceed even closer to her. Don't just stand there; do something! A voice in Bridget's head screamed. Reacting on this impulse, Bridget grabbed the arrow's wooden base and flung it towards Jasmine. Bridget instantly regretted her actions as she saw the arrow pierce into Jasmine's sickly green arm. Bridget could not believe her eyes as she saw a gooey white liquid squirt out of Jasmine's arm.

"What's wrong with you?" Bridget cried in horror.

"What's wrong with me? The question should be what's wrong with you?" Jasmine seethed as she took a tissue out of her pocket and held it against her cut.

"You were going to attack me!" Bridget exclaimed.

"No I wasn't. I was just trying to scare you; you know, get you back for upsetting Primrose earlier today."

"How was I supposed to know it was just a joke?" Bridget quietly asked, more to herself than to Jasmine. Bridget looked at the arrow which was now lying on the floor. It was just a piece of wood and metal now, but seconds ago it was a deadly weapon. Bridget looked up from the floor as she heard the other kids arriving.

Jasmine picked up the arrow with her cut arm, which had magically stopped squirting the white goo, and gave Bridget a challenging look. "Just leave me and my sisters alone," she hissed, before joining the others.

Bridget was still so shaken up by the events, which occurred just minutes ago, that she could hardly hold the bow and arrow steady. On her first attempt to fire the arrow, it had dropped in front of her feet and on the second try it did not go much further.

"Try to hold your hand steady," the coach instructed her. Bridget tried, but it was no use; she just could not keep her hands steady. "Why don't you let someone else have a turn?" the coach said with a smile, while taking the bow and arrow from Bridget and handing it to Jasmine. "Don't be nervous," the coach whispered to Bridget as she passed by him. "We are all rooting for you." Bridget knew that the coach was wrong. "Have you ever shot a bow and arrow before?" the coach asked Jasmine.

"No," she confessed.

"Okay then," the coach said with a smile. "First you place your hand here and raise the bow to..."

"I don't need any instructions," Jasmine said bluntly.

"But...but you said you've never used a bow and arrow before. You need basic instructions," the coach stuttered.

"Uh, no I don't," Jasmine replied cheekily as she placed the arrow against the bow and shot it towards the target board. Everyone gasped as the arrow landed directly in the center of the target board.

"You were just joking about never using a bow and arrow before," the coach said in relief. "You were just joking," he repeated, as if trying to convince himself that Jasmine's rudeness was just part of the joke.

"No joke," Jasmine said sharply. "I've never touched a bow and arrow before today."

"That...that must have been beginners luck then," the coach stumbled with his words.

"Give me another arrow and you'll find out."

Bridget could not believe the way in which Jasmine was talking to the coach. She watched in amazement as the coach handed Jasmine another arrow. Everyone was quiet as Jasmine prepared to shoot again. It seemed as if everything was in slow motion from the time Jasmine released the arrow to the time the arrow hit the end of the original. No one said anything as they looked at the long arrow, which was really two arrows combined, sitting in the center of the target board.

Jasmine snatched another arrow from the coach's hand and did the same thing again. Now there were three arrows attached to each other on the target board.

"That's incredible. That's unbelievable!" the coach cried. "I've never seen anything like it before!"

Neither have I, Bridget thought as she quietly crept out of the gym. But it's not incredible; it's down right scary.

* * *

Bridget did not say a word during dinner that night. Of course her mother did not notice. Mrs. Rye was an accountant for the biggest car dealership in their city. She took her job very seriously and often acted like she was at work even when she was at home. Bridget and her mother did not have a close relationship, to say the least.

When Mrs. Rye's cell phone began to ring, Bridget had an epiphany. She would look in the new telephone book that had been delivered to their house just yesterday. Surely the Walkers will be listed in it, Bridget reasoned. She looked across the table to see her mother having an argument with the person on the other end. Bridget knew that her mother had taken the telephone book into her den last night. Since Bridget was not allowed in her mother's den without permission, she waited for her to get off the telephone. She tried to make eye contact with her mother and she even coughed loudly, but her mother would not look at her nor get off the telephone. Bridget knew her mother would be on the phone for hours so she quietly left the table and crept into her mother's den. She quickly found the telephone book and looked under the name Walker. She sighed as she saw about fifty people with that last name in her city.

Unhappily, Bridget left her mother's den and grabbed her jacket. She needed some time to think; Bridget knew that she would get that chance on a stroll around the block.

\* \* \*

"I'm back from my walk," Bridget called out as she wiped her muddy shoes on the front door mat. "That is if you even noticed I was gone," she added under her breath.

"Come into my den right now!" Bridget heard her mother call. Bridget cringed as she remembered leaving the telephone book open on her mother's desk. She tried to make herself look small and ashamed as she stood at the entrance to her mother's den.

"I presume this is your doing," Mrs. Rye said with a serious face as she pointed to the telephone book that lay open on her desk.

"Yes," Bridget replied quietly.

Mrs. Rye sighed when she saw the pitiful look upon her daughter's face. "You should have asked me if you wanted to use anything from my den. You know that my office is off limits. I'm not angry that you used the telephone book, but I am angry that you defied my orders."

I didn't follow your orders? Bridget thought in bewilderment. I'm your daughter not your employee. Bridget felt the blood in her veins boil. "I apologize," was all that she said.

113

"Your apology is accepted," Mrs. Rye replied in a serious tone. "However, you will have to be disciplined. I think an appropriate punishment would be for you to clean out and organize the library."

"Yes mother," Bridget replied spitefully. As she turned around and prepared to leave, Bridget thought about how different her mother was compared to her. Mrs. Rye was very strict while Bridget liked to let loose every once in a while. Everything about her mother said professionalism. She even referred to the family's small room, which was filled with less than one hundred books, as a library. However, in this case Bridget did not care about her mother's exaggeration; she was just glad that she did not have to clean out a real library.

"Bridget," Mrs. Rye said sternly. Bridget turned around and gave her mother a tight smile.

"Sorry," Bridget apologized as she took the telephone book from the desk and placed it back into its original position. That telephone book had caused a lot of trouble and had not even reaped any information on the Walkers.

Bridget knew that it would be no use to leave the cleaning of the "library" until later. She knew that her mother would check in on her precisely one hour from now. Bridget sighed deeply as she opened the door to the library. As she stepped inside, darkness filled her eyes. Her fingers swept over the wall until they bumped against the light switch. As she waited for her eyes to adjust to the changing lights, she tried to remember the last time she had been in this room. When her eyesight returned to normal she realized that the book shelves were already filled and that there were only a few books scattered on the floor. When Bridget approached the bookshelves, she realized that they, along with the books, were extremely dusty.

"It's a good thing I brought the duster along," Bridget muttered as she began to dust the top of the bookshelves. She let out a loud sneeze as the dust went up her nose. She silently cursed her mother for making her clean out the room. Before she began to dust again, Bridget pulled the neck of her sweatshirt protectively over her mouth and nose.

After the bookshelves and the books were dust free, Bridget began to put the scattered books, which lay on the floor, on the bookshelves. She picked up a long thin book and grumbled. The book was entitled: "Victorian Age: The Meaning of Flowers".

"I've had quite enough flowers, thank you very much," Bridget said aloud, while thinking about the Walker sisters. Bridget was about to put the book on the shelf when curiosity got the better of her. "The meaning of flowers," Bridget repeated the book's title with new interest. She suddenly had the urge to see what the book said about the Holly, Poppy, Jasmine, and Primrose flowers. Flipping to the index, Bridget ran her finger over the "J" section until she saw the word Jasmine. She quickly turned to page forty-eight. A vision of a beautiful white and pink flower filled her eyes. "Jasmine," Bridget read out loud, "expresses the sentiment of preciseness. Originally found in..." Bridget stopped reading; her heart missed a beat. Her mind was racing as she re-read the sentence. "Jasmine expresses the sentiment of preciseness." Images of the day's events flashed in Bridget's mind. She remembered Jasmine's comment about her innate instinct to know where things are. Even more evident to Bridget's newfound theory of Jasmine was the fact that she shot three arrows with exact precision. It was as if Jasmine was born with the ability of accuracy.

Not wanting to believe such an absurd thing, Bridget quickly looked up the flower Holly. "Holly expresses the sentiment of foresight," Bridget read aloud. She remembered Holly's prediction about the janitor's tardiness with fear. Holly seems to be able to foretell what is going to happen, Bridget realized.

Bridget's mind was unable to form any logical thought as she turned to the page dedicated to Poppies. "Poppies express the sentiment of oblivion." As Bridget's fingers flew over the pages in search for the Primrose, she had visions of Poppy standing in confusion while asking what was going on. "Poppy really is oblivious," Bridget whispered with a shiver. Bridget's eyes were now filled with the image of small yellow flowers. "The Primrose," Bridget read slowly, "expresses the sentiment of early youth." Bridget felt as if she were going to faint as images of Primrose whining and crying circled her head. Bridget's head rose from the book. She felt her whole body go cold then tingle in fear. She did not even react to the thump that the book made when it fell from her hands and onto the floor.

"They are flowers...the Walker sisters are flowers. Well, that explains the green arms and legs," she laughed out loud. Bridget was in too much shock to realize her state of mind.

* * *

Bridget was not surprised when she found herself having trouble getting to sleep that night. She tossed and turned for hours until falling into a restless sleep at around 3:00 AM. Bridget dreamt that it was summer and she was walking peacefully around beautiful beds of colorful flowers. All the flower beds were arranged by color and size. The light colored flowers were in a small bed and were near the entrance of the park. Suddenly, Bridget found herself running towards the flower beds that were larger and contained dark purple, dark blue and black flowers. All Bridget could think about was getting to the exit gate that was located behind the dark, large flower beds. Bridget knew that she could not leave by the entrance, even though that seemed like the logical thing to do. As Bridget ran towards the exit, the dark colored flowers began to grow at an alarming rate. The stems of the flowers turned into a ghastly shade of green and slithered towards Bridget. Bridget jumped from the stem's grasp and continued to run. She was so close to the exit that she could see the rust, which was just beginning to form, on the black gate. Just a few more feet and she would be free. Bridget screamed as a stem wrapped itself around her ankle and pulled her down. Bridget hit the ground with a hard thud. All she could see were small yellow and red stars on a black background. Then her body went numb as the stem squeezed her to death.

Bridget's eyes flung open. Sweat lay on her forehead, matting her bangs. It was just a dream, Bridget told herself. That thought calmed her down and regulated her heartbeat. She smiled, knowing that she was safe, knowing that she was safe from the deadly flowers of her dream. However, one glance at her backpack on the floor reminded her of the reason she had dreamt about killer flowers in the first place. Bridget numbly arose from her bed. "A living nightmare," she commented quietly to herself.

* * *

"You look awful!" Lauren exclaimed when she saw Bridget walking down the hallway.

"Then I look how I feel," Bridget muttered. Bridget had only known the Walkers for twenty-four hours but in that little time they had turned her life upside down. All during breakfast, she had contemplated telling Lauren about her startling discovery. However, before leaving her house that morning, she decided to say nothing. Bridget was sure that Lauren would think she was lying, or worse, absolutely crazy.

"What's wrong?" Lauren asked with a pout. "Don't you feel well?"

"Obviously not," Bridget snapped. As soon as her aggression was released, she regretted it. Bridget cringed when she saw the hurt expression on Lauren's face.

"Okay, I'll back off," Lauren said as she threw Bridget a confused glance, and then walked away.

Bridget sighed. The day had not started off well. "My life won't get better until I get rid of the Walkers," Bridget quietly seethed. Bridget's thoughts were cut short by the ringing bell. In fear and determination, Bridget walked into the room that contained the Walker sisters. As Bridget closely watched Holly, Poppy, Jasmine, and Primrose, a plan of action formed in her mind.

Everything seemed to move fast as the morning came to an end. Bridget did not know if she was shaking from fear or excitement as she ran out of the History classroom and towards the science lab. Bridget carefully peeked into the science room and saw a teacher talking to a student. Without thinking her plan over, Bridget ducked down low, hurried into the classroom and hid behind a large table.

"I'm saddened to say that I will be recommending a three day suspension to the principal," the science teacher said.

Bridget's whole body began to tingle in fear. Is he talking to me? She thought in horror.

"But I said I was sorry. I didn't really mean to cut Amanda's hair," the boy who was talking to the teacher cried.

He hasn't spotted me, Bridget realized thankfully.

"I'm sorry but my decision is final," the science teacher replied to the boy.

Bridget backed up against the desk as much as she could and watched tensely as they left the room. Bridget did not waste a second as she sprang into action and opened the chemical cupboard. She knowledgeably grabbed for the spray bottle that was marked "plant poison" then quietly crept out of the science room; making sure that the door was locked behind her. As Bridget held the spray bottle filled with plant poison, she smiled to herself. I'm glad I paid attention to the horticulture unit in science class, she proudly thought.

Bridget made a beeline to the lunchroom and searched for the Walker sisters there. Her heart started to beat faster as she realized that they were not there. Out of the corner of her eye, Bridget saw a sad looking Lauren walking towards the lunchroom doors that lead outside. "I bet they're outside!" Bridget exclaimed out loud, referring to the Walker sister. She ignored the curious stares that her peers were casting upon her and ran pass Lauren and out the door.

"Hey!" Bridget heard Lauren shout out in surprise. Bridget ignored her friend's call and ran towards the four girls who were sitting on a bench in the distance.

It was sunny outside, but a cool wind blew against Bridget's face. Bridget ignored the uncomfortable feeling and tightened her grasp on the spray bottle of plant poison. Her heart raced in excitement as she realized that it really was the Walker sisters who were sitting on the bench. Of course it's them, Bridget smirked. No normal person would eat outside on a day like this. Bridget's skin crawled as she imagined what Holly, Poppy, Jasmine, and Primrose would eat for lunch.

"Hi Bridget!" Primrose called out in her little girl voice. "Hi Lauren!" she added.

"You followed me!" Bridget snapped at Lauren as she turned around to face her friend. "Go! Go back to the lunchroom!" she commanded.

"No!" Lauren shot back. "I'm not leaving until you tell me what is wrong."

"Leave. It's for your own good," Bridget pleaded.

"You're really starting to scare me," Lauren muttered with a quivering chin.

"I'm scared too," Holly said suddenly. "Tell me what you are hiding behind your back Bridget. I can't foresee your actions because your mind is so muddled. Even you don't know what you're going to do next."

"Oh yes I do," Bridget cried, revealing the spray bottle of plant poison and thrusting it towards the Walker sisters.

"What's that?" Poppy asked in confusion, referring to the spray bottle in Bridget's hands.

"You really live up to your name, Poppy," Bridget said, feeling fully in control. "So do your sisters."

"What is going on?" Lauren shrieked in fear.

"Tell me," Bridget continued, ignoring her friend's protest. "How were you created? How do you turn a flower into a person?"

"You've gone crazy!" Lauren cried in frustration.

"No, I haven't," Bridget said passionately, while glancing at Lauren for a moment. "I'm not crazy but whoever invented the Walker sisters is. They're flowers. They're walking talking flowers."

"They are just regular teenagers," Lauren pleaded with Bridget.

"She's not crazy," Jasmine said calmly. "In fact, she is completely right about us being flowers. However, she is wrong about our maker. Mrs. Walker wasn't crazy; she doesn't even know what has happened."

"What did happen?" Bridget demanded, still holding the spray bottle high.

"You humans know nothing," Jasmine laughed bitterly. "You have no clue that you are being watched by every flower and tree. We're all alive and experience the same emotions that humans do." The smirk on Jasmine's face faded. "No. We don't have the same feelings as humans; we're better than humans and can feel more joy and pain than you could ever imagine. We, the flowers and the trees, are superior to humans in every aspect but one; we cannot walk."

"You're walking now," Bridget observed in disgust.

"I guess humans are smarter than we give them credit for," Jasmine mocked.

"You're meant to stand for precision, not cruelty," Bridget proclaimed.

"Cruelty? Cruelty?" Jasmine shrieked. "Don't you dare talk to me about cruelty! Humans are the cruelest creatures on the planet. You stand on us. You cut our stems and put us in small vases. You even cut our heads off then press them in books!"

"So humans are horrible to plants- I get it," Bridget mocked Jasmine. "But that doesn't explain how you have transformed into a human."

"I don't have to tell you anything," Jasmine hissed.

"Stop it!" Holly yelled. "I can see how this will end and it's not pretty. I'll tell you how we grew our bodies if you put that bottle down," she bargained. Curiosity got the better of Bridget as she lowered the spray bottle. "Just keep it down," Holly warned. "That plant poison could kill us."

"That was the plan..." Bridget stated.

"Well it doesn't have to be," Holly interrupted.

119

"We don't have to tell her anything," Jasmine said, making the interruption this time.

"Yes we do," Holly said knowledgeably. "We grew into humans from the drop of blood that belonged to the only human that ever truly loved us. Mrs. Walker grew Poppy, Jasmine, Primrose, and myself from a seed and cared for us with the utmost love. She lavished us with plant food and sprinkled us with water each day; she never, ever tried to cut us. One day she cut herself on a sharp blade of grass that grew nearby. Drops of blood landed on Poppy, Jasmine Primrose, and I. Then the next thing we knew, we had grown into humans. The love of the woman who cultivated us gave us life.

"Is...is this for real?" Lauren asked in a shaky voice.

"Yes," Holly replied.

"It's not normal!" Bridget cried out suddenly, lifting the spray bottle up once again.

"Don't hurt us. Just leave us alone," Primrose pleaded.

"There's no point in begging," Jasmine said, putting an arm protectively around Primrose's shoulder. "Humans can't be reasoned with."

"You're flowers masquerading as human entities. Do you really think I can just look the other way?" Bridget cried in frustration.

"Yes," Holly replied calmly. "Yes you can."

"I...I can't," Bridget stuttered.

"Yes you can," Lauren said, almost in tears.

Bridget's eyes fell upon the Walker sister. She saw the familiar look of anger on Jasmine's face, but this time she realized the cause of her anger. Jasmine has seen terrible things happen to her species; she felt as if she could never trust a human. No longer wanting to see the pain that Jasmine harbored, Bridget turned her eyes towards Poppy. She almost laughed when she saw the confused, yet innocent, expression that played upon her beautiful face. Bridget's eyes then traveled to Primrose. She's just a child, Bridget realized in sadness. She suddenly felt terrible for causing her so much fear. Next, Bridget's eyes turned to Holly. Holly wore a grateful expression on her face. It only took Bridget a second to realize why Holly, the one blessed with the power of foresight, was smiling. She knows what is going to happen, Bridget realized.

"Okay," Bridget muttered as she lowered the spray bottle. "Okay."

A smile broke out on Primrose's face as she ran to give Bridget a hug. "Thank you," she whispered.

"Thank you," Bridget whispered back.

* * *

The three remaining months of the school year went by quickly as Bridget spent them getting to know Holly, Poppy, Jasmine, and Primrose. Bridget was the most surprised with Jasmine and her change of attitude. Although Jasmine still claimed to hate some humans, she admitted to being quite fond of Lauren and even Bridget.

Bridget, along with Lauren and her four new friends, became inseparable as the weeks of summer passed. They spent their days playing games, telling stories, swimming in Lauren's pool, and window shopping at the local mall. As the summer days came to an end, Bridget noticed a change in the Walker sister's behavior. However, Lauren did not seem to notice the change as she continued to talk excitedly about the upcoming school year.

"Hurry up," Lauren begged Bridget as they walked to school together on a cool September day. "I promised the Walkers that we would meet them in their garden by 8:30. It's already 8:37!" Bridget obediently followed Lauren, but she did so with a heavy heart. She felt as if something was not right.

"Holly, Poppy, Jasmine, Primrose!" Lauren called out when she and Bridget had entered the garden in which the Walker sisters resided. "Where are they?" Lauren asked in confusion. Before Bridget had a chance to reply an old woman came out of a nearby house.

"Oh my! You two frightened me," exclaimed the plump old woman with graying hair.

"I'm sorry," Lauren apologized. "We were just looking for our friends." Bridget shot Lauren a warning glance. The last thing they needed was for this woman to ask why they were looking for their friends in a garden.

"I haven't seen anyone here," replied the woman with a smile. Bridget and Lauren watched as the old woman bent down to give some nearby flowers plant food. "Oh no!" she suddenly exclaimed.

"What's wrong?" Bridget asked with a pounding heart.

"Oh no," the old woman repeated again. "I've been looking for my favorite small collection of flowers since last spring. I thought they had grown legs and walked off," she absurdly exclaimed. "But now I've found them and they're dead." As the old woman stepped aside, a holly, poppy, jasmine, and a primrose lay flat on the ground. They were shriveled and decaying.

"No!" Lauren cried out loud, upon seeing the state of her friends. "I agree that the loss of a flower is sad, but come on…it's not like they were people." The old woman cast a look at Lauren, as if to say she were crazy, and then walked back to her house.

"That wasn't Mrs. Walker, was it?" Lauren asked, still obviously shaken up.

"I suppose it was," Bridget replied sadly.

"Well, she didn't look very concerned about her flowers!" Lauren cried in confusion.

"She hasn't truly experienced the power of flowers," Bridget explained, "but we have."

"Do you think they will come alive next spring?" Lauren asked, while trying to hold back the tears that threatened to come sliding down her cheeks at any given moment.

"I guess we'll just have to wait and see," Bridget replied as she stared at a long sharp blade of grass.

\* \* \*

# The Secret Oracle of an Egyptian King

# The Secret Oracle of an Egyptian King

"Go...go away," seventeen-year-old Vaughan Riley stuttered. His eyes grew large as the mummy took no heed of his request, but advanced forward instead.

"It's all over for you," the mummy rasped in a dry voice. The cloth that covered the mummy's face moved up and down as it talked.

"What do you want from me?" Vaughan cried, a bit louder than he had intended to.

"You know what I want," the mummy rasped in that same dry tone. "I want my treasure...now!"

"I'll never give up the treasure!" Vaughan protested in bravery. "I've spent my whole life looking for the treasure. Do you really think I would just hand it over to you?"

"You'll hand it over to me or I'll take it," the mummy threatened. "Either way it will be returned to me."

"No!" Vaughan yelled as he backed away from the moving mummy.

"Stop that right now!" Dr. Riley shouted as he entered the room. Vaughan and the mummy stopped and stared at Dr. Riley.

"Did we disturb you?" the mummy asked in a friendly voice as it pulled the white strips of cloth from around his head. "Sorry," it added in a sheepish voice, before Dr. Riley had a chance to respond.

"Aren't you two a little old to be playing dress up?" Dr. Riley asked sourly, while ignoring the question that had been asked.

Vaughan looked down at his explorer outfit, which consisted of a wide brimmed brown hat, a dark green shirt, brown shorts, and a waist belt that held a small chisel. He then looked at his best friend, Danny, who was wrapped in toilet paper. "We're not playing dress up; we're actors," Vaughan protested, trying to hide his embarrassment over the realization that perhaps they were a bit too old to be playing make-believe.

"I don't care what you call it," Dr. Riley snapped. "Just stop it right now." With that said, Dr. Riley marched out of the room.

The two boys said nothing as they picked up the toilet paper trail that had begun to unravel when the "mummy" was about to attack the great explorer, Vaughan Riley.

"Um, can I make an observation?" Danny asked quietly, finally breaking the silence.

"Sure," Vaughan answered, positive that he knew what his friend was about to ask.

"Is your dad alright?" Danny carefully inquired. "It's just that he hasn't been acting like himself lately."

"I've noticed," Vaughan sighed. "I guess he is stressed about the grand opening of the King Rhinkuhtan exhibition tomorrow." Vaughan suddenly lost that feeling of embarrassment as excitement began to overpower him. He smiled as he thought about the event which had led Danny and himself to dress up in the first place. Vaughan's very own father, Dr. Riley, had discovered the tomb of King Rhinkuhtan. Well, I guess the other archaeologists helped find the tomb also, Vaughan thought generously.

Vaughan, along with his father, had moved to Cairo, Egypt ten years ago when Dr. Riley was offered a job working with a team of Egypt's finest archaeologists. When Vaughan had found out that he was moving to Egypt he was overwhelmed with excitement. This excitement had not disappeared; Vaughan loved visiting pyramids and looking at all the artifacts that his father had found.

"You're probably right," Danny said thoughtfully. "After all, this is one of the biggest discoveries your dad has ever worked on."

Vaughan nodded in agreement as he picked up the last trail of toilet paper. After my dad sees how great the exhibition at the museum is, he'll relax and become the friendly father that I once knew him to be, Vaughan reassured himself.

* * *

Vaughan shifted uncomfortably beneath his dark blue suit which he had outgrown last year. Up until just recently, money had been tight in the Riley household. There had been no time to buy a new suit for the big occasion. Vaughan's eyes met Danny's, who laughed and pointed at him. Vaughan struggled against the urge to stick out his tongue at him. Vaughan, along with his father, the four other archaeologists who had helped Dr. Riley find the tomb, and the museum curators, were all standing in front of the newly opened King Rhinkuhtan exhibition. The guests had all been amazed over the golden artifacts. However, it was the item under the velvet cloth which was the main attraction. Under the dark purple velvet cover was the mummified body of King Rhinkuhtan, Cairo's king. Although Vaughan had already seen the mummy, he felt a rush of excitement surge through him. He looked up at his father, expecting to see a wide smile on his face, but what Vaughan saw shocked him. Dr. Riley looked nervous and very guilty. He looks how I do when caught touching newly unburied treasures, Vaughan thought silently.

"And now, without further ado, I present to you the mummified body of King Rhinkuhtan," a museum curator announced.

Vaughan stepped aside as his father and the four other archaeologists marched up to the velvet rug and pulled it off. The bright flashes from cameras that snapped in front of him blinded Vaughan. After everyone had got a picture of King Rhinkuhtan's mummified body, the question and answer period began. The museum curators and the archaeologists were guided to a high table at the front of the main entrance hall while Vaughan was forced to sit with the crowd. Vaughan did not mind being treated as an unimportant individual; he would much rather be part of the crowd than in the centre of it any day.

"You looked pretty nervous up there," Danny stated as Vaughan sat down beside him.

"Thanks for noticing," Vaughan replied sarcastically, while rolling his eyes. "Actually," he said in a serious tone, "I was more concerned about my dad than myself."

"He looked even more nervous than you! And he kept looking around the room; it was like he was trying to find someone or was waiting for something bad to happen. Have you found out what is bothering your dad yet?"

"Not yet," Vaughan replied, shaking his head. "Ever since he found the tomb he has been acting so strange. He has really drawn into himself and shut me out in the process. I just don't get it. Finding King Rhinkuhtan's tomb is the best thing that could happen in his career; so why isn't he happy?"

"I wish I could help but I don't think I can. You and your dad need to have a serious talk about things."

"I think I'll take your advice," Vaughan said nodding. "Thanks for being so helpful."

"It's the least I can do," Danny said with a sly smile. "After all, if it weren't for your dad's ticket I wouldn't be seeing the King Rhinkuhtan display until tomorrow night."

Everyone became silent as the question and answer session began. "My question is for Dr. Riley," said a short plump man who held a mini tape recorder in his left hand. Vaughan's dad nodded at the man in acknowledgment. "Your team's discovery of King Rhinkuhtan's tomb is one of high importance. The amount of gold objects that King Rhinkuhtan had buried with him increases this importance tremendously. Could you please briefly describe the process which led you to find the tomb?"

"It was a long process," Dr. Riley said in an unhappy, monotone voice. Vaughan's face reddened as the people in the crowd began to giggle. Why is my dad acting so weird? Vaughan asked himself for what seemed like the hundredth time that day. "We began the excavations when our monitors picked up large empty spaces beneath the sand. The process of just finding the entrance to the tomb required the most sophisticated machinery as well as a lot of human strength. When we found the entrance to the underground tomb, finding the tomb of King Rhinkuhtan was not too difficult."

"It was surprisingly easy," one of the woman archaeologists spoke up. "We were prepared to deal with traps and false tombs, but we found no such thing. I have been involved in many excavation projects and I have never seen a pyramid quite like this one."

"If the pyramid was poorly designed, how can you be sure it really is King Rhinkuhtan's tomb?" the plump man inquired.

"It is King Rhinkuhtan's tomb!" Dr. Riley suddenly screamed as he jumped up from his chair. "We've done carbon testing on the mummy and it is King Rhinkuhtan!"

Vaughan looked at Danny in shock. Danny returned his friend's stare, while murmurs of confusion echoed throughout the room. Vaughan heard his father's teammates trying to calm him down.

"I'm...I'm sorry," Dr. Riley stuttered to the plump man. "I just wanted to make sure that you realized your accusation. It's...it's not true. The tomb belongs to King Rhinkuhtan." Dr. Riley hurried down from the stage and ran from the room. Vaughan sprang from his seat and ran after his father.

"Dad, wait up!" Vaughan shouted as he followed his father to their minivan.

"Get inside now," Dr. Riley shouted to Vaughan, while holding the door open for him. Vaughan jumped into the van and closed the door.

Dr. Riley put the key into the ignition and sped off. Vaughan said nothing as they rushed home and then into their house.

"Mind telling me what just happened?" Vaughan asked breathlessly as he thumped down on the kitchen chair.

"I...I can't," Dr. Riley answered as he locked the door and looked fearfully outside the window.

"When did you obtain a stutter?" Vaughan asked in annoyance.

"There is obviously something going on. You might as well tell me now because I will find out eventually."

"They're coming; I know that they're coming."

"You are really starting to scare me," Vaughan said with a quivering chin. "Who's coming?"

Dr. Riley turned to face Vaughan for the first time since they had entered the house. "I don't know," he said sadly.

"Tell me," Vaughan pleaded.

"No, you don't understand, Vaughan. I really don't know who it is."

"Okay," Vaughan said slowly, while trying to get his head around the situation. "You don't know who is after you, but do you know what that person wants?"

"They want the lie to be kept forever. They want everyone to keep on believing that King Rhinkuhtan was the true ruler of Cairo."

"Do you mean to tell me that King Rhinkuhtan wasn't the ruler? Of course he was! It's written in all my history books at school. Everyone knows that King Rhinkuhtan was Cairo's ruler!" Vaughan felt his cheeks flush in fear. All of Cairo's citizens admired King Rhinkuhtan; he was known for being fair and helping even the lowest of peasants. If what his father was saying was actually true, many people would be very upset.

"He's not," Dr. Riley said, shaking his head. "When it was my turn to help load the contents of the tomb into a transportation lift, I found something. I found a scroll written in ancient hieroglyphics. I was able to read most of the hieroglyphics; the scroll told the story of how the real King Rhinkuhtan was killed by his servant and how that servant successfully impersonated him. No one knew except for the servant's brother who was also a servant to the real King Rhinkuhtan. The servant's brother did not like what was happening, but he said nothing due to the fear that the imposter King Rhinkuhtan would have him killed.

For the whole time that the imposter King Rhinkuhtan ruled, the brother kept quiet. But on the day that the imposter King Rhinkuhtan died, the brother wrote of what really happened on the scroll and buried it along side the "king". He hoped that one day someone would find out the truth."

"Why didn't the brother verbally tell the truth after the imposter King Rhinkuhtan had died?" Vaughan asked in awe.

"He was afraid that people wouldn't believe him and then punish him for telling lies about the recently deceased king."

"Okay, so you found a scroll that changes the course of Cairo's history, but you still haven't told me why someone would be after you."

"Someone was watching me the day that I discovered the scroll. They jumped me just seconds after I had finished reading the scroll. I fought off the man who had attacked me and ran away. I managed to hold onto the scroll, but I didn't see who attacked me since he was wearing a black mask over his face. He must have been a part of the excavation process since he was able to gain access to the tomb." Dr. Riley stopped talking and paused for a minute. "Then again, when I ran out of the tomb there was no one to ask for help. Perhaps the man had beaten up the two security guards, thus gaining entrance that way." Dr. Riley threw his hands up in confusion. "I don't know! I just don't know! The only thing I do know is that I brought the scroll home with me and put it in a safe."

"Why would you do that?" Vaughan asked in shock, amazed that his father would take an ancient scroll.

"I didn't mean to steal it," Dr. Riley protested. "I don't even want to look at the thing now. I only brought the scroll home to protect it. When I tried to take it to the carbon-testing lab, I was attacked again. This time a dagger was flung at me. Luckily it missed hitting me. On the dagger was a note that said I was to burn the scroll and tell no one. I was so frightened that I put the scroll back into the safe and told no one. You are the only other person who knows."

"So that's why you have been acting so strange lately," Vaughan realized. At least one thing was making sense to him.

"I didn't want to tell you, Vaughan," Dr. Riley said, shaking his head. "Now I am afraid that we are both in danger."

"What are we going to do?" Vaughan asked numbly. On the one hand, Vaughan was stunned and excited about the action movie situation his father and he were in. On the other hand, he only liked to pretend he was in danger; he didn't actually want to die!

"I can't tell the other archaeologists or even the police. I will be thrown in jail if they find out."

"It's obvious that the person who is after you wants the scroll destroyed, so why not do it? Why don't you just burn it? It will protect us, not to mention protecting Cairo's citizens from the shocking fact that their beloved King Rhinkuhtan was a fraud as well as a murderer."

"I can't destroy a ten thousand year old artifact!" Dr. Riley practically screamed. "I took an archaeologist oath that stops me from ever bringing harm to an artifact."

"Well then, I don't know what to do. But I do know that you better do something. I have a feeling that the bad guy will be back." As soon as Vaughan had finished his sentence a loud bang on the front door startled both Vaughan and his father. They looked at each other in fear.

"Don't answer it," Vaughan pleaded. Dr. Riley didn't have a chance to reply as a voice boomed from behind the door.

"It's Andy. Are you in there Dr. Riley?" the voice from behind the door asked. Vaughan and his father let out a sigh of relief. It was just Andy, one of Dr. Riley's teammates. Vaughan's father opened the door and let Andy in.

"Is everything thing alright, Dr. Riley?" Andy asked in concern, after he had been ushered into the house and then had the door closed shut behind him.

"Certainly, why do you ask?" Vaughan's father replied as he shot Andy a fake smile then turned towards the window to look fretfully out.

"What happened to you at the museum?" Andy inquired. "Everyone is wondering," he added.

"I...I felt sick," Dr. Riley lied. "I think I ate some expired clams or something. You better go incase it is contagious."

"Your excuse isn't making much sense," Andy said suddenly. "Are you sure there isn't something on your mind?" Vaughan felt his chest tighten as he watched Andy closely. There was something about Andy's cocky tone and expression that made Vaughan nervous. "Talk to me, Riley," Andy said slyly, while walking closer towards Dr. Riley. Vaughan felt his whole body tingle in fear.

"Could you please leave Andy? I'm really not feeling well," Dr. Riley said in a funny voice, as if he were testing his friend.

Andy shook his head lightly back and forth. "No, I don't think so," he hissed, coming closer to Dr. Riley. Vaughan watched in horror as Andy reached into his dark brown jacket and revealed a sharp looking dagger.

"Andy, no," Dr. Riley said in disbelief.

"Oh yes," Andy replied as he leapt towards Vaughan's father. Vaughan did not even have time to think as he ran towards Andy and kicked the dagger out of his hand. Andy looked stunned for a moment then he dived for the dagger. But Vaughan was faster; he grabbed the dagger and held it in front of him. "Put the dagger down," Andy said, with less confidence than he had before.

"Not until you tell us what is going on. How could you attack my dad like that?" Images of the countless hours that his father and Andy had spent together while working on the King Rhinkuhtan dig filled Vaughan's head.

"I wasn't going to hurt your father," Andy protested.

"Then why did you bring the dagger?" Dr. Riley asked in anger.

"To threaten you," Andy replied angrily.

"Why would you threaten me?" Dr. Riley pried.

"You know the truth about my ancestor. I had to stop you from ruining my reputation. I don't want that darn scroll. In fact, I want it to be destroyed forever."

"Your ancestor...?" Dr. Riley exclaimed.

"You want everyone to think you're so great because you're related to a king," Vaughan interrupted his father, directing his comment towards Andy.

"No," Dr. Riley said abruptly. "I would have guessed in an instant that Andy was behind all of this if I had known that he was a descendant of King Rhinkuhtan. Why do you want to protect a name that people don't even know you bear?"

Vaughan watched as Andy's face went pale. "Wait," Vaughan said suddenly. "He's not an ancestor of King Rhinkuhtan. That's absurd! In my history book it said that King Rhinkuhtan died without any offspring. He didn't have any kids!" Vaughan was still holding on tightly to the dagger. He liked the way it made him feel powerful.

131

"You're right!" Dr. Riley exclaimed, shaking his head as if he were angry with himself. "There's no way that you can be a descendant of King Rhinkuhtan. You were just a middle class archaeologist until we found King Rhinkuhtan's tomb. What's really going on, Andy?" Andy had just opened his mouth to answer when a loud crash from upstairs made all three of them jump. "What in the world was that?" Dr. Riley asked with wide eyes.

"My backup," Andy said, regaining his confident smile.

Vaughan felt breathless as he ran towards the door and tried to unlock it with his free hand. Realizing that he needed both hands to escape, he dropped the knife and opened the door. Vaughan felt awful for leaving his father, but he needed to get help from the police; there was no way that they could fight Andy and his backup alone.

Vaughan's legs and lungs ached; they cried to Vaughan, threatening that if they did not rest soon they would collapse. Vaughan ignored the threats.

"You have to help me," Vaughan yelled as he stumbled into the police headquarters. Everyone who was in the building looked up at Vaughan in shock then rushed to his side. "Get all your officers to 1786 Old Egypt Road now! I have an emergency. My father is being held up by at least two men."

The police officers did not ask any questions until they were in the car, driving with the sirens on, in the direction of Vaughan's house. "Why is your father being attacked? What state was he in when you left him? Do you know who is attacking your father?"

Vaughan answered the questions as thoroughly as he could, but his head was spinning from fear. It seemed to take only a second to get to Vaughan's house. He was told to stay in the car while the police officers burst into the house. Vaughan watched from the safety of the car, praying that his father would be alright and, if he was alright, that he would not be in too much trouble for taking the artifact. Vaughan could not hear much from inside the car. His whole body tingled from fear and from the urge to get out of the car and see what was happening. Horror surged through his body as he saw Andy and one other native Egyptian being dragged from Vaughan's house in handcuffs. Vaughan looked on in admiration at the four police officers who had the two men restrained. It looked as if they really had a hassle getting the two bad guys into those handcuffs. Vaughan's admiration was cut short when he saw his own

132

father being escorted out of their house in handcuffs. Vaughan could not sit still any longer. "Why is my dad in handcuffs?" he yelled in a panic.

"Because he stole from King Rhinkuhtan's tomb," Andy said through a bleeding lip. "If I'm going down he's coming with me!" Andy yelled as he was shoved into a police car that had just arrived.

Vaughan looked at his father in fright. "No," he protested. "You've got it all wrong. My dad was just protecting the scroll. He's not the bad guy!" Vaughan's mouth dropped open as the police officers ignored his cries and proceeded to put Dr. Riley into the police car.

"It's going to be okay," Dr. Riley reassured Vaughan. But Vaughan was not reassured. He knew his father was lying to him. "You did what you had to," Dr. Riley added, seeing that he had not convinced his son.

"You better come with us," a police officer said to Vaughan.

Vaughan's heart raced. "I'm not being arrested, am I?"

"No," the police officer said with little sympathy. "But we can't leave you here alone." Vaughan felt numb all throughout the car ride back to the police station. The events that had just happened were too much for him to contemplate; he stared out of the window and tried to think about nothing.

* * *

The police confiscated the scroll. Dr. Riley was forced into telling the police officers the location of the safe and the combination to access it. The story of Dr. Riley, Andy, and, most importantly, the fake King Rhinkuhtan leaked out quickly onto the streets of Cairo where the citizens responded in an uproar. They needed someone to blame for the deterioration of the history that they had once been so proud of; Dr. Riley and his team of archaeologists seemed like the most suitable people.

Dr. Riley had been charged with harboring an ancient artifact and was fined significantly. Dr. Riley was no longer in trouble with the police, but his reputation was permanently scarred. Vaughan noticed a big change in his father's attitude. He was more withdrawn than ever before. He even refused to leave the house.

"I'm going to the grocery store now," Vaughan called to his father as he took the shopping list and money from inside the kitchen cabinet.

"Hurry back," Dr. Riley said, emerging from his study.

"I will," Vaughan promised as he walked out the door and shut it behind him. Vaughan took a deep breath of the hot, dry air. He was thankful to get out of the house. His father insisted that he spend most of his time inside the house, thus away from the multitude of people who were angry with the Riley's. Vaughan was beginning to wish that September would come so that he could go to school; there was no way that his father could keep him away from school.

Vaughan quickened his pace as he walked through downtown Cairo. He felt the eyes of his neighbors burrow into him. Why are they mad at me? I didn't do anything, Vaughan thought in a fleeting moment of spite for his father and the neighbors. Even Danny seemed to be ignoring him. It felt like something from the past when he heard someone quietly calling his name. Vaughan spun around and noticed Danny sitting on a nearby bench, wearing sunglasses and a wide brimmed hat.

"Over here," Danny whispered again.

"It's not that hot," Vaughan said bitterly.

"Please don't be mad at me," Danny pleaded, once Vaughan had sat down beside him. "I wanted to see you, but my mom and dad wouldn't let me. They said I shouldn't talk to the people who ruined Cairo's history.

"I didn't ruin Cairo's history!" Vaughan exclaimed. "The real King Rhinkuhtan's servant did!"

"I know it's not your fault," Danny said with a sympathetic smile. "That is why I've been hanging out here all day; I was hoping that you would pass by. I wanted to ask you if you heard about the excavation plans."

"Excavation plans?" Vaughan asked in confusion. "What excavation plans?"

"I guess you haven't heard then," Danny said, while biting his lower lip. "The Cairo museum has decided to hire a new team of archaeologists to excavate the real King Rhinkuhtan's tomb."

"Hold on a minute," Vaughan said, trying to get his head around the information that he had just obtained. "How do they know where the real tomb is? And why won't the museum hire the team that discovered the fake King Rhinkuhtan's tomb?"

Danny looked at Vaughan in sorrow. "You really have been hiding under a rock," he said sadly. "The direction to where the real

King Rhinkuhtan is buried was written on the scroll. As for the reason for the new archaeology team," Danny paused and sighed, "I don't know how to say this so I'll just spit it out bluntly; everyone in Cairo knows that your dad and his team of archaeologists will never be given the chance to dig for artifacts again. No one believes that they can be trusted."

"That's crazy!" Vaughan yelled as he jumped up. "My dad made a mistake, but he isn't a thief."

"I know that," Danny replied passionately. "It's just too bad that the rest of Cairo doesn't."

Vaughan glared at his friend then turned around quickly and ran towards his house. He wasn't really angry with Danny; Vaughan knew that he was just speaking the truth.

"What took you so long?" Dr. Riley asked as Vaughan came barging into the house. "And where are the groceries?" he asked in annoyance.

"Forget the groceries," Vaughan said abruptly. "I just found out that the Cairo museum has hired a new team of archaeologists to dig up the real King Rhinkuhtan's tomb. The directions to the tomb were written on the scroll. Why didn't you tell me that, dad? And why didn't you tell me that you would never work as an archaeologist in Cairo again?"

Dr. Riley offered no reply, but shook his head sadly instead. "I was so afraid that this would happen. I mean, I knew that Cairo would want the real King Rhinkuhtan's tomb excavated but I thought, perhaps, I would be assigned to the job. I've been a fool," Dr. Riley said, placing his head on his hands. "I'm sorry for not telling you about the scroll as soon as it happened. I was afraid and confused. I wasn't thinking clearly."

"It's okay, dad," Vaughan said, trying to sound reassuring. "But what will happen to us now?"

"We'll have to move from this place. It is true that I will never be hired here again. Perhaps we can go to Alberta and I could get a job at the National Dinosaur Park."

"Your passion lies within mummies and pyramids, not dinosaurs," Vaughan said sadly.

"I know, but we have to make the best of things." Dr. Riley ruffled Vaughan's hair. "Come on; let's go get the groceries together.

We can't hide in here forever." Vaughan gave his father a weak smile then followed him out of the house.

* * *

The months slowly rolled by and Vaughan regretted his wish for the new school year to begin. No one seemed to like him anymore; even the teachers, especially the history teachers, who gave him the cold shoulder. Vaughan's only friend was Danny. Vaughan was very grateful for Danny's company; he even harbored new feelings of respect for Danny since he had also become an outcast due to association. Vaughan was sure that he would miss Danny when he moved. The Riley's house had been up for sale for two months and had just received its first offer. Vaughan would be thankful to get away from the cold stares, but he would miss looking at the beautiful Cairo desert and pyramids. The ill treatment of the Riley's had gotten worse during the past few weeks as the new archaeologist team found and began the excavation of the real King Rhinkuhtan's tomb.

"Vaughan, Vaughan!" Danny shouted to his friend one morning in early October. "Did you hear the news?"

"What news?" Vaughan inquired.

"The team of archaeologists found the real King Rhinkuhtan's tomb last night. They entered the tomb late last night then disappeared. All eight of them disappeared!"

"Disappeared?" Vaughan asked with wide eyes, suddenly grateful that his father was no longer working as an archaeologist in Cairo. "Did they find their bodies?"

"No, that's the really weird part," Danny explained. "There were tons of video cameras recording the opening of the tomb. Then at exactly 11:23 PM last night, the time that the seal to the tomb's entrance was opened, everything went black. All the safety lights burst into a thousand pieces! The archaeologists and the people recording the events had to make their way out of the tomb in the pitch dark. When they got outside everyone was there except for the eight archaeologists! I can't believe you haven't heard about it! Everyone is talking about it."

"No one talks to me, remember?" Vaughan replied.

"Oh," Danny said awkwardly. "Anyway," he continued, "they sent a bunch of people into the tomb to find the archaeologists, but they came back empty handed. It's like the eight of them disappeared into

136

thin air. The museum is calling for a new team of archaeologists to continue the excavation."

"This is ridiculous!" Vaughan exclaimed, while throwing his hands in the air. "First my dad is targeted by two psychos, and then eight archaeologists disappear. Why won't the museum just give up on the excavation?"

"A lot of people believe that there is a curse on the tomb. They believe that the tomb your father found belonged to the real King Rhinkuhtan. They think their king is angry at his people for doubting him."

"Oh, enough!" Vaughan exclaimed, while throwing his hands up in the air again. "I just don't care any more. My dad and I will be getting out of Egypt in a few weeks and you know what? I'll be glad to go. I'll miss you, but not all the superstitious nonsense."

As Vaughan and Danny walked silently to school, Vaughan felt joy surge through him. It's over, he told himself. I'm not going to worry any longer. Vaughan smiled to himself; he had no way of knowing that he would soon be worrying about his very survival.

\* \* \*

Vaughan quickly broke his promise of not worrying as he tossed and turned that night. He would slip into a restless sleep only to be wakened by a terrifying dream. Vaughan kept on having nightmares about his father and himself being run out of Cairo by angry mobs of people. Vaughan had almost fallen back to sleep when he heard a loud scream coming from down the hall.

"Dad!" Vaughan cried as he jumped out of bed and ran to his father's bedroom. As soon as he had entered his father's bedroom, he flicked on the light switch. It took Vaughan's eyes a few seconds to adjust to the sudden change in light, but when he could see clearly, he let out a blood-curdling scream. Right in front of him stood the native Egyptian, who had been arrested along with Andy, holding a dagger towards Dr. Riley. Vaughan's sudden entrance stunned the man, but only for a few seconds.

"Don't move a muscle," the native Egyptian commanded in a thick ancient. This was not a problem for Vaughan as fear kept him stiffly in place. "If both of you do as I say, no one will get hurt." Vaughan nodded like a mechanical toy, obediently followed the Egyptian man out of the room, and then out of the house. "I want the both of you to walk in front of me," the man ordered.

"Where are we going?" Vaughan asked, somehow knowing what the answer would be.

"We're going to the real King Rhinkuhtan's tomb," he hissed evilly.

One of us should make a run for it, Vaughan realized to himself as he and his father walked side by side. He would not be able to catch us both if we ran in different directions. However, the image of the Egyptian man catching even one of them was too much for Vaughan to contemplate as he continued to walk.

It was dark outside and neither of them knew where the real King Rhinkuhtan's tomb was. We're walking towards the original excavation site, Vaughan thought, realizing that the newly dug tomb was near there also. Vaughan found out that he was right as they neared the heavily guarded excavation site.

"How will we be able to get inside?" Dr. Riley asked the Egyptian man.

The native Egyptian said nothing as he turned to Vaughan and Dr. Riley and then smiled. Vaughan almost passed out when he saw the rotten remains that used to be teeth. His teeth weren't like that before, were they? Vaughan questioned himself. It was unlikely that Vaughan would have noticed the man's teeth, under the circumstances in which they had met. However, it would have been hard to miss such an unusual feature.

"Stay here," the Egyptian man finally spoke. Vaughan and Dr. Riley watched in horror as an odorous, dark yellow gas seeped from the man's mouth. Vaughan began to panic when he realized that he could not move his body. The weird gas from the Egyptian man's mouth had frozen Vaughan and his father in place. All they could do was watch in fear as the Egyptian man walked up to the guards and blew in their faces. All the guards stood frozen in place. If he was able to, Vaughan would have widened his eyes as the man proceeded back towards them. The Egyptian man looked deep into Vaughan's eyes; Vaughan stared back at the two glowing coals inside the man's eye sockets. He felt himself melting; he felt himself regaining control over his movements. Vaughan wanted to run for help; to tell the police about the escaped criminal and his weird features.

"You're going into the tomb. Stop thinking about running away," the Egyptian man threatened Vaughan.

He can read my mind, Vaughan thought in horror. What in the world is going on?

"You'll have the answers once we get inside the tomb," the Egyptian man said, reading Vaughan's mind once again. Vaughan and Dr. Riley followed the native Egyptian as he led them into the deep tomb. The ground under Vaughan's feet sloped down at a sharp angle. He felt as if he were going to fall over. As the threesome walked deeper into the underground walkway, the air began to heat up and get heavier. The only light came from the dull, newly installed, safety lights that littered their path and the glow from the Egyptian man's eyes. They soon came to an opening in the wall. The remains of an old stone door lay on the ground at the entrance.

"Go inside," the Egyptian man commanded. Not knowing what else to do, Vaughan and Dr. Riley followed the man's instructions. The room looked old and dusty. There was nothing in it. The Egyptian man walked into the room behind Vaughan and Dr. Riley. The two Riley's watched in amazement as the man pried his fingers into a small crack in the wall and spread the walls apart. The whole room shook and sand began to sprinkle on them as the walls revealed a doorway. "Follow me," the Egyptian man instructed.

Vaughan followed the man, but he was no longer scared. He had seen too much; he no longer doubted the possibility of anything. Vaughan felt his confidence dwindle as he saw eight people, who he presumed were the new archaeologist team, sitting in a corner of the room. The archaeologists huddled together in fear when they saw the Egyptian man. However, they were not the only ones in the room. In the corner, the area where the archaeologists seemed to be avoiding was a mummified body.

"Please," Dr. Riley started to beg.

He's going to get us out of this mess, Vaughan thought thankfully about his father's pleading. "Please, I'll do whatever you want if you just tell me who you are."

Vaughan felt his mouth drop open.

"I'll tell you who I am, but it will cost you your life!" the Egyptian man answered passionately. "I am King Rhinkuhtan's servant."

"You...you can't be. You died thousands of years ago. I just excavated your mummified body!" Dr. Riley protested.

"My mummified body may be in the Cairo museum, but my real body, my body that walks, is alive!"

"You're not a mummy, you're a dummy!" Vaughan yelled. "A mummy can't come back to life. What do you really want, weirdo?"

"Vaughan, be quiet right now," Dr. Riley warned.

"Let the kid think whatever he wants to do. It doesn't matter," King Rhinkuhtan's servant hissed. "You'll all be dead soon enough."

"Before you kill us," Dr. Riley pleaded desperately. "Tell us the story of what happened to the real King Rhinkuhtan."

"Alright," the fake king replied. "I'd love to tell my brilliant plan to someone other than my ungrateful brother. I locked the real King Rhinkuhtan in this very room. Do you see that pathetic excuse for a mummy over there?" the king's servant asked, pointing to the mummy that was in the corner. "That's the real King Rhinkuhtan. He doesn't look so great anymore does he?" the fake King Rhinkuhtan laughed evilly. "I locked him in this room in early October. That is when a poisonous gas seeped through these walls. This phenomenon occurs every ten thousand years. And guess what? It's that time of year again." The servant laughed, producing a horrible dry sound.

"How do you walk once again?" Dr. Riley further pressed on.

The fake King Rhinkuhtan stopped laughing. "The cause of my rebirth is unknown. I remember the day that I died then a long darkness in between. Then I arose on the day that my mummified body was found by you and your archaeologist friends. I overtook Andy with my newfound powers and commanded him to get the scroll for me. But he failed and I had to take action for myself."

"But you were arrested. How did you get out of jail?" Vaughan demanded.

The king's servant laughed. "I can move walls that weigh thousands of pounds, getting past some thin metal bars and police officers were not much of a task."

"How did you fool your nation?" Dr. Riley asked, with a bit too much enthusiasm.

"I was fine impersonator," the servant boasted. "I tricked everyone into believing I was the real King Rhinkuhtan. Only my brother, who witnessed the murder, knew the truth. But he said nothing out of fear. I was a better king than the real one anyway; I was great to my nation. I took care of everyone, especially the poor. My brother never appreciated me," the servant complained. "I woke up from my ten thousand year slumber to find that he had written the true story of what happened. How could he betray me like that?" The fake king shook his head sadly. "What could have been if he had only believed in me."

"Why would he ever believe in a murderer?" Vaughan yelled as rage surged through his body.

"Enough!" the servant shouted. "It is not my fault that you are in this situation. "If Dr. Riley had just destroyed the scroll, no one would have found out the truth. Now that the truth is out all I can do is take my revenge on those who let the secret out." The fake king backed out of the small room. "Goodbye," he said with an evil smirk as the wall began to close behind him.

"No!" Vaughan cried as he ran towards the wall. But it was too late. The wall closed shut. Vaughan pried his fingers into the small crack but he did not have the strength to open it. He turned and faced the eight frightened archaeologists.

"I wish I hadn't taken this job," one of them muttered in fear.

"I wish I had never moved here," Dr. Riley said in defeat.

"Don't give up," Vaughan encouraged. "If a ten thousand year old mummy can come back to life we can surely find a way out of here. We just need to work together."

"We're too weak," one of the eight archaeologists complained. "We have been trapped in here for a day now. We were almost out of air when the mummy opened the wall."

"You'll be even weaker if we don't get out of here before the poisonous gas comes," Vaughan observed. He watched as no one moved. Even Dr. Riley looked hopelessly at Vaughan. "What is wrong with you people? Don't you want to live?" Vaughan cried as he turned passionately back to the wall and attempted to pry the wall open once again. Beats of sweat formed on Vaughan's forehead as he sunk his fingers deeper into the sandy wall and tugged with all his strength. "What's that noise?" he asked suddenly as he heard a hissing noise. When he did not receive a reply, he turned and looked at the others who were staring up at the ceiling in horror. As Vaughan's eyes looked up he felt his heart stop. Seeping through the ceiling was a dark yellow odious gas.

"The poisonous gas!" one of the archaeologists screamed. The scream was contagious as the other seven archaeologists began to scream also. Dr. Riley sat silently as if to die in dignity. I'm not going to scream nor sit quietly; Vaughan resolved as he pulled his t-shirt over his nose and began to work on the wall again. A few minutes had passed and the archaeologists were still screaming. Vaughan's ears rang from the sound of the archaeologists and from the hissing sounds of the poisonous gas. He was being to feel sick, but he still pried at the door. Suddenly, the archaeologist's screams began to take on an even more frightened tone. Vaughan ignored the screams as he closed his eyes and pulled at the walls even harder. Vaughan's eyes flew open as he felt the walls being moved apart. Then Vaughan finally began to join in on the screaming. Reaching from behind Vaughan was a pair of mummified arms.

Vaughan stumbled backwards and fell onto the mummified body of King Rhinkuhtan. The king made no sound as he moved away from Vaughan and spread the walls apart. The yellow gas that had begun to fill the air soared out of the small room and dispersed into the other room. Vaughan felt as if he could breathe a lot better now. When the archaeologists saw the open wall, they got over their weakness very fast and jumped up from the floor. The archaeologist, who had complained about being weaker than them all, was the first to leave the room. He was in such a hurry that he pushed the mummy over. The other archaeologists followed their friend, but in doing so they trampled over the mummy.

"Are you alright?" Vaughan cried as he leaned on the ground next to the mummy. He could not believe that he was asking a ten thousand year old mummy how he felt!

"Avenge my death," it replied in a dry voice, before its head fell lifelessly to the ground.

"Let's get out of here," Dr. Riley said coughing as he dragged his son from the room. They raced out of the tomb and into the fresh air. The hot dry air of Cairo had never felt so good to Vaughan.

"What in the world is going on?" Vaughan asked for what felt like the hundredth time that day.

"I agree. It's unbelievable," Vaughan's father replied. "We'll talk about it later, but first we need to find that impostor before he hurts anyone else!"

"But he could be anywhere," Vaughan protested.

"I'm sure he's still in Egyptian. No king, regardless of how he achieved the throne, would abandon his nation." Dr. Riley's face suddenly lit up. "I know where he is," he cried.

"Where?" Vaughan begged for the answer.

"He's gone to collect his treasures."

Vaughan and Dr. Riley arrived at the Cairo museum half an hour later. Although Vaughan had wanted to run, Dr. Riley had made him walk. He said that they needed to take deeps breaths of air to get rid of any gas that might have got into their lungs. He had reassured Vaughan that they would be alright since they had not been exposed to the gas for a long period of time.

When they arrived at the museum's entrance, Vaughan wished that they had gone home instead. As they got closer to the museum they saw that it had been broken into. There were frozen guards all over the place. Vaughan gulped as he realized what the fake king had done to them.

"Wait here," Dr. Riley instructed Vaughan as he crept into the museum. Vaughan peered from outside as he watched his father move closer to the servant. The servant was smashing open the displays that contained King Rhinkuhtan's gold items. Vaughan's heart rate accelerated as he watched his father pick up a heavy platinum bowl, which was sitting on a nearby pedestal, and walked slowly and quietly towards the servant who was picking small pieces of gold up from inside a broken display case. Vaughan watched in horror as his father raised the platinum bowl above the fake king's head, threw it, and then missed his target completely. The servant had bent over to pick up a piece of gold that he had dropped. The platinum bowl went smashing down on the glass display case instead.

"How did you escape?" the fake king yelled, grabbing Dr. Riley and pushing him towards the nearby display case that held the mummy's body. "You'll just have to take my place inside this display case forever."

Vaughan's mind raced as he ran into the museum and towards this father and the fake king. He felt an unfamiliar surge of strength course through his body. He felt as if he had more power and strength than ever before. Vaughan grabbed the servant around his waist and threw him against the display case. Dr. Riley went stumbling backwards and hit into a pedestal that was holding an ancient plate. The plate went flying to the ground, crashing into a thousand pieces. The loud noise distracted the fake king for a moment. Vaughan took advantage of the servant's shocked state and flipped him into the display case with his mummified body. Then he shut the lid of the display case tightly. Vaughan and his father watched in amazement as the fake king struggled and shouted. Vaughan's mouth hung open as the servant began to shrivel. The decaying mummy lay lifeless in his display case. As Vaughan watched the fake king die he felt his newfound strength being taken away from him. "I took your revenge," Vaughan whispered to the real King Rhinkuhtan.

"We better get out of here before the guards awaken," Dr. Riley said. Vaughan nodded then quickly followed his father back to their house.

\* \* \*

"Let's just go to bed and talk about everything in the morning," Dr. Riley said, once they had got safely to their home. "We'll need all the rest we can get. The news about tonight's events will be all over Cairo by tomorrow morning. I bet those archaeologists are already at the police station, telling them what had happened."

"They probably won't believe them. Even I don't believe it," Vaughan added.

"You're in shock. So am I," Dr. Riley admitted. "Come on," he said to his son, leading him up the stairs, "you need to get some sleep."

"There's just one thing I have to do first," Vaughan said with a wide smile on his face.

"What do you have to do?" Dr. Riley asked in surprise.

"I have to make a telephone call," Vaughan replied as he walked towards the phone. Dr. Riley nodded then said goodnight. "Hi Danny, it's me," Vaughan said as the person on the other end of the line answered the telephone. "Sorry for calling you so late, but I have a really big story that I bet you haven't heard yet."

\* \* \*

# Cold Territory

## Cold Territory

Dale Stone crashed his ice pick into the icy mountain with his right hand. Then he did the same thing with his left hand. Dale pulled himself up with the two ice picks and kicked his spiked boot a few times before doing the same thing with his other foot. Dale rested for a moment to catch his breath. He looked down to see many feet of the icy mountain beneath him. He smiled to himself as the familiar feeling of pride and excitement pulsated through his body.

Dale Stone lived for climbing mountains. He used to work full time as a dentist, but now he only worked part time. He took the other half of the year off to go mountain climbing. Dale Stone was born and raised in British Columbia, Canada where he had climbed just about every mountain there. Dale had become restless in British Columbia and decided to travel further. He had been climbing mountains in Asia for a month now. He had one more month left in Asia until he had to return to Canada and resume his job.

With one hand, Dale took a thick nail from the pouch around his waist and drove it into the ice. Then he used the same free hand to clip a rope around the nail. He did this to protect himself incase he would fall. But of course the great mountain climber, Dale Stone, would never fall; the rope was just merely a precaution.

Dale took a deep breath as he began climbing higher up the mountain. He was in Asia climbing a 2000-foot icy mountain. Dale grunted as he continued to move up the mountain. The weight of his backpack was beginning to wear him down. He raised his head and calculated that the ledge was about twenty feet above him. With the promise of a rest on the ledge, Dale continued to push himself harder. He had just driven his left ice pick into the mountain and had started to dig his foot into the ice when he suddenly lost his footing. Dale felt his other foot slip in the aftershock. He swung from the two ice picks, trying desperately to hold onto them. Dale's arms began to ache and his fingers began to tremble. "Hold on, Dale," he motivated himself, just before his fingers slipped from the ice picks. "No," Dale screamed as he plummeted down the icy mountain.

His body crashed back and forth into the icy mountainside as he continued to fall. Dale felt himself pulled upwards after he had fallen past the second last nail that he pinned into the mountainside. He used the rope to pull himself upright. Dale sighed as he saw his two ice picks, sticking into the mountain a few feet above him. Holding onto the rope with one hand, Dale took the two small emergency ice picks from his pouch and began to make his way back up to where he was before the fall.

When Dale had finally reached the ledge successfully, he cursed himself. He could not believe that he had fallen from the mountain. Dale's self-defeating thoughts soon vanished from his mind as he looked upon the beautiful scenery in front of his eyes. Vast snow covered mountains appeared as far as Dale's eyes could see. At the top of the snow was a pure shade of white, but near the bottom it appeared dirty and grey. Although the mountains were a few miles away from the main city, the pollution traveled and stuck to the mountains. Dale was angered at the people who polluted, but he felt helpless as he told himself that there was nothing he could do about it. He took a deep breath and slowly released the air from his lungs. His breath appeared as small white clouds in front of his face, and then they drifted off. It was chilly on the mountain, but the bright sun warmed his body. Dale closed his eyes as he readjusted his sun proof glasses then got ready to climb the rest of the mountain.

Dale sweated under his heavy clothing and from the weight of his backpack. A cold wind beat on the small portion of his face that was exposed. He grunted as he pulled himself up to the top layer of the mountain. With one last surge of strength, Dale flung himself onto the top.

Pride swelled within his chest as he lay on the cold icy snow and stared into the blue sky. White puffy clouds covered the tips of the higher mountains in the distance. "I'll conquer you next," Dale promised as he pointed his index finger towards one of the particularly high mountains. A wide smile played upon his face. Even though he was uncomfortable, Dale had never felt better.

Dale walked over to the center of the mountain to set up his portable self-timed camera. He smiled widely and held a Canadian flag proudly in his hands as the camera snapped the first picture. Dale had just started to get ready for the next picture when he heard a loud cracking noise. "Huh?" Dale exclaimed in confusion as he looked down towards his feet where the noise was coming from. Dale's eyes widened in horror; the snow was beginning to crack in jagged edges around his

147

feet. "Jump!" Dale yelled to himself. He did not have time to move as the icy snow gave way under his feet. The visions of beautiful mountaintops and blue skies disappeared from Dale's eyes as he felt himself falling into the mountain.

A few seconds later, Dale landed with a thud on lightly packed snow. He shut his eyes tightly as pain and adrenaline coursed through his body. When the pain began to subside, Dale opened his eyes then screamed in horror. "I'm blind!" Dale yelled in a high pitch voice that only a dog could hear.

Complete whiteness surrounded Dale. He turned his head from left to right, but he could still see nothing but whiteness. "Oh," he moaned as he felt a migraine creeping deep inside his skull. He was no longer concerned about the pain that coursed through his arms, back, and legs as he shakily stood up; all he cared about was regaining his sight. Dale's heart fluttered in hope as he began to see some fuzzy shapes. As he looked down at his hands, he was able to see the silhouette of them. Taking heed of the chance that his regained eyesight yielded, Dale began searching around him for anything that might have fallen down alongside himself.

It did not take him long to find his backpack. My eyesight is getting better; Dale realized with a sigh of relief as he clung tightly onto his backpack and began searching the floor again. Dale bent down and picked up his special sunglasses that lay in front of him. He gasped as he placed them upon his face. Even though his eyesight was still poor, his eyes had improved greatly. Dale suppressed gasping again as he gazed at his surroundings. Everything around him was a sparkling shade of white. "It's the most pure snow I have ever seen," Dale spoke quietly in amazement.

Dale's eyes gazed up and down the white snow walls as he twirled around. He was in a small room that contained two exits. One of these exits was a dark hole in the snow wall, while the other exit was about fifty feet above his head. At the very top of the mountain there was a hole that appeared very small. "I must have fallen through there," Dale said out loud. "I could have broken every bone in my body or even died!" Dale looked down at where he had fallen. It looked as if the snow, that broke his fall, was lightly packed so that if someone fell they would not be seriously hurt. Does that mean that I'm not alone down here? Dale asked himself with a shiver. Upon thinking about life down here, a new fear was conjured in his mind; how would he get out of here? And where is here?

Although his eyesight was still adjusting to the bright snow, his eyesight was good enough to see fairly well. Dale checked his equipment; he had fallen down with everything except his two ice picks. "Well, if I'm inside the middle of the mountain I might as well explore a little," Dale reasoned out loud. He felt excitement overpower his panic. "I've just made a huge discovery." He smiled to himself as he secured his belongings in his backpack and pouch then headed to the oval shaped hole in the icy wall. Despite the excitement that he felt, Dale gulped as he stepped into the pitch-blackness.

Dale could feel the brightness of the previous room leave him as he limped slightly in the dark. He took off his special sunglasses, which made the room a bit lighter. However, it was still very dark as he bumped into an unseen wall. "Oh no," he exclaimed in panic as he turned around and bumped into another wall. "The room's closing in on me," he shrieked in horror. Dale closed his eyes and waited to be crushed by the cold icy wall.

He opened his eyes minutes later when he realized that he was still alive. Dale let out a whoosh of air that he had been holding in. Then he brought his hand to the cold wall and began to walk until he felt an opening in the hard snow wall. Not knowing whether the path led him deeper into the middle of the mountain or if it would lead him back to the room, in which he had fallen into, Dale stepped forward. He sighed as brightness filled his eyes once again. Dale was back where he had started.

"Up!" Dale cried suddenly, realizing that the only way out was through the hole in which he had fallen though. He immediately regretted not retrieving his large ice picks from the mountainside. He had been too afraid of falling again so he just scaled the rest of the mountain with the small emergency ice picks. I'll be able to get out of here with the small ones, Dale thought as he reached into his pouch. The longer his fingers rummaged in the pouch, the more anxious Dale became. His face flushed in fear as he realized that the ice picks had been left at his side while he admired the clouds. In a panicked fury, Dale ran towards the tightly packed snow and dug his spiked boots hard against the wall. Pain shot through his left foot and traveled to his head, but he ignored the feeling and dug his other foot into the wall. Dale felt all the muscles in his body ache and tense up with the extreme pressure as he began to advance up the wall. He had only got up the wall by a few feet when he came tumbling down. Dale landed hard on his back and once again, felt the familiar feeling of pain shoot through his body.

He took off his backpack, which was digging uncomfortably into his back, and removed a bottle of painkillers and a bottle of water. Dale took out an energy bar and nibbled on it slowly. As he ate silently, he thought about the disastrous situation that he was in. As Dale sat on the snow floor, the cold temperature of the mountain began to settle into his exposed face. He huddled himself tightly while thankfully realizing that it was actually warmer inside the mountain than it was outside.

It seemed airless and silent inside the mountain. Dale could only hear a quiet ringing in his ears, the deep breathes of air he took in, and the beating of his heart. It's actually kind of peaceful down here; Dale thought as he placed his backpack against the corner of the wall and leaned against it. Dale could feel that his eyes were getting heavy and that his head was beginning to tilt down towards his chest. He closed his eyes and fell into a restless sleep.

* * *

Dale began to slowly wake up. He muttered nonsense to himself as he, still half asleep, kicked his legs. Dale felt warm and cozy underneath a thick soft blanket.

"Huh?" Dale cried out loud as he regained full consciousness. He remembered falling down the middle of the mountain and into the bright cave. He also remembered going to sleep with just his backpack for comfort; Dale knew that he did not have a blanket. "Where did this come from?" Dale inquired out loud as he ran his hand over the smooth blanket. He suddenly jumped up and grabbed his backpack; he knew that he was not alone in the mountain's icy stomach. He ran into the dark tunnel, determined to find a way out. As soon as Dale had stepped into the darkness, he collided with a heavy object.

He felt his head spinning as he heard a deep voice say, "I thought I heard you talking." Dale stumbled back into the brightness as the person, who had just spoken, advanced forward. He stared in shock as the brightness revealed the man behind the voice.

The man stood at about six feet tall. He was clothed in the same material from which the blanket was made; it was wrapped tightly around

150

his body like it was robe. His face, which was a pale shade of blue, and his long stringy white hair and beard made Dale sick to his stomach.

"Who...who are you?" Dale stuttered in shock.

"I'm Yurick," the man replied, smiling and offering his hand towards Dale's. However, Dale did not see Yurick's hand as he stared at his smile instead. Yurick's teeth were made from light blue jewels. "Aren't you going to shake my hand?" Yurick asked with a booming laugh. Dale's hand numbly found Yurick's, but he never took his eyes off the strange man's face.

"Are we in the middle of the mountain?" Dale hurried to ask.

"Yes," Yurick replied casually as he walked over to the blanket that had been in the corner and began to fold it neatly. "I was surprised to find you down here," Yurick admitted. "I don't usually check this room, but I'm glad that I did. You didn't hurt yourself when you fell through, did you?"

"No, I...I'm fine," Dale replied, still stumbling over his words.

"Oh good," Yurick said with a smile, revealing his sparkling blue teeth once again. "Did my blanket keep you warm?" he inquired further.

"Yes," Dale answered, regaining some of his composure. "How long have you been down here for? Do you still have your ice picks?"

Yurick laughed in amusement. "I lost my ice picks twenty one years ago; it would be pointless to search for them now."

"Twenty one years!" Dale yelled. "How could you have possibly survived down here for that long?"

"I was taught," Yurick said proudly.

"By whom? Are there more people down here?"

"Not anymore," Yurick said sadly. "It's just you and me. The real inhabitants of the Palace of Ice are dead."

Dale closed his eyes and prayed for his head to stop spinning.

"You don't look very well," Yurick observed. "Would you like some fresh ice water?"

"No," Dale said, slowly opening his eyes, "but I do want to know all about the Palace of Ice and its inhabitants."

"Are you sure? It's such a sad story."

"Tell me," Dale pleaded, suddenly realizing that he really had made a discovery of a lifetime.

151

"Alright," Yurick agreed, unfolding the blanket and spreading it on the ground. He sat on it and motioned for Dale to do the same. Dale obediently followed Yurick's gesture and waited anxiously for him to start talking.

"I was an avid mountain climber," Yurick began, "and I remember being particularly anxious to tackle this mountain. It was an unusually hot day when I started my climb, but I didn't want to turn back because I had traveled from very far away. It was hard work to get to the summit, but I finally did it. I was standing on the middle of the mountain, looking at the beautiful scenery and feeling very proud. Then I heard the cracking of ice. The next thing I knew I was laying at the bottom of the mountain. However, I had not fallen down the mountainside; I was actually inside the mountain's stomach! I had broken my leg because of the fall. There was no snow there when I fell," Yurick further offered. "I remember lying on the cold ice floor in complete agony. I knew I was a goner. I don't know how much time had passed, but when I saw the community of mountain inhabitants, nothing else matter. They called themselves Iceneeks. They looked like normal human beings, only shorter, bluer, and with teeth made from jewels. Surprisingly, the Iceneeks spoke English and reassured me that I would be alright. They moved me through that dark tunnel and into the most beautiful place I had ever seen. The Iceneeks nursed me back to health and then taught me how to survive in the Palace of Ice."

"Wait," Dale interrupted. "Why didn't you try to get out?"

"Once my leg had healed I tried to climb out several times, but I just kept on falling down. The Iceneeks didn't have the right equipment that would help me escape, so I finally gave up."

"You mean there's no way out of here?" Dale shrieked in rising panic.

"Of course there isn't," Yurick said angrily. "I've tried everything. Although I love this place, I miss the real world. I'm so lonely down here."

"What happened to the Iceneeks?" Dale asked in curiosity and in hopes of learning something that may help him escape from the mountain's stomach.

"I'm so ashamed," Yurick said, barely audibly. "It wasn't my fault," he protested, "I never meant to hurt them."

"I believe you," Dale said cautiously, realizing that he was dealing with someone whom he had just met, in the middle of the mountain, and who proclaimed to have killed a whole community of people.

"The change in temperature caused me to develop a bad cold and cough. Once again, the Iceneeks nursed me back to health, but in doing so they caught my cold. I guess their bodies weren't used to my foreign germs because they began to die in the order which they caught my cold. Oh, I still feel guilty about it to this very day." Yurick buried his head into his hands.

Dale didn't know what to say. He planned to give Yurick a reassuring pat on the back as he raised his hand. However, he lowered it as he felt unsure about Yurick's disposition. "Show me the rest of this place," Dale urged instead.

"Alright," Yurick agreed, perking up a bit. Dale watched as Yurick neatly folded the blanket once again and then he followed him towards the dark tunnel's entrance. "Stay close to me," Yurick warned. "It's very easy to get lost in these tunnels."

Dale nodded then silently stepped into the darkness. Dale felt the air getting warmer and the pressure getting higher. He moved slowly, putting one foot just inches before the other. Yurick's heavy breathing did nothing to calm Dale's nerves.

Dale followed Yurick as he made quick and jagged moves. As his speed increased, Dale had a hard time keeping up. Yurick's quickened speed and turns eventually led to a bright light at the end of the tunnel. Dale tried to peek around Yurick in the hopes of catching an early glance at the shimmering light. However, Yurick was too large, so Dale waited anxiously until he emerged from the tunnel after Yurick.

"Oh, whoa," was all Dale was able to mutter. He narrowed his eyes in the brightness, but he dared not close them. Pure white ice walls, decorated in flawless blue and red gems surrounded Dale. A pond in a far corner shone light blue. It looked as if there were sunbeams projected from underneath the pond; and this light made the gems twinkle and shine.

The room itself was very large and contained a lot of appliances that a normal house would have. There were chairs, tables, and beds. The only difference was that the furniture was made out of ice and had a thick blanket covering them.

"This place is magical!" Dale exclaimed in awe.

Yurick laughed. "Although it may look magical, I assure you that it's not. It's more a matter of survival," he added with a wink.

"How do you eat?" Dale asked in a rushed, anxious voice.

"I catch my food through the pond," Yurick explained. "I catch fish, seals, and any other animal that happens to be passing by. I use my tourmaline gem spear to catch them."

"Your *what* spear?" Dale asked in confusion.

"My tourmaline gem spear. The handle is made from a long icicle while a tourmaline gem is used as the spearhead." As Dale followed him towards the spear and the pond, Yurick went on to describe the spear further. "The Iceneeks taught me how to make a spear. First you model the icicle into the length that you desire and then you gently put the already heated tourmaline gem at the end of the icicle. You have to wait a few days for the tourmaline gem to attach itself properly, but after that the spear has a fifteen year usage."

"Where did all the gems come from?" Dale inquired as he looked hungrily at the glistering tourmaline gem in Yurick's hands.

"Why, they grow here!" Yurick exclaimed as if Dale had just asked the silliest question possible. "There are only two types of gems that grow down here, but they grow in abundance," Yurick explained as he urged Dale to follow him to the wall. "The tourmaline gem grows here," he said, pointing to a cluster of the familiar looking blue gems that were buried deep inside the icy wall. Dale bent down to touch another cluster of tourmaline gems that were poking through the wall. They were cold and very jagged. Dale suddenly understood how the tourmaline gem could rip through the thick skin of a seal.

"And these," Yurick said, interrupting Dale's thoughts, "are star rubies." Dale looked at the gem, which Yurick was pointing to. It was a deep shade of red and shaped like an oval. However, most interestingly were the white lines in the ruby, which appeared to make a cross.

"They really are beautiful and I bet they are very rare. Why didn't the Iceneeks collect them and sell them?"

Yurick stopped looking at the wall and turned his wide eyes to Dale's face. "An Iceneek would never use a gem other than for survival. And they definitely wouldn't sell the gems even if they could get out of the Palace of Ice."

"Why?" Dale asked simply.

"Why? Why?" Yurick repeated in horror. "Because this place is cursed by the spirits of past Iceneeks, that's why!"

Dale looked at Yurick and laughed. "Yeah, right," he smirked. "I think you've been down here far too long." Yurick looked at Dale intensely then raised his spear. Dale's eyes widened as Yurick ran towards him with the dangerous looking tourmaline gem pointed forwards. Dale let out a scream then leapt towards the ground. He covered his head with his hands and waited to be pierced to death.

Dale looked up in surprise as he heard the splashing of water and Yurick exclaim, "I've got one! I knew a fish had entered the pond because of the changing reflection upon the walls." Yurick proudly held up the tourmaline gem spear which held the squirming fish in place. "Hungry?" he asked.

Dale licked the plate, which had contained cooked fish, clean. Dale usually had good table manners, but there was something about eating from a pure ruby plate, which made him forget about manners.

"Enjoyed that, didn't you, Dale?" Yurick asked with a laugh. Dale nodded, his head still buried in the plate. "It's about time we got some sleep," Yurick suggested, noticing that the light from the pond was no longer bright. Dale looked around him and saw that the room was darker but that the gems still glittered brightly. Dale felt as if he were floating through a star filled sky late at night.

"You can take that bed," Yurick said, pointing to a small bed that was covered in blankets. Not knowing what else to do, Dale followed Yurick's instructions. Still fully clothed, he got under the thick fur blanket and shut his eyes. He heard Yurick nestle into a nearby bed. "Dale?" Yurick asked suddenly.

"Yes?" Dale replied, trying to sound sleepy.

"I know you must be sad, but I want you to know that there is nothing to worry about. I'll teach you how to adapt and survive in the Palace of Ice. I'll even make you an outfit like mine tomorrow."

Dale said nothing. He wondered if Yurick really thought that those words would be reassuring to him. Dale shook his head as if trying to erase the thought from his mind. It doesn't matter what Yurick thinks, Dale silently told himself, because before sunrise I'll be out of here.

155

Dale was still wide-awake an hour later. He lay anxiously in his bed, listening to the rhythm of Yurick's snores. Then, ever so quietly, Dale climbed out of bed and headed towards the tourmaline gems and star rubies that he had seen against the wall. He kneeled down beside the cluster of gems and stared at them greedily. They shimmered and shined even in the dim light.

Dale's hands shook as he reached out and wrapped his hand around a star ruby. The top of the star ruby was still attached to the frozen wall, but Dale had already thought of the solution to that problem. He removed the matches that he has transplanted from his backpack to his pocket earlier that evening. Dale struck the match and heated the ice around the precious gem. He let the brunt match fall to the ground then he carefully rocked the star ruby back and forth until it came loose. As Dale held the heavy gem in his hands, a smile played upon his face; he suddenly felt very powerful.

An unrhymed snore from Yurick made the feeling of immortality disappear. Dale quietly placed the star ruby into his backpack and worked at removing several more. Next, he moved onto the tourmaline gems, which came out easier than the star rubies had. Once Dale had all the gems that he could carry, he crept towards the tunnel and prayed that he would be able to find his way out.

Dale had great difficulty maneuvering himself throughout the tunnels, but after fifteen minutes and with a lot of bumping into the walls, he was able to find the room in which he had fallen. Dale looked up at the roof, but was unable to see the spot where he had fallen through. This room is a lot darker than the other, Dale thought with a shiver. He stood beside the pile of snow and walked sideways to the wall. He then took the two tourmaline gems, which he held in his hands, and drove them as silently as possible into the icy wall. Dale was happy to learn that the sharp edge of the tourmaline gem entered somewhat easily into the wall. Dale had put on his climbing gloves and was still wearing his spiked boots. He was glad that he had these items with him. He would need them desperately to climb out of the mountain's stomach.

Dale drove the second tourmaline gem into the icy wall then lifted himself up. He dug his boots into the wall, the right, and then the left. Dale was moving up the wall more slowly than he had hoped to, but it was a very difficult climb. As Dale reached the top, he urged himself not to look down. He realized the dangers of being so high off the ground without the proper safety equipment.

Getting over the mouth of the mountain was the hardest part of the climb. Panic shot through Dale's body as he swayed back and forth for a few seconds. His feet searched for a place to sink into. Dale's body was the shape of a sideways "U" as he used his last surge of energy to throw himself up and over the hole in the middle of the mountain.

Dale scrambled away from the hole. He stuffed the two tourmaline gems, which he had used for ice picks, then grabbed his emergency ice picks which he had left on the mountain top earlier that day. Too afraid to get close to the hole, Dale left his camera and the tripod and hurried to prepare for the climb down the mountain.

With only the moonlight to provide light, Dale finally made it to the bottom of the mountain. "I'd rather be on this side," Dale muttered to the wall, meaning for his words to be spoken to Yurick. Dale smiled as he thought about the pile of gems, which were weighing heavily in his backpack, and began his long walk back to town.

* * *

Dale spent the remaining days inside his hotel room, while anxiously waiting for the day when he could return home. He had considered calling his airline and asking for an earlier flight. However, he did not want to draw attention to himself and he thought that fleeing the country might do just that. Instead, Dale protectively watched over his precious gems. He had cushioned each star ruby and tourmaline gem individually in wrappings. Dale then carefully packed them into his luggage. He hated the thought of having them out of his eyesight and exposed to the possible danger of theft, but he knew his best chance of smuggling the gems was through this method. Dale knew that the gems could not be taken on the airplane in hand luggage.

Dale's anxiety increased as the day of his flight home approached. On the night of his last day in Asia, Dale could not bring himself to sleep. He stared at the ceiling and counted the tiles. When this did not bring sleep to his eyes, he stared at the old peeling wallpaper and counted the small red flowers that decorated it. The red flowers became fuzzy and Dale's eyelids closed. He had just entered into the first stages of sleep when a dark shadow passed over his eyes.

"Huh?" Dale cried as he woke up in a fright. His heart raced as he looked around the room; everything was the same as it had been before. Dale quickly glanced at his luggage and was relieved to see that it was still there. Feeling better, but still shaken up, Dale sat back down in bed. He closed his eyes and listened to his heart beat calm down. It was just a shadow from outside; probably a cat or something like that. Dale's hypothesis satisfied him as he turned on his side and pressed his face into the warm pillow. I can't wait until my gems and I are safely home, Dale thought with a smile as he imagined the situation.

"Give them back," a hoarse voice said suddenly. Dale sprang back up in bed, his eyes wide in fear. "Give them back to whom they belong," the hoarse voice said again. Dale swung his whole body around in the bed and surveyed the room. He saw nothing. "Give them back to me," whispered the voice.

"Who are you?" Dale screamed, while covering his head with his hands and rocking back and forth. A loud knocking from behind Dale made him shake uncontrollably. "Go away," Dale screamed from behind his hands.

The knocking came louder this time. "Be quiet," said an angry voice from behind the wall. Dale took his hands away from his face when he realized that the knocking was coming from a disturbed neighbor.

"Did you hear a voice?" Dale called to his neighbor. He repeated his question when he did not receive an answer.

"Are you talking to me?" the voice behind the wall asked.

"Yes," Dale replied. "Did you hear that voice just a minute ago?"

"I didn't hear anything but you yelling some sort of question," the neighbor responded. "Is everything okay in there?" he said in a somewhat concerned tone.

"I...I'm fine," Dale reassured him. "Sorry to disturb you. I just had a bad dream."

"Well, just try to keep it down," the neighbor said. Dale heard a squeak as his neighbor settled back in his bed.

Dale did the same thing as he tried to convince himself that he really did have a bad dream and that there were no voices in his room. However, he was not fully convinced. He spent the night worrying and falling into short, restless sleep patterns.

* * *

Dale did not hear any more noise that night, but he was very tired as he dragged himself out of bed the next morning. His flight was scheduled to leave at 10:00 AM. Dale was feeling weak and anxious. Although he wanted to get home, he was very nervous about going through the airport's security. He had heard from many people that the airport had very strict security rules. Dale shuddered as he thought about what would happen if the security guards caught him. "Don't be so negative," Dale scolded himself out loud. "You're not going to get caught."

"Next in line please," called out the security guard as she motioned for Dale to step forward. Dale removed his watch and flung in onto a nearby dish before stepping through the metal detector. "Thank you; enjoy your flight," the woman said, handing Dale back his watch, after he had successfully gone through the metal detector.

"Flight 521 to Vancouver, BC now boarding," a loud voice called through the intercom. Dale held his ticket in his hand and proceeded to the boarding area. He had just got in line when he felt a pair of hands clasp heavily down on his shoulders.

"Huh?" Dale exclaimed out loud, startled by the sudden attack.

"Hand over your bag," the police officer, who had grabbed Dale, demanded. Dale did not have a chance to succumb to the man's demand as the bag was roughly torn from his hands. Dale's heart raced. He was so thankful that he had not put any of the gems in his hand-traveling luggage.

Dale watched as the officer unzipped his bag and rummaged around in it. The officer's eyes widened, then he called into his walkie-talkie for backup. Dale did not have a chance to voice his confusion as another officer approached the scene and dragged Dale away from the line. Dale felt a hundred pairs of curious eyes watch him as he was escorted away.

"What's going on here?" Dale finally choked out as he was pushed into a dark room. The officer reached into Dale's bag once again. However, this time he revealed a star ruby.

"We received an anonymous tip," he said in a thick accent. "We were told that you had stolen many precious gems from our country."

"I didn't put that star ruby in my bag," Dale said truthfully.

The officer gave Dale a dirty look. "The rest of your luggage is being sent here," he sneered.

"This isn't fair. You have to let me go." Dale felt the panic rising in his chest. Although he was surprised to see the star ruby in his hand luggage, he knew exactly what would be found in his other luggage.

"Isn't fair?" the officer mocked nastily. "I'll tell you what's not fair! How would you like it if outsiders visited your country, then stole precious gems from your museum?"

"Museum?" Dale muttered. "I never took any precious gems from a museum. I found them."

The officer looked at Dale in disgust. "How dare you insult my intelligence!" he bellowed. "Do you take me for a fool? Star rubies cannot be found anywhere but in the museum. The last cluster was excavated over two hundred years ago."

"But I've found lots of clusters of them, as well as tourmaline gems," Dale pleaded.

"Ah, so you admit it," the officer exclaimed through narrow eyes. "Last night the museum was broken into and stripped of all its star rubies and tourmaline gems." The officer stopped talking as two more men, who were carrying Dale's luggage, entered the room. Dale wished he could be swallowed up by the floor as the officer opened his luggage, unwrapped numerous packages, and revealed the star rubies and tourmaline gems. One of the officers nodded to another. The next thing he knew, a blindfold had been placed over his eyes and he was being lifted away by the two men.

"Where...where are you taking me?" he stuttered in shock.

"Where thieves like you belong," replied an officer as he shoved Dale outside then into a car. Dale squirmed in an attempt to break free, but an officer tied a thick rope around Dale and the seat.

"You can't do this to me," Dale shrieked. "I have rights. I deserve a trial."

"A trial?" one of the officers mocked. "There is no trail for thieves like you. You get thrown straight into prison."

"No! I demand my lawyer." In a fury, Dale kicked out his leg and made contact with one of the men. Dale heard the man stumble backwards and yelp in pain. Dale also heard another man approach him and then he felt a hard object being smashed against his head.

When Dale woke up his head was pounding from the blow he had received earlier. He opened his eyes to see blackness. The room was so dark that Dale thought he was still wearing the blindfold. However, when his eyes adjusted to the change in light, he realized that he was free of any constraints. Dale slowly got to his feet and examined his surroundings. He was in a small room that was built from large gray stones. In the corner was a thin mattress lying on the floor; a thin torn blanket lay in a heap on top of it. In the other corner were a single toilet and a few sheets of toilet paper. Although the room was dark and gloomy, the thick metal bars, which locked Dale in, produced the most fear.

"Let me out of here," Dale yelled as he leapt towards the bars and shook them forcefully. He grabbed at the cluster of chains, which kept the bars closed, and tugged at them with all his might. The chains made a loud clunking noise against the bars, but they did not come loose. "Let me out of here," Dale yelled again.

"Why should I?" came a cold voice from behind Dale.

Dale shivered furiously. He was positive that there was no one else in the jail cell a minute ago. When Dale tuned around, horror filled his eyes. He stood facing a blue looking man who was clothed in the same type of outfit that Yurick had been wearing. "Are you an Iceneek?" Dale asked, not really wanting to know the answer to his question.

"Of course I am," the Iceneek snapped. "I'm the ghost of the Iceneek that was chosen to protect the Palace of Ice from thieves. It is my duty to make sure our precious gems stay where they belong."

"You put that star ruby in my hand luggage," Dale realized, hardly believing what he was saying.

"Yes," the Iceneek confessed. "And I did a lot more than that. I broke into the museum and hid their star rubies and tourmaline gems. I then called the police department and told them that you were responsible for it and where you could be found."

"Listen, I'm really sorry that I stole your gems. I'll put all of them back- I promise." Dale felt beads of sweat dripping down his face. He could not believe that a ghost had set him up.

"It's too late to make amends," the Iceneek sneered, "Besides; I've already taken the gems back to the Palace of Ice. I have no further use for you. The police, however, will definitely need you. Now that the star rubies and tourmaline gems have been stolen yet again, they will

161

think you have an alias. They'll be asking you a lot of questions which you won't be able to answer. I suppose you're smart enough to figure out what the consequences of that will be."

"No," Dale choked. "Please don't let them hurt me."

"The police are very proud of their heritage. They hate it when foreigners steal from them," the Iceneek hinted in a sinister tone.

"Please...I'm sorry," Dale pleaded. "Just don't let them hurt me."

"Stop repeating yourself; it's annoying," the Iceneek scolded. Dale became quiet. "I see that you are truly sorry and so I'll offer you a choice," the Iceneek said. "You can stay here and take the punishment which the police give you, or you can come back with me to the Palace of Ice."

"Will I have to live in the Palace of Ice forever?" Dale asked with wide eyes.

"Yes, but at least you'll live," the Iceneek hinted.

"After what I've done to you, why would you want me to live in your beautiful palace?" Dale asked suspiciously.

"I don't make the rules," the Iceneek replied. "I truly wish that you had never fallen down the middle of the mountain, but it is too late to change that."

Dale stared at the Iceneek, examining every one of his features. His face was hidden in his dark hood, so all that Dale could see was an outline of a pale blue face and the brightness coming from his teeth. "Alright," Dale agreed. "I'll go back with you."

Dale watched in amazement as the Iceneek stepped closer to him and revealed the most beautiful tourmaline gem Dale had ever seen. Dale let out a startled cry as the Iceneek brought the tourmaline gem smashing down on his head. Dale felt no pain. The next thing Dale knew was that he was back in the Palace of Ice, lying on the same snow mound that he had first fallen on.

"Hello, Dale," Yurick said in an unfriendly voice.

"Where's the Iceneek?" Dale asked, feeling as if he may need the Iceneek's protection.

"He's gone. Iceneeks only come to fulfill their duties when something goes wrong."

"Oh," Dale said simply.

"You shouldn't have stolen those precious gems," Yurick scolded.

"I know," Dale said sincerely. "I wish I had never taken them. But please understand, Yurick, that I am truly sorry."

"Don't apologize to me," Yurick said.

"But I feel badly for leaving you," Dale protested.

"Then make it up to me. Tell me how to get out of here."

Dale looked at Yurick in surprise. "You can't leave," he exclaimed.

"Yes I can, but only if you tell me how. I'm not going to steal any gems," Yurick added, when he saw Dale give him a suspicious gaze.

"You can't leave me down here. I don't know how to survive."

"I'll teach you everything you need to know if you tell me how to get out of here."

"I don't want to live down here all by myself," Dale protested.

"You should have thought about that before you stole the gems. Surely you knew that you would be punished." Dale stared silently at Yurick. "Either you tell me how to get out or I'll kill you," Yurick threatened.

"Alright," he agreed, not knowing what else to do.

* * *

Yurick spent the next four weeks teaching Dale everything that he would need to know to survive.

On the day of Yurick's departure, Dale was surprisingly relieved. Yurick had become bad tempered and just plain annoying. I guess being so close to freedom can really change a guy, Dale thought to himself as he watched him disappear through the mountain's opening.

Dale had just turned around and prepared to walk through the tunnels when he heard an unhappy voice mutter, "Dale, you've done it again." Emerging from the dark tunnel, surrounded in a bright blue light, was the Iceneek who has put Dale in jail, then rescued him from it.

"What...what have I done?" Dale asked, while remembering Yurick telling him that Iceneeks only return when they had a duty to fulfill.

"You have let Yurick escape," the Iceneek said angrily.

"So?" Dale asked in confusion. "Wasn't he allowed to leave? I thought I was the only one who wasn't allowed to leave."

163

"You fool!" the Iceneek bellowed. "We wanted to keep Yurick here because he knows all of our secrets. We told him that there was no way out so he would stay here forever. Now, he has gone back to the outside world and there is nothing that I can do about it."

"Why not?" Dale questioned. "You certainly found me quick enough."

"Yes, but you did something wrong. Yurick is innocent."

"I'm sorry," Dale said pathetically.

"Well, I can't punish Yurick but..."the Iceneek stopped and stared at Dale, "I can punish you."

Dale backed up against the cold wall and shut his eyes. Although he could not see the Iceneek, he heard his words perfectly clear. "I think it would be for the best if you become one of us. You cause too much trouble when you are alive." Dale shut his eyes tighter as he felt a cold wave surge through his body.

When he opened his eyes, everything was bright. As his eyes adjusted to the brightness, he realized that he was high in the sky, looking down at the mountain. The Iceneek, who had taken him there, came to rest on the cloud that Dale was sitting on.

"We spend our days looking over the mountain which contains the Palace of Ice," the Iceneek explained. "I know that it's very boring just looking at mountains, but you broke the rules and now you have to pay the price."

"Look at mountains forever?" Dale muttered. The Iceneek gave him a sad nod with his head. "That's too bad," Dale said, trying to suppress a smile, "I really hate looking at mountains!"

\* \* \*

# Curses Never Die

# Curses Never Die

"The kids were an absolute handful today," Erin commented, referring to the kids in their snorkeling instruction class.

Nineteen-year-old Erin and her older brother Justin had lived in Hawaii their whole lives. They both attended the University of Hawaii where they studied environmental science. This summer, like every other summer for the past six years, Erin and Justin held snorkeling lessons on their own private beach. They lived with their mother who was the author of the popular book series entitled The Adventures of a Hawaiian Girl. Erin and Justin had enjoyed the luxuries of being rich since they were very little.

"For sure," Justin replied, rolling his eyes. "I can't believe that Samantha thought it was funny to pretend to drown! I think I lost ten years off my life when I saw her floating face down in the water." Justin shuddered then flicked his soaking wet hair out of his eyes.

Both Erin and Justin had dark brown eyes and hair. They were tall, slender and well tanned from the countless hours spent in the sun.

Erin sighed. "Remind me why we started giving kids snorkeling lessons?" she asked.

"For our love of kids and the water," Justin laughed.

This time Erin rolled her eyes. "You got the latter part right."

"Dinner is ready," the housekeeper shouted, interrupting Erin. Erin and Justin ran towards their large three story house with bags of dripping wet snorkeling equipment.

\* \* \*

That night Erin tossed and turned in her sleep. She kept dreaming about Samantha. In her dream Samantha had drowned for real. Erin called to Samantha, but she did not respond. Erin dove into the water and swam to Samantha's floating body. She pulled Samantha's head up to the surface then screamed in horror when she saw the girl's dead blue face.

Erin sat straight up in bed and breathed heavily. "It's just a dream. Samantha is fine," Erin whispered aloud. Hearing her own voice calmed her down a little bit. She looked at her bedside clock, which read 2:31 AM, before lying back in her bed. Sweat clung to her nightshirt, making Erin extremely uncomfortable. It took an hour but Erin finally fell into a peaceful sleep. Erin had no clue that she wouldn't be sleeping peacefully for a very long time to come.

* * *

"Are you ready to dive with the best diver that the world has ever seen?" Justin asked in a cocky voice.

"I would love to. Do you see that person anywhere?" Erin asked, while placing her hands over her eyes and pretending to look around the vast sea.

"Very funny," Justin said, sounding hurt.

Erin laughed then really did look around the sea. Erin and Justin were one hundred feet from shore, bouncing up and down according to the sea's gentle waves, on their white and blue boat.

"Let's get geared up," Erin said suddenly, not being able to resist diving into the sea's dark blue waves any longer. Erin and Justin checked their equipment thoroughly then put it on.

"Remember to stay close to me," Justin instructed, after he had attached an oxygen tank to his back. "We have never dived so far from the shore before."

Erin nodded before jumping into the clear water. Her eyes quickly adjusted to the darkness as she swam deeper into the water. Erin loved the feeling of peacefulness that being deep under the water yielded. She saw some large fish in the distance and headed towards them. Unfortunately, they would swim away as soon as she tried to approach them. Erin was so engrossed in the scenery that she got a fright when she saw a dark figure approach her. It only took her a few seconds to figure out that it was Justin.

Justin was waving at Erin, indicating that he wanted her to follow him. Erin gave up chasing after the fish and obediently followed her brother. Although it seemed like Justin just wanted to show her something, Erin knew that she should obey his signals just in case something was wrong. Erin and Justin had spent hours practicing underwater signals on dry land.

Erin came to a stop beside Justin then gasped as she saw the deep chasm that lay in front of them. Erin turned to Justin to give him a surprised look from behind her diving mask. She knew that they were both thinking the same thing; that the presence of the chasm was a great discovery. Erin peered down into the chasm and shivered. It looked extremely deep. Her eyes turned back to Justin as she saw him trying to

167

get something from the pouch that was clipped to his waist. She continued to watch Justin in interest as he pulled out a flashlight and shined it into the chasm. Erin almost fainted when she saw what was down there.

The light from Justin's flashlight illuminated a mossy covered ship. Justin slowly moved his flashlight around the exterior of the ship. Erin and Justin's eyes met in bewilderment. How long has the ship been down there? How did it get there? Why hasn't anyone found it before? All of these questions ran through Erin's head. She was so wrapped up in how she could get the answers to her questions that she hardly noticed Justin take a flying leap off the edge then plunge into the chasm.

"No!" Erin shouted from behind her mask. She felt her whole body go ice cold as she watched Justin descend towards the shipwreck. She could not believe that he would jump like that without notifying her first.

In anger, fear, and confusion, Erin jumped after Justin. Her body really did go cold as she descended into the dark water. She had to turn on her own flashlight to its highest setting just to see where she was going.

As Erin continued to slowly swim downwards, she spotted Justin's flashlight. She swam towards him, while thinking about the trouble she would give him. When Erin had approached Justin she shined the flashlight on him then screamed.

Instead of seeing Justin's familiar face, Erin saw a large ugly fish that had long sharp teeth. Although its massive teeth were unusual, it was the small round ball of light, which hung on a string of flesh in front of the fish's face that really frightened Erin. She had never seen anything like it before. Erin felt her heartbeat increase as the fish stared at her then quickly swam away. She shivered in fear as she continued to search for her brother in the murky water. How could he have got so far from my view? Erin thought anxiously as she remembered the rule of always keeping you diving partner within eyesight. Not knowing where else to look, Erin descended even further as she headed towards the shipwreck.

Erin felt the water pressure get heavier. She checked her depth meter and oxygen indicator. Erin was relieved to see that she could descend about fifty more meters before she would run into any problems with her oxygen supply. Erin felt a bit calmer when she spotted Justin just a few meters away. She hurried after him but stopped in horror as she watched him enter the ship. He knows better than to enter a sunken ship, Erin screamed internally. She was very angry at her brother's stupidity. He knows that a ship, which has been under deep water for a long time, can easily cave in when it experiences a disturbance. A disturbance like Justin could definitely make the ship collapse, Erin thought anxiously.

She approached the ship and looked at it closely. She lifted her arm forward and gently scraped away the underwater moss that had gathered on it. This ship must have been down here for hundreds of years, Erin thought as she rubbed the thick moss from her hands.

As Erin waited for Justin to emerge, she studied the side of the ship. She was hoping to find something that would indicate how the ship had gone down.

The minutes passed slowly but Erin soon realized that Justin had been in the ship for half an hour. Where is he? She thought desperately. She knew that Justin had to come out of the ship within the next ten minutes if they hoped to get to the water's surface without running out of oxygen or getting the bends. Erin wanted to take a deep breath of oxygen, but she swallowed in fear instead. She knew that she could not afford to use up more oxygen than necessary. Swallowing in a small nervous way, Erin carefully entered the ship.

The darkness of the ship was so dense that Erin's eyes could not fully adjust to it. Her only refuge came from the flashlight that now appeared dim. Erin moved slowly through the debris that appeared in the beam of her flashlight. Where are you Justin? Erin thought angrily. Erin carefully maneuvered through the ship, realizing that it was a lot bigger than it looked. Everything inside the ship was a mess. Covered in that familiar thick moss, planks of wood and furniture littered the ship's floor.

Erin looked at the oxygen indicator and began to panic. They had to be out of the ship in four minutes if they wanted to make it out of the water alive. This thought made Erin quicken her pace. She had to suppress a deep sigh when she saw the end of the ship's hallway. Erin was sure that every door she had passed had been shut. This meant that Justin was not in the ship or that he had gone into a room then became trapped inside it.

Erin felt her ears ringing as she began to see dots in her eyes. She felt herself struggling to breathe. Logically, Erin knew that she still had enough oxygen left in her tank. However, it was the thought of running out of air and dying in the sunken ship that made her panic to a point where she felt like she could not breathe. Everything went black just as a hand grabbed her from behind.

The fright of being touched so unexpectedly startled Erin out of her fainting fit. "Justin!" She screamed when she had turned around. Of course he could not hear her but Erin was sure that he knew she was furious at him. Erin began flinging her arms wildly towards the ship's exit. She waited for Justin to swim to the exit but he didn't. Instead he motioned for Erin to follow him inside the room that he had just come out of. Erin, understanding what Justin wanted her to do, shook her head and pointed to her oxygen indicator. To Erin's surprise, Justin began pulling her towards the room. She struggled to escape Justin's grasp, but he was too strong. Erin gave up as Justin pushed her into the room and pointed towards a bright light.

As Erin carefully approached the object, she realized that the light was coming from inside a box. She watched as Justin rushed past her then reached for the box. He pulled on the lid of the box once then waved Erin over to him. He can't open the box so he wants me to help him, Erin thought, figuring out Justin's message to her. Well Justin, if we don't get out of here right now we'll both need help, Erin thought angrily.

Catching him off guard, Erin roughly shoved Justin towards the door. Justin hesitated as he stood at the door's entrance, starring at the glowing box. However, he snapped back to reality when Erin shoved the oxygen indicator in from of his face. Erin knew that she had got her message across as she watched Justin's eyes go wide in fear.

Moving at an efficient pace, Erin and Justin made it safely out of the shipwreck and the chasm. They slowly swam to the surface of the water. There were only three more meters to go when their oxygen tanks ran out of air. They held their breath until they reached the surface.

Erin ripped off her mask and gasped for air. Although she was furious at him, she allowed Justin to help her aboard the boat. She felt dizzy as she rested her head in between her knees. Erin lifted her head to see Justin sitting nearby with a dreamy look on his face. She narrowed her eyes at him and thought about the trouble she would give him when they got home. However, right now all Erin wanted to do was rest.

\* \* \*

"You have committed so many wrong acts today that I don't even know where to began," Erin scolded Justin, after they had arrived home and had time to recuperate. Now that she was feeling physically better, Erin let Justin have the trouble she promised she would give him. "Actually, I do know where to begin," Erin continued. "Your first mistake was to jump into that chasm without signaling to me first. You know that staying together is the first rule of deep sea diving. Your second mistake was entering that shipwreck. It could have collapsed on you! And why didn't you check your oxygen indicator? If it weren't for me you would be a breathless corpse in that ship!"

"Erin, calm down," Justin said soothingly. "You are getting too upset. You should see your face; it's the shade of an overcooked lobster."

"Welcome back Justin's concern," Erin said, personifying her brother's emotion. "Too bad you weren't concerned about me when we were in that chasm!" Erin shrieked.

"I am really sorry," Justin said sincerely. "I just got so excited when I saw the shipwreck. I forgot that you were even with me. I was so engrossed in the ship that nothing else mattered." Justin took a deep breath then continued. "Don't you realize how special our discovery is? It is obvious that no one else has ever found it. I bet we are the first people to enter that ship since it went down."

"Why did it go down in the first place?" Erin asked, her curiosity overcoming her anger at Justin. "I didn't see any signs of destruction; other than what the salt water and water pressure have done."

"I never noticed any disturbance that would have brought such a large ship down either," Justin admitted. "But who cares how it went down? I would rather know what was inside that glowing box."

"Maybe it was a fish," Erin said, while thinking about that scary fish with sharp teeth and the light attached to its head.

"Huh?" Justin questioned in puzzlement. "I don't think there's any living thing inside the box. The object has probably been locked up since the ship went down."

"Well, we'll find out soon enough," Erin replied, a little bit embarrassed over saying that a fish was trapped in the box. However, she forgave herself quickly as she thought about the frightening day that she had had.

"I'm glad you agree. To tell you the truth, I didn't think you would want to go down there again since you were..."

"Excuse me?" Erin interrupted in shock. "Go down there again? Are you crazy? I'm not going down there again!"

"But you just said we would find out what is in the box," Justin protested.

"Yes I did," Erin admitted. "But I meant that we would find out when we reported the shipwreck and when a professional diver checks it out."

Justin's face went a pale shade of white. "We're not telling anyone," he threatened.

"What?" Erin gasped, taken back by her brother's tone of voice. He has never spoken to me like that before, she thought in fright.

"We can't tell anyone," Justin continued in the threatening voice. "I found that shipwreck and that box is mine."

"It doesn't belong to you," Erin said quietly, still frightened by the intensity of her brother's voice.

Realizing that he was upsetting his sister, Justin spoke in a calmer voice as he said, "Erin, I discovered that shipwreck. It is mine to explore. Now I realize that you may be concerned, but there's no need to be. With all things in consideration, the ship is in great shape. It won't collapse. I'm not asking you to come with me to the shipwreck again, but I will ask you to keep this to yourself. I'm going back down and there's nothing that you could say that would change my mind."

Erin looked at Justin with fear in her eyes. "It should be a professional that goes down there," she argued.

Justin shook his head in disagreement. "I've been diving since I've been old enough to talk. I'm practically a professional."

"Dinner's ready!" the housekeeper shouted to Justin and Erin.

Erin looked at Justin as he gave her a pleading look then headed towards the dinning room. Practically isn't a sure enough word for me, Erin thought in worry.

* * *

Erin groggily woke up the next morning and turned her head to look at the digital clock that sat on her bedside table. She sat straight up in bed in a panic when she saw 10:10 AM written on the clock. Without even getting dressed, Erin ran out of her bedroom, down the stairs and to the boat. She prayed that Justin had not already left for the shipwreck.

Erin let out a breath of air when she saw that the boat was still stationary at the dock. She was a bit annoyed at herself for waking up so late and taking the chance that Justin had already left. She had decided late last night, while she was tossing and turning restlessly, that she would accompany Justin to the shipwreck. Although all her logical senses were telling her to stay away from the chasm and to tell a deep sea diving professional about the shipwreck, her emotional senses were telling her to be loyal to her brother. He seemed so intrigued and enthusiastic about the sunken ship and the mysterious glowing box that Erin could not bring herself to crush his feelings. Erin also knew that she would never forgive herself if something happened to Justin while he was exploring a shipwreck under her knowledge.

"What are you doing here?" Justin asked as he emerged from inside the boat, while carrying his diving equipment in his hands. "Did you change your mind?" he asked curiously.

Erin nodded. "I would never let you dive alone."

"I was hoping you would think that," Justin smiled. "So are you ready to dive?"

"No," Erin replied, while shaking her head.

"But you just said..." Justin's voice trailed off, revealing his surprise.

"I know what I said," Erin replied smiling. "I have to eat breakfast first. There's no way that I'm diving on an empty stomach!"

* * *

Erin was no longer feeling confident about her decision as the boat neared the coordinates of the shipwreck. "Are you sure you still want to go through with this?" Erin asked uncertainly as Justin anchored the boat.

"Yes," he replied intensely.

Erin sighed. "Remember that you promised to stay within an arms length of me at all times and that we are just going to carefully explore the ship for a few minutes and see if we can open that glowing box."

"I remember," Justin said, rolling his eyes at Erin. "Don't worry so much. I just want to see that box again."

"You and your glowing boxes," Erin teased with a smile. However, she stopped smiling as she saw Justin put an unfamiliar tool into his underwater pouch. "What was that?" she asked in confusion.

"What do you mean?" Justin asked, trying to sound innocent.

173

"Don't play ignorant," Erin scolded. "I'm referring to the tool that you just put in your pouch."

"Oh that," Justin stalled for time. "It's just a mini crowbar."

"Why would you bring..." Erin did not need to finish her question when she saw the look of guilt on Justin's face. "You're going to break into that glowing box!" she exclaimed in disapproval.

Justin lowered his head in shame. "I want to see what's inside the box."

"I thought we were going to try and open it with our hands. That box is probably an antique. We can't destroy it."

"Don't lecture me," Justin scoffed. "Let's just dive."

Erin did what her brother said but she felt that familiar feeling of anger for him returning.

The water sparkled in the sun, creating a blinding reflection. Erin adjusted her diving mask then jumped into the water on the cue that Justin gave her.

Erin and Justin swam deep into the water until they reached the chasm. While holding hands, Erin and Justin leaped into the chasm then swam towards the shipwreck below. Although she had seen it yesterday, it felt like Erin was viewing the ship for the first time. She could not get over the vastness of it. Erin carefully followed Justin into the ship. She was not surprised when he headed straight for the room that held the glowing box.

Erin watched as Justin struggled to open the box with his hands until he motioned for her to help him. As Erin got closer to the box she realized that the light, which was escaping through the cracks in the box, was very powerful. Erin tried to help Justin lift the lid from the box, but she was unsuccessful in doing so.

Erin took a step back as Justin took the mini crowbar from his pouch and brought it to the glowing box. When Justin lifted the mini crowbar up high, Erin grabbed her brother's arm before he could smash it down on the antique box. She glared at Justin, warning him not to completely destroy the box. Justin nodded in understanding as Erin lowered the mini crowbar and gently pressed it against the edge of the lid. Justin twisted and turned the mini crowbar until the lid began to rise. Even though her eyes were on the box, the vibrations from beside her told Erin that Justin was wriggling about in anticipation. She watched as Justin's fingers pried in between the lid and the box then flung it open.

174

"I'm blind!" Erin screamed suddenly. She moaned in pain as her eyes ached from the sudden brightness that came from within the box. Although she still could not see properly, Erin could tell that the bright object in the box was becoming less intense. Her heart began to slow down as she realized that she was no longer blind. Erin squinted, trying to get rid of the dots in her eyes, as she looked upon the object in the box in amazement.

Inside the box lay a large glowing diamond that constantly changed from a deep shade of red to dark purple then to royal blue. Not in any museum or in any movie had Erin ever seen such a beautiful diamond. She felt so overwhelmed by the diamond's beauty that she yearned to touch it. Her fingers ached with anticipation as her arms stretched out to grab the diamond. However, Justin's hands reached for the diamond first. Erin watched in extreme jealously as Justin wrapped his hands around the diamond and brought it close to his face. Behind his diving mask, Justin's face reflected the colors that the diamond shone. The diamond was so large that Justin needed both of his hands to hold it up. Reluctantly, then graciously, Justin handed the diamond to Erin. Erin loved the feeling of the diamond's hard coolness in her hands. She felt hypnotized as the diamond changed from red to purple to blue then back to red again. The diamond changed colors in this pattern and never varied.

When Justin took the diamond from Erin, she snapped out of the hue-induced trance and checked the oxygen indicator. She tapped Justin on the shoulder, indicating that they should leave now. Justin nodded as he put the diamond safely in his pouch. Normally, Erin would have insisted that he put it back where he had found it; she hated it when people took things that did not belong to them. However, Erin wanted to keep the diamond as much as Justin, so she said nothing.

Justin pushed his way through the water and towards the door. He was about to step through the doorway when suddenly the door shut in his face. Erin's heart missed a beat as she saw the bubbles pulsating around the door. She watched in horror as Justin unsuccessfully tried to open the door. Erin shot through the water until she was at the closed door. She tried to push the door, but it would not budge. She then tried to pull the door, but that did not work either. Erin felt like pounding on the door and kicking it, but she knew she couldn't do that incase the whole room caved in. In desperation, Erin tried to push the door again, but of course nothing happened. Erin tuned to Justin with tears in her eyes. Justin gave Erin a warning sign, indicating that she must not cry. Then he smiled soothingly at her. What in the world could he be smiling about? Erin thought frantically. We are going to run out of oxygen and die down here. Erin soon realized why Justin was smiling when she saw him pull out the mini crowbar that he had used to open the box. He began carefully chopping away at the moss-covered hinges of the door. Erin stood still as Justin worked quickly, but precisely, on the hinges. She hurried to help Justin gently lower the door as it came loose. Without waiting a second longer, Erin bolted through the door and out of the ship. Soon Erin and Justin were safely aboard their own familiar white and blue boat.

Erin and Justin did not say much as they sat on their boat, still dressed in their wetsuits. They stared in awe at the diamond in Justin's hand. Every so often Justin would hand the colorful diamond to Erin, who would happily receive it.

"Where are we going to keep it?" Justin asked, breaking the long spell of silence.

"We really shouldn't keep it," Erin replied, biting her lower lip. However, the look on Erin's face clearly described her intention to keep the diamond.

"It's really special," Justin commented as he looked closely at it. "Perhaps we should hide it in my room," he suggested.

"I don't think so," Erin replied through a tight smile. "I have a better idea," she added, "let's kept it in my room."

"No way!" Justin cried. "Why should we keep it in your room? The diamond belongs to me more than it does to you. I was the one to find it after all."

Erin's mouth hung open. "So, are you saying that you're keeping the diamond for yourself? If it weren't for my dedication to silence, we wouldn't have the diamond right in front of us now."

"Well, that would be your fault, wouldn't it?"

Erin felt her blood boil. She did not like her brother's tone of voice whatsoever. "This isn't going to work," she noted.

Erin watched Justin's face go pale in fear. "Sure it will," he answered, trying to sound polite and considerate. "We will put the diamond in a place that we can both agree on."

"Sounds fair," Erin said slowly. "But we are back at square one; where should we keep it?"

"We could get a safe in a bank," Justin suggested.

Erin shook her head. "The bank would need to know what they are storing. They would ask too many questions. Besides, do you really want it stored away in a place where we can't see it?"

It was Justin's turn to shake his head next. "No. Not at all! Maybe we should hide it at the bottom of our closets. You can hide it in yours for a week then I will hide it in mine for a week. That way the chances of someone finding it are less."

"It's not ideal, but if it's the best that we can come up with...Okay, lets hide it in my closet first."

Justin gave Erin an angry look then laughed. "Okay," he agreed. "You can have it first. Besides, we have the rest of our lives to look at the diamond."

\* \* \*

Erin and Justin spent the following day staring at the diamond. They came up with wild possibilities of where the diamond had come from and why the ship had sunk.

"I have another theory," Erin said, referring to the origin of the diamond. "Perhaps the ship came from a far away country where the inhabitants had to flee because of environmental reasons or because of a repressive government. The inhabitants gathered up all the diamonds, which grew in abundance there, then fled to Hawaii. However, the ship and its crew were caught in a fierce storm that killed all the people. Then the ship sank, never to be seen again, until we came along." Erin smiled to herself, obviously pleased with her theory.

"Nice story. However, if the ship had been in a hurricane, or some other disaster, why wasn't it damaged?"

"Good point," Erin replied.

"I liked the part of your theory that claimed there to be more diamonds on the ship," Justin said suggestively. "After all, I only looked in that one room because the door was slightly ajar. Perhaps there are more diamonds in the other rooms."

Erin's eyes sparkled in excitement, but then clouded over in concern. "It might not be safe to open the other doors," she protested.

"I think it would be fine," Justin argued. "We broke down that door and nothing happened."

"True," Erin agreed. "But it was scary, not too mention weird, how that door just slammed shut and wouldn't open again."

"That was probably caused by the water movement as I approached the door," Justin explained.

"I suppose you're right," Erin smiled greedily. "Let's go," she said, wrinkling her nose in excitement. Erin and Justin put the diamond safely in a box in Erin's closet then ran down the stairs.

"Where are you two going in such a hurry?" the housekeeper asked, coming out of the kitchen with a large bowl and spoon in her hand.

"We're going for a ride in the boat," Justin replied.

"Be sure to tell me when you take the boat out," the housekeeper advised. "Your mother wouldn't be very happy if you two were using the boat without telling someone first." Erin and Justin nodded their heads before walking quickly out the door and to their boat.

Images of thousands of beautifully colored diamonds filled Erin's head as she dove into the water with her brother and headed down into the chasm. When they had reached the ship's entrance, Erin followed her brother carefully through the doorway. As Erin entered the ship, she began to find it difficult to breath. She gasped for air and felt a heavy pressure coming from her tank. Erin began to panic as she saw millions of small bubbles coming from behind her. The pipe to my oxygen tank has a leak, Erin realized with intense fear. Erin swam to Justin and pulled his arm.

As Justin turned around, Erin saw an angry expression on his face. However, that look of anger quickly changed to fear when he saw Erin's leaking pipe that lead to her oxygen tank. Justin quickly dug into his pouch and pulled out a knife and a short piece of a thick metal cylinder. Erin felt water leaking into her mask as Justin worked on fixing the pipe. Erin felt herself being able to breathe easier once Justin had cut the broken pipe in half and attached the metal cylinder in between the two pipes. However, Erin still had water in her mask that was beginning to circulate throughout the oxygen tank. Justin took Erin's hand as they swam back up to the surface.

"Didn't you check your equipment?" was the first thing that Justin said as they took off their diving gear.

"Of course!" Erin shrieked, still terribly frightened over what had happened in the water. "I checked all my equipment thoroughly. I

178

always do," Erin said frantically, while suppressing the tears that were filling up in her eyes.

Justin shot Erin a sympathetic look then embraced her in a hug. "I know you do," he said suspiciously. "So, what is going here?"

*  *  *

It was three days after the accident with the oxygen pipe when Justin approached Erin with regards to the shipwreck. "Do you want to go back down?" he asked her bluntly.

Erin looked up from the magazine that she was reading. She got up and closed the door behind Justin. "I do," she replied timidly. "But I have to confess that I am a bit scared to dive again."

"I've replaced that pipe already," Justin explained. "And I have checked all the diving gear about a hundred times each. I promise you, Erin, the equipment is perfectly fine."

"I thought the equipment was perfectly fine the last time I went diving," Erin replied.

"This time it's more than perfect," Justin tried to persuade Erin. "Trust me."

Erin thought about it for a moment then sighed. "Okay," she agreed with a little smile.

After Justin had promised her a hundred times that the equipment was safe, Erin got into her wetsuit and geared up for some deep sea diving.

It was not long before Erin and Justin were in the shipwreck, exploring the rooms carefully. The anxieties that Erin had felt earlier disappeared as she shone her flashlight over the contents of one room. It contained a single moss covered bed and dresser. Erin and Justin searched the room but did not find anything of interest there. The following six rooms were all like the first. Erin felt herself losing hope in finding a room full of colorful diamonds.

Justin gently pushed Erin towards the exit of the room. Erin followed Justin out of the room and into a larger one. She had to stop at the entrance of the large room because Justin would not move out of the way. Erin nudged Justin, indicating for him to move, but he would not budge. In annoyance, Erin gave Justin a hard push which sent both Erin and Justin flying into the room. As Erin regained her balance and looked upon the room, she screamed from behind her mask.

179

Erin had discovered why Justin had stood still in the doorway. He must have been staring at this wall in shock, Erin realized as she looked upon it in terror. Engraved deep within the wall was the warning, "they have stolen the cursed diamond. God help us all who are aboard this ship."

This has to be some sort of joke; Erin thought as she approached the wall and rubbed her hands over the writing. Chunks of moss came off the wall and floated through the water. Erin re-read the words and shuttered. Let's go, she motioned with her hands to Justin. Erin suddenly did not feel like exploring the ship anymore. Justin nodded in agreement then began to make his way through the ship.

What Erin saw next was so shocking that it seemed to happen in slow motion. Everything was fine as Justin swam through the water, but things went wrong when he passed the last door. Justin had forgotten to shut the door and as he swam in front of it, the door suddenly sprang off its hinges and slammed right on top of Justin's right leg. Erin watched in horror as her brother lay lifelessly on the ship's floor.

Oh no, Erin moaned silently as she swam quickly to Justin. She looked at his face and was relieved to see that his eyes were open. He looks terrified and his mask is slightly broken, but at least he's alive, Erin told herself as she struggled to lift the door off of her brother. Erin grunted and groaned as she tried to lift the door. It took a few minutes, but Erin eventually lifted the door up high enough so that Justin was able to propel himself from underneath it. Once he was out of harm's way, Justin reached for Erin and pointed to his leg. His leg is broken, Erin realized unhappily. She helped Justin stand up on his unhurt leg then she put his arm around her shoulders. Slowly, she managed to swim with Justin until they were out of the ship and the chasm. Erin kept on checking to see if the chip on Justin's mask had got any bigger. She was afraid that the pressure of the water may crack the glass. Erin did not want to think about how she would handle that situation if it happened.

Once they had reached the surface safely, Erin helped Justin aboard the boat. She took off his mask and his other diving equipment. "How does your leg feel?" she asked in concern.

"Sore," was all Justin said as he lay on the ground, clutching his hurt leg.

Erin pulled up the anchor then started the boat's engine. She went as fast as she could to get Justin back to shore and to see a doctor.

* * *

"How does it feel?" Erin asked a week after the accident.

"It feels better," Justin admitted. Justin had not broken his leg after all, but had got a bad sprain. He had not been able to walk on his right leg since. Erin had told her mother and the housekeeper that Justin had sprained his leg by bashing it into a rock as they were diving. Both her mother and the housekeeper were furious at Erin and Justin for diving without telling anyone first. Their diving equipment had been taken away immediately. Erin never told anyone about the shipwreck that she and Justin had found.

"I keep on thinking about that message on the ship's wall," Justin said suddenly.

"So have I," Erin confessed.

"I believe it," Justin said firmly. "There is no way that the two accidents which occurred under the water were coincidences. I think the diamond did it."

Erin looked at Justin then sighed. "I've been thinking the same thing," she said. "What should we do? If we tell anyone that we found that ship, we will get in so much trouble for going back and exploring it. And what if the ship is also cursed and a deep sea diver explores it and gets killed? I would never forgive myself!"

"I heard of this guy," Justin said in concentration. "His name is Dr. Otter and he specializes in anthropology of the Hawaiian region. If anyone knows anything about our diamond it will be him."

"Can we really trust him with our diamond?" Erin asked cautiously.

"I can't tell you for sure, but I do know that I don't care about that diamond as much as I use to."

"Neither do I. To tell you the truth I haven't even looked or touched the diamond since your accident."

"Then it's settled," Justin said with finality. "We will go see Dr. Otter as soon as I can walk again."

* * *

Justin was able to walk reasonably well two weeks after the decision to see Dr. Otter was made. It was a warm, but cloudy morning, as Erin and Justin made their way to Dr. Otter's house. "I hope he's in," Erin whispered to Justin as they rang the doorbell and waited for Dr. Otter to answer.

181

"I heard that he will travel to all sorts of different places for long periods of time then when he gets home, he stays in his house for months, looking over all the treasures that he has found." Justin stopped talking as a man answered the door. "Um, Dr. Otter?" he asked in uncertainty.

"Yes. What can I do for you?" Dr. Otter asked as if he were in a great hurry.

"My brother and I have found something. We were wondering if you would take a look at it." Erin inquired.

"I usually require advanced notice to look at found items, but since you are already here I guess I can take a quick look. What is it that you have found?"

"I was hoping you could tell us that," Justin said as he carefully took the colorful diamond from his backpack and handed it to Dr. Otter.

"Oh no," Dr. Otter uttered in sheer horror as he backed away from the diamond in Justin's out stretched hand. "Where in the world did you find the cursed diamond of Vastor?"

"The cursed diamond of Vastor?" Erin asked, confused and scared at the same time.

"Take that diamond away from my sight and I will answer your questions," Dr. Otter said shakily. Justin obediently put the diamond back in his backpack and waited for Dr. Otter to speak.

"You must be deep sea divers," Dr. Otter said in a calmer tone of voice.

"Yes," Erin began to reply, but Justin kicked her foot with his. He gave her a warning look that told her to be quiet.

"We're not going to tell you were we got it," Justin said stubbornly.

"You don't have to," Dr. Otter replied reasonably. "In fact, I don't want to know where you found such an evil item."

"Is it really cursed?" Erin asked with wide eyes.

"Oh yes," Dr. Otter replied quickly. "Do you know the story behind the diamond?"

"No," Erin and Justin answered at the same time.

"I suppose you wouldn't. If you knew, you wouldn't have touched the diamond in the first place. You see, this diamond belonged to one of the most sacred tribes in Hawaii over two thousand years ago. During this time a great man named captain Vastor sailed the sea. He caught food for the inhabitants of Hawaii. One day when captain Vastor

182

was out catching fish from his boat, he saw another boat in the distance. When he got closer to the boat he noticed that it was sinking at a rapid pace. Being the truly brave man that he was, Vastor jumped into the water and saved the lives of eighteen people. Vastor did not know this at the time, but he had just saved the life of the head leader of Hawaii's most sacred tribe. As a reward, the tribe gave Vastor the colorful diamond that you now possess. However, the tribe was so afraid that Vastor would be killed by thieves that they put a curse on it. Whoever stole the diamond from Vastor would be cursed and plagued with bad events only to die a horrible death. Everyone in Hawaii knew about the horrible curse so no one ever tried to steal the diamond from Vastor. When Vastor died he was buried with the diamond. Hundreds of years later, some foolish grave robbers took the diamond then fled in a ship. However, the curse had not died with Vastor. All the men in the ship were killed and the ship sunk and was never seen of again."

Erin gulped loudly. "We never knew about the curse. After we took the diamond bad things started to happen. How can we stop the curse?"

"The only way to avoid the curse of the diamond is to get rid of it. You should put it back where you found it. Please leave now. I do not want to be so close to the cursed diamond." With that said Dr. Otter hurried back into his house and shut the door.

Erin turned to Justin in desperation. "We have to get rid of the diamond," she said softly. "I know," Justin said sadly.

"I guess we should head back to the ship one last time and return the diamond," Erin said as they began to walk home.

"I don't want to take the chance of getting hurt in that ship again, do you?"

Erin shook her head. "But we have to get rid of it," she protested.

A wide smile grew on Justin's face. "I know exactly how to get rid of it," he said, trying to suppress a gleeful laugh.

\* \* \*

"Here is the one million dollar check," a man said as he handed the check to Justin. Erin stared at awe at the large sum of money written on the check. She could not believe that the check bore her and Justin's name.

183

Justin had come up with a great way to get rid of the diamond, thus relieving them of the curse, as well as finding a way to fill up the joint bank account, that Erin and Justin had just set up, at the same time. They had sold the diamond to the National Hawaiian Museum. The CEO of the museum was skeptical about buying the diamond from young adults and Erin and Justin were sure that they were not paid a fair price for the diamond, yet they were still extremely happy.

Erin and Justin could not help but giggle when the news of the museum's new precious diamond, which has been bought from two anonymous Hawaiian residents, spread all around the island and raised mass interest. Everywhere they went they saw posters advertising the grand opening of the diamond exhibit.

"That's one event that I won't mind missing," Justin commented as he walked by a large museum promotion poster with Erin.

Erin said nothing, but nodded in agreement. She could not shake the growing feeling that they had been wrong to sell the diamond to the museum. Although the million dollars in their secret bank account had made Erin happy at first, it was now a constant reminder of the not-so-noble transaction that she and her brother had made. Erin said nothing to Justin about the feeling of guilt that plagued her since he seemed so happy and confident with their decision.

When the night of the grand opening at the museum came, Erin and Justin locked themselves in Erin's room and played board game after board game. Erin was thankful that all the tickets to the grand opening of the diamond exhibit were sold out when their mother tried to buy a ticket. Even Justin seemed uneasy.

Erin and Justin had just started their fourth game of Chinese checkers when they heard a loud gasp from downstairs. Erin and Justin bolted out of the bedroom and down the stairs. They came to a complete stop when they saw what was on the television.

"Hawaii cable one news is covering the unbelievable accident that took place at the National Hawaiian Museum's grand opening of the diamond display. At 7:35 PM tonight, just less than half an hour before the display was to be opened; a fire broke out and spread quickly throughout the whole museum."

Erin's and Justin's mouth hung open as they watched the television flash images of the black mess and dying flames that used to be called a museum.  Erin noticed the CEO of the museum running frantically in the background.

"The entire museum and all that it contained has been completely destroyed.   That is over thirty five million dollars in antiques," the news anchor said.

"What a loss," Erin and Justin's mother said, shaking her head. "I was so shocked to see these images when I turned the television on," she explained.  "I'm glad I didn't get a ticket to the event after all!"

"If you have just joined us," the news anchor said, once he had returned back on the screen.   "I am at the National Hawaiian Museum which has just burnt down."  The news anchor stopped talking as a man hurried up to him and whispered something in his ear.  "This just in," the news anchor said, once the man had left the screen, "one item has not been destroyed.   Ironically, this item is the diamond that was to be presented tonight."

Justin grabbed for Erin's hand in fear.  The feeling of his cold hand chilled Erin down to her bones.  Erin felt Justin shaking as a picture of the undamaged diamond, which was glowing a deep shade of red, filled the screen.

"It was either them or us," Erin said evilly.

* * *

# Long Live the Bonsai

# Long Live the Bonsai

"Go long, Cad," Cody called to his twin sister Caddy Phillips.

"You won't be able to throw the football to where I am now," Caddy protested.

"Just go long," Cody instructed. "I've eaten my oatmeal; I'm feeling strong."

Caddy laughed at Cody's joke and then moved back.

Caddy was born on the twenty-sixth of July at 7:10 PM. Her brother had been born six minutes later. The Phillips twins would be sixteen years old in just twenty more days. Although they were different genders, Caddy and Cody looked very much alike. They both stood tall at five foot seven inches and had athletic builds. They even shared the same color of blue eyes and red hair. Caddy dyed her hair a darker shade of red and wore it long and in layers. Cody's hair, on the other hand, was a slightly lighter shade of red. Just like their looks, Caddy and Cody shared just about everything else. This pleased their parents and confused their friends. However, Caddy and Cody didn't care about what other people thought because together, as brother and sister and best friends, they could accomplish anything.

"Okay, that's far enough," Cody called out as Caddy reached the edge of their front lawn. Maybe I was a little too cocky, Cody thought as he twirled the football in his hands. Taking a deep breath and closing his eyes, Cody stepped forward and threw the football with all his strength. He opened his eyes a second later to see the football heading straight towards their elderly neighbor, Mr. Tennessee. Mr. Tennessee, who had just driven up his driveway, was getting out of the car. "Mr. Tennessee!" Cody yelled, amazed at the power of his own strength, "move out of the way!"

Cody's warning alarmed Caddy. She turned around to see Mr. Tennessee being helped out of the car by his daughter, Sophia. Caddy also saw the football heading straight towards them. Without thinking twice, Caddy ran towards them and caught the ball, just inches away from Mr. Tennessee's head. Mr. Tennessee looked on in interest, either unaware or in apathy towards the fact that he had almost been hit by flying cowhide. Sophia, on the other hand, was fully aware and very upset.

"You little monsters," Sophia yelled as Cody, who wore a guilty expression, approached the crime scene.

"I am so sorry," Cody said, elongating the word sorry. "I swear, I never meant to throw the football so far."

"I don't care if your actions were intentional or not," Sophia argued. "The fact is that you almost hit my father with it."

"We'll never play football in the front yard again," Caddy promised.

"Is that meant to make me feel better? You'll just end up hitting him when he's relaxing in his backyard. I can picture the football flying over the fence, not giving my father a chance to get away."

Caddy stared with her mouth open. She knew what she and Cody had done was bad. However, she also knew that it was done unintentionally, and perhaps more importantly, had been stopped by her fast thinking.

"Oh, let them be," Mr. Tennessee finally spoke. "No harm was done. I'm sure they've learned their lesson."

"We have," Cody promised. Caddy nodded in agreement.

"Well then," Mr. Tennessee said. "It's over and done with. It was nice seeing you two again," he added, with a hint of laughter in his eyes as he was guided towards his house.

"It's a good thing you're moving, father," Sophia said, shooting Caddy and Cody one last glare.

Caddy turned to her brother, not knowing whether to scold him, compliment him on his improved throw, or laugh in relief.

"I didn't see that coming," Cody commented with wide eyes.

"Neither did they," Caddy added with a laugh, while suppressing her feelings of guilt.

* * *

Later that day, the Phillips were sitting around their dinner table eating an Italian inspired meal. Caddy was just about to ask for the spaghetti when someone knocked on the door. Mrs. Phillips got up to answer it and came back with a surprised expression on her face.

"Mr. Tennessee's daughter is at the door. She wants to see you two," Mrs. Phillips said, looking at Caddy and Cody. "She was quite short with me. What's going on?"

"I guess we'll find out," Caddy said, before Cody's guilty conscious could make him say anything incriminating. "Better not keep her waiting," Caddy added, getting up and pulling Cody with her.

"Quick thinking," Cody whispered to her.

"Twice in one day. I'm on a roll," Caddy joked dryly. Caddy stopped talking when she saw Sophia waiting impatiently. Caddy plastered on, what she hoped was a friendly smile. "Hello, Sophia," she said, pushing Cody out the door and closing it behind them. Whatever Sophia had to say, she didn't want her parents to hear it.

"I've just gotten a call from my husband. Our youngest daughter has a cold and keeps crying for me to come home early. I was planning to stay the whole weekend to help clean out the attic for my father. However, I won't be able to." Sophia sighed as if she were about to do something she really didn't want to. "Perhaps you two can clean out the attic instead. This will give you a chance to redeem yourselves," she added quickly, like she was the one doing them the favor.

"Sure!" Cody replied enthusiastically. "I love looking through old junk."

"This isn't for your own pleasure," Sophia scolded. "It's to help my father with his move."

"Of course," Caddy amended. "When should we come?"

"Tomorrow morning at 9:00 o'clock."

Cody groaned. He hated getting up early, especially during the summer break.

"We'll be there," Caddy promised.

"Thank you," Sophia said almost humbly. "My father will appreciate it."

"Don't you mean you'll appreciate it?" Cody said, when Sophia had walked away.

When Caddy and Cody entered the kitchen, Mrs. Phillips didn't hesitate to ask them what Sophia wanted. "She asked us to help Mr. Tennessee clean out his attic," Caddy replied, sitting down to finish her cold spaghetti.

"And what did you say?" Mrs. Phillips inquired further.

"We said yes," Cody answered.

Mrs. Phillips smiled at her husband. "We have two really great kids," she said, squeezing Caddy's and Cody's hand affectionately.

"You sure do," Cody replied a bit too quickly.

190

"Thanks," Caddy said, feeling more than just a little guilty.

* * *

"Wake up, Cody," Caddy said, while standing over her brother's bed. "It's 8:40. It's about time we got going to Mr. Tennessee's house." Caddy stared at her brother. For a moment she thought he might be dead. "Cody!" Caddy yelled, leaning over her brother's limp body. Cody immediately sat up.

"What!" he yelled back. He looked startled and angry.

"We have to go to Mr. Tennessee's house, remember?"

"Oh yeah," Cody said, rubbing the sleep away from his eyes. "You didn't have to scare me to death though."

"Yes I did," Caddy argued. "You would have slept until noon if I hadn't wakened you."

Cody stuck his tongue out at his sister and Caddy mimicked his gesture.

The Phillips twins arrived at Mr. Tennessee's house at 9:06 AM. Mr. Tennessee opened the door and greeted them with a smile.

"It's very nice of you two to help me," he said, stepping aside so Caddy and Cody could come in.

"We want to help," Caddy replied with a reassuring smile.

Mr. Tennessee led Caddy and Cody towards the attic. Even though the Phillips and Mr. Tennessee had been neighbors for five years, Caddy and Cody had never been in his house. The living room and dinning room were pretty much bare. Only opened boxes, a chair and a small table were left.

"It's a real mess up there," Mr. Tennessee commented as they reached the stairs to the attic. "I need you to wipe the dust off the boxes and bring them down the stairs. We can sort through the items and decide what to do with them after."

Cody nodded his head. "No problem," he said enthusiastically.

"Don't lift anything too heavy. I don't want you two to get hurt," Mr. Tennessee said as he walked back down the hall.

Cody ran up the stairs to the attic then cried loudly. Caddy heard her brother's cry then a loud thud.

"Cody?" Caddy called, running quickly up the stairs. "Are you okay?"

Cody groaned in reply.

Although the attic was dark, Caddy could see the silhouette of her brother on the floor. She placed her hands on the wall and swept them over the coldness in search of a light switch. She flipped the light switch on when she found it. Caddy saw her brother, holding his leg, and a large box in front of him. "Silly thing," Caddy commented as Cody stood up.

"The stupid box shouldn't be lying at the entrance," Cody complained, glaring at the box that had tripped him.

"You shouldn't go running into dark rooms," Caddy advised.

"How was I supposed to know it was there?" Cody asked in disbelief. "I bet Sophia put it there on purpose."

"She did not," Caddy replied, rolling her eyes. "Do you need to go home?" she asked, looking at Cody as he rubbed his leg.

"No. I'm okay," Cody said. "The pain is dying down but I'm sure I'll be left with quite a bruise."

Caddy and Cody began dusting the attic. They opened up the two windows to avoid suffocating on the flying dust. Although the attic was small, it was packed with boxes and other odds and ends.

"Look at this," Cody shouted suddenly. Caddy put down the box that she was carrying and walked towards Cody. He was bent over a box. "Baseball cards!" he exclaimed, holding up a handful of cards.

"You made me come over to see some silly cards?" Caddy sighed and picked up the box once again.

"They are not silly," Cody protested. "They are worth a lot of money. They are even in plastic sheets." Caddy ignored her brother and continued to transport the boxes down the stairs.

It was a little after noon when Caddy and Cody emerged from Mr. Tennessee's house. They found him sitting on a wicker chair on his porch.

"How are the two workers?" he greeted in a friendly tone.

"Great," Caddy replied, a little bit out of breath from all the work she had done. She had done a lot more work than Cody had. He had been too busy looking at the baseball cards. "We're just going to head over to our house for lunch," she explained.

"Oh, there's no need for that," Mr. Tennessee said, dismissing the idea.

"But we're really hungry. We need to eat," Cody protested, amazed that Mr. Tennessee would want them to work through lunch.

"You'll just have to starve then," Mr. Tennessee said evilly. "I won't allow you to leave this house." Cody gasped and Caddy's eyes went wide. Mr. Tennessee continued to stare at them in a sinister manner. Then he began to chuckle.

He's crazy, Cody thought in fear, getting ready to make a quick getaway.

"I'm just jesting," Mr. Tennessee explained.

"You're what?" Cody asked with wide eyes.

"He's kidding," Caddy explained, beginning to calm down.

"You seemed to think I was going to keep you as my prisoners," Mr. Tennessee told Cody. "I couldn't resist pulling a prank. What I really meant is that I have a frozen pizza that can be ready in ten minutes. Would you care to join me?"

A smile broke out on Cody's face. "Sure," he replied.

After Caddy, Cody, and Mr. Tennessee had finished their pizza, they went upstairs to empty the contents of the boxes that had been taken down from the attic. Caddy went into the attic to get the few remaining items while Mr. Tennessee and Cody decided what to do with the items that were already brought down. Caddy reached for the last remaining box. Behind the box, lying on the ground was a small tree in a pot. The pot and the tree were covered in such a thick layer of dust that Caddy couldn't see what it looked like. Caddy carried the pot to the window and began to dust it. She could soon see that the pot was black. She moved her hands around the small pot. It was round, smooth, and surprisingly warm. The tree, which sat in the middle of the pot, was in dire need of water. It was a miniature hemlock surrounded by small yellow pebbles. Caddy placed the tree on top of the remaining box and carefully took it downstairs.

"I'll take great care of them," Caddy heard Cody say to Mr. Tennessee. She saw Cody happily holding baseball cards in his hands.

"Cody," Caddy scolded as if he were a five year old. "You can't take those."

Mr. Tennessee chuckled. "Of course he can. I want him to have them. They would just get thrown out or given to a charity otherwise."

"Charity begins at home," Cody said, sticking his tongue out at Caddy.

Caddy rolled her eyes. Sometimes Cody can be so immature, she thought to herself. "Look what I found in a corner of the attic," she said, taking the spotlight away from Cody. She held up the ailing tree.

193

"Oh my," Mr. Tennessee said suddenly. "How in the world did it ever get up there? And more importantly," he quickly added, "how has it survived so well?" Mr. Tennessee took the tree from Caddy and examined it.

"Didn't you put it up there?" Caddy asked in confusion.

"No. I haven't seen it in five years." Mr. Tennessee took a moment to ponder then said, "I remember the last time I saw my bonsai tree..."

"Your what?" Cody interrupted.

"My bonsai tree," Mr. Tennessee began to explain. "It's a small tree that is kept in a pot. The tree, which is a hemlock in this case, is kept small by cutting its roots. If properly taken care of, a bonsai tree can live for years. I once heard a tale that the bonsai tree and its owner were connected."

"Connected? How?" Cody interrupted again.

"I'm not sure. I can't remember the rest of the tale. It must not have been too exciting if I can't remember it," Mr. Tennessee said with a wink. "The last time I saw my bonsai tree was when I was taken to hospital for pneumonia. Sophia looked after my house while I was in the hospital for a few weeks. When I came home the bonsai was gone. I didn't ask Sophia about it since she had been such a great help; I didn't want to bother her any further. I thought she had broken it. I wonder why she would hide it in the attic? That is very peculiar."

"What else would you expect from a weird lady?" Cody muttered under his breath. Caddy shot her brother a glare.

"I can imagine it being a beautiful tree once," Caddy commended, turning her eyes back to the bonsai.

"It was. I am so surprised that it survived through such a difficult time. I guess it's just like its owner after all."

Caddy gave the suddenly sad looking Mr. Tennessee a sympathetic smile. "You should nurse it back to health," she advised, trying to take Mr. Tennessee's mind off his own health problems.

"I would love to see it flourish," Mr. Tennessee replied. "However, I won't have any time. I'll be too busy talking to my new friends in the retirement home and participating in their organized activities. I would be honored if you took it though." Mr. Tennessee handed the bonsai tree to Caddy. Caddy knew that Mr. Tennessee was trying to act brave.

"Thank you. I'll take great care of it."

Cody felt the urge to throw Caddy's comments back in her face and say, you can't take that. However, there was something sensitive in the words that were being exchanged by his sister and Mr. Tennessee. Cody decided to say nothing.

\* \* \*

It was a rainy Monday morning, two weeks after Caddy and Cody had waved goodbye to Mr. Tennessee and four weeks since Caddy was given the bonsai tree. With all the free time that summer vacation yielded, Caddy spent it taking care of the bonsai tree and learning how to do so properly. She gave the hemlock tree a much needed trim and watered it. Although she liked the bonsai tree very much, there was something weird about it. According to all her research, it was impossible for a bonsai tree to survive the conditions in which it had been exposed to. Caddy stared at the hemlock tree, remembering how shriveled and ill it had looked just a month before. Now it was a luscious dark green hemlock tree surrounded by sparkling yellow pebbles. It looked as if it hadn't suffered a day in its life.

Caddy turned her head towards the window and stared out. She felt very happy sitting at the bay window with the bonsai tree resting on the window's ledge. She watched the rain pour down and listened to the music it made as it hit the window. Caddy's eyes closed in contentment. Caddy felt as if she were being carried away just like the river of rain that was being swept down the street. Before she closed her eyes, something out of place appeared in the street. Caddy shut her eyes, thought about what she had just seen, then opened her eyes widely.

"No way," she muttered. "It can't be." Caddy leaned forward and pressed her face against the glass. "Mr. Tennessee is dancing in the rain!"

Caddy heard a big laugh from behind her. "I thought I heard you say that Mr. Tennessee is dancing in the rain." Cody chuckled again. "What did you really say?" he inquired.

"Um, Cody," Caddy said slowly. "That's what I said."

"Yeah right," Cody laughed again, while walking towards the window. "Mr. Tennessee dancing in the street while it's pouring rain? You need to get your eyes checked, Cad." Cody stopped talking as his eyes fell upon Mr. Tennessee, who was indeed running around the street and splashing in puddles like a four year old.

"He must have gone crazy," Caddy concluded. "I'm going to bring him in." Caddy ran out the front door without bothering to put on a jacket. Cody followed closely behind.

"Mr. Tennessee!" they yelled in unison as they approached the old man. Mr. Tennessee looked up and smiled widely.

"Hey, guys!" he yelled through the pouring rain. Caddy and Cody stared at Mr. Tennessee in shock. His eyes shone a bright blue and his skin had a dozen less wrinkles then it did a month ago.

"Why aren't you in the retirement home?" Caddy shouted over the pouring rain.

"More importantly," Cody added, "why are you outside in this weather? Are you lost?"

"I was lost," Mr. Tennessee admitted thoughtfully. "But I've found myself now. I've found the person that I used to be." Mr. Tennessee turned his head towards the sky and opened his mouth.

What's he doing? Caddy silently asked herself. "Do you feel alright?" she voiced her concern out loud.

Mr. Tennessee closed his mouth and lowered his head. Then he spat a mouthful of water onto Caddy's face.

Cody stared in shock at Mr. Tennessee then at his sister. Normally in a situation like this, Cody would have laughed hysterically. However, it wasn't as funny under the circumstances.

Caddy wiped her face with her already soaking wet sleeve. "Let's go inside and get you dry," she said through clenched teeth. She couldn't believe that Mr. Tennessee, a man who was well into his seventies, had just spat water all over her face.

Mr. Tennessee suddenly became sullen. "Alright," he said finally. Mr. Tennessee motioned for Cody. Cody was confused at Mr. Tennessee's sudden weakness but he held out his hand to him anyway.

Caddy, Cody, and Mr. Tennessee slowly made their way to the Phillips' house. Caddy stepped over a large puddle and proceeded to open the door. Her hand had barely touched the doorknob when she heard Cody's startled cry then a loud splash. Caddy twirled around to see Cody lying face down in the large puddle, which she had stepped over seconds ago. Mr. Tennessee stood over Cody and let out a deep laugh.

"Mr. Tennessee pushed me!" Cody shrieked in bewilderment. His wet face looked up at Mr. Tennessee in complete confusion.

196

"I'm sorry," Mr. Tennessee apologized with a chuckle. "It was just too tempting. I do hope that I didn't hurt you." Mr. Tennessee stooped down and pulled Cody up. Cody was shocked to feel the strength that Mr. Tennessee had, while Caddy was shocked to see her brother lifted up so easily. Cody was no lightweight at one hundred and forty-six pounds heavy.

"No hard feelings?" Mr. Tennessee said sincerely to Cody, while holding his hand out to him as a sign of repent.

Cody didn't return Mr. Tennessee's gesture. Instead, he looked skeptically at his hand. "You're forgiven," Cody said, remembering that he was talking to an elderly man.

Caddy ushered Cody and Mr. Tennessee into the house where they all proceeded to change into new clothing. Mr. Tennessee wore a pair of Cody's denim shorts and a black t-shirt that bore a symbol of an evil looking mushroom man. In other words, he looked absolutely ridiculous.

"What happened to you?" Caddy inquired as the three of them sat in the living room. Mr. Tennessee suddenly sprung up from his chair and began talking excitedly.

"I just couldn't stay in that retirement home any longer. It's so boring! If you're not sitting all by yourself in the bedroom, which is more like a walk-in closet, you're being forced into knitting contests or multiple rounds of Bingo. That retirement home is more stagnant than an abandoned bird bath."

"I like Bingo," Cody interjected.

"Not after playing it with an announcer who can hardly pronounce the letter "B" you wouldn't," Mr. Tennessee argued.

"If you hate it so much, why don't you move in with your daughter instead?" Caddy asked sympathetically.

"Are you joking?" Mr. Tennessee cried. "Living with Sophia would be even worse than living in a retirement home. Sophia's more stagnant than that abandoned bird bath I mentioned earlier."

A laugh escaped Cody's lips. Caddy glared at him in response. "If you don't want to live at the retirement home or Sophia's house, where do you want to go?"

"Next door to this place," Mr. Tennessee said sadly.

Caddy felt her heart break. "Why did you sell your house in the first place?"

197

"Sophia insisted," Mr. Tennessee replied gravely. "She said it wasn't safe for me to live in such a big house by myself. I did agree with her because I hadn't been feeling the best. Although my mind begged for me to stay, my body told me differently. However, everything has changed now. I feel great; I feel like I did when I was an active forty year old."

"Why the sudden change?" Cody inquired with interest.

"I have no clue," Mr. Tennessee admitted. "My strength has been increasing since you two left my house over a month ago."

"That is really weird," Caddy thought out loud. "Have you been put on any new medication?"

Mr. Tennessee shook his head. "I don't take any medication whatsoever."

"You must be doing something different," Caddy protested. "Elderly people don't just become the physically active people that they were when they were forty!" Caddy coughed awkwardly. "Sorry," she added, concerned that she might have offended Mr. Tennessee.

"Well, I'm the exception, baby," Mr. Tennessee replied. The room suddenly became deadly silent as Caddy looked at Mr. Tennessee in surprise.

Did he just call me baby? Caddy thought to herself. "I'm sure the past few weeks have been shaky for you," Caddy said in realization. "Have you talked to Sophia lately?"

"Yes. I talked to her just minutes before I escaped from the retirement home. She's more concerned about me than ever. She thinks my new burst of energy indicates that there is something wrong with me."

"We can't change Sophia's mind, but we will visit you and help you form a reasonable plan of action," Caddy offered.

"Visit me where?" Mr. Tennessee asked through narrowed eyes.

"The retirement home."

Mr. Tennessee sighed. "Alright, I'll go back, but only temporarily."

Caddy gave Mr. Tennessee a half smile. "Our mom should be home in an hour. She'll drive you to the retirement home. In the mean time, I'll call the retirement home and tell them that you're safe."

Cody and Mr. Tennessee sat in silence after Caddy disappeared down the hallway. Cody fiddled in his seat and looked around the room, wondering what to say to Mr. Tennessee. "The bonsai tree that you gave Caddy has started to bloom again," Cody said quickly, upon seeing the bonsai tree that sat on the window's ledge.

Mr. Tennessee walked quickly towards the plant. "Caddy's done an excellent job reviving it." He stared thoughtfully at the bonsai after he had praised Caddy's work.

"Is something wrong?" Cody asked, afraid that Mr. Tennessee had fallen ill.

"No," Mr. Tennessee replied slowly. "Everything's fine."

\* \* \*

"I don't understand why Mr. Tennessee doesn't like it here," Cody commented to Caddy as they walked into the beautifully furnished gathering room in the retirement home. It was a week since Caddy and Cody had seen Mr. Tennessee, but they were sure to keep their promise to him. "It's amazing," Cody said as he stepped off to the side to see a cage that contained a green and yellow budgie. Caddy proceeded to the front desk to ask for Mr. Tennessee's room number. "Hello, pretty birdie," Cody cooed at the bird as he stuck his index finger into the cage. "Ouch," he exclaimed as the bird snapped at him then dug its beak into Cody's finger.

"That's Little Old Nasty who just bit you," an elderly man said as he walked towards Cody and the bird cage.

"I wish someone had warned me earlier," Cody commented, while looking at his hurt finger. Cody was just about to introduce himself to the man when he heard Caddy calling him.

"He's run away again!" Caddy cried when she had reached Cody's side. "Why does he keep on doing this?" she asked in desperation.

"You must be talking about Mr. Tennessee," the elderly man interrupted. "We were all waiting to see what crazy stunt he would pull off next."

"You mean he's been acting strange in front of his friends as well?"

"The word strange doesn't do any justice for Mr. Tennessee. He's down right crazy. It's been getting worse lately. He's got more energy than all of the staff put together." The elderly man paused for a second and looked closely at Caddy and Cody. "How do you know him?" he asked suspiciously. "Are you his grandchildren?"

199

"No. We're his neighbors," Caddy replied quickly. "Can you tell us what kind of things he has been doing lately?"

"Well," the elderly man began, "there was the incident at the Bingo game last night. He pretended to eat some of the mark pieces. He put on a great big act. He was chocking and coughing unstoppably. The staff was ready to have the shorts sued off them when they reached Mr. Tennessee and saw him lying lifelessly on the floor. Then suddenly he spat the mark pieces in the staff member's faces and laughed like a crazy hyena. All of this was followed by the staff chasing him around the retirement home. It was half an hour before they caught him."

Caddy and Cody were shocked. In all the years they had known Mr. Tennessee, he had never played a prank like that. "We better get going," Caddy said suddenly. "The lady at the front desk is casting us unfriendly glares. I think she wants us to leave."

"That lady is an old prune. Take no heed to her glances. Won't you stay and play a game of checkers?"

Caddy cast the man a sympathetic smile as she shook her head. "We have to find Mr. Tennessee."

"Thanks for the story about Mr. Tennessee," Cody added, before they left the building.

"I just wish it was a fictional story," the elderly man replied quietly, while shaking his head in disapproval.

"I guess we should start looking for Mr. Tennessee ourselves. Where should we start?" Caddy sighed and looked down the street, wondering where to begin the search.

"Before we start running all across town in search for him, what did the receptionist say to you?"

"Just that Mr. Tennessee was not in his room this morning and that they were treating it as a runaway. The staff at the retirement home has already organized a search party and the police have been notified."

"This is serious," Cody muttered.

"I know," Caddy replied, tugging on Cody's arm to get him moving. "That's why we have to start our own search right now!"

Caddy and Cody spent the whole day looking for Mr. Tennessee. They only stopped once for a quick lunch, that consisted of a club sandwich, at the mall. They had searched the entire mall as well as roamed the streets and checked all the parks. However, Mr. Tennessee was nowhere to be found.

"It's getting late," Cody observed as they peered over the fence and into the property of the lawn bowling club. "We better go home."

Caddy sighed for what seemed like the hundredth time that day. "I feel responsible somehow," she said suddenly.

"For what?" Cody asked in surprise. "For Mr. Tennessee's disappearance?"

Caddy nodded. "Don't be so silly," Cody scolded his sister. "We've been nothing but kind to him. If there's anyone to blame it's the retirement home's lousy security system and Sophia's attitude."

"I guess," Caddy said, not fully convinced. Caddy couldn't help but feel as if she were connected to the disappearance of Mr. Tennessee.

An occasional car whizzed by as Caddy and Cody walked along the light gray pavement. They reached the end of the road where the forest began; it was a place devoid of houses and people. Caddy and Cody were about to turn the corner and head back to their house when Caddy saw someone out of the side of her eye. She could see an old man peering at them from behind a tree just on the outskirt of the forest. As soon as he saw Caddy looking at him, he turned around and ran into the dense forest.

"Someone's watching us," Caddy proclaimed, a bit too happily. "It must be Mr. Tennessee!" she cried as she began to run towards the forest.

"Caddy!" Cody screamed, running after his sister. "It might not be Mr. Tennessee." Cody broke through the forest's edge just seconds after Caddy had, but the forest was so dense and Caddy was such a good runner that he could no longer see her. "Caddy!" Cody yelled louder than what he thought was humanly possible. "Caddy, where are you?" Cody stood still and listened. He hoped to hear Caddy call back to him or even better, reappear. However, all he could hear was the rapid beating of his own heart. Cody had just started to run again when he heard Caddy scream. The scream was close and getting louder by the second. Cody stood frozen in fear as the sound of trees being flung out of the way rang in his ears. He felt as if the sound was all around him.

"Ahhh!" Caddy screamed as she catapulted out of the trees and bumped into her brother.

"What is it?" Cody asked in a hurry.

"Just run," Caddy advised him. Cody stood frozen in place until someone else broke through the trees. Then Cody's eyes widened in

201

surprise. There was a man standing right in front of him. The man wore dirty old overalls which Cody presumed were once white. The man's face was covered in dirt; he had a long black beard to complete the ensemble.

Cody let out a scream as the man reached for him with a grubby hand. Cody spun on his heels and ran in the direction which he had come. Cody's feet thumped hard against the ground as he prayed for them to move faster. He broke out of the forest and saw Caddy waiting anxiously for him. When Caddy saw Cody she grabbed his hand and dragged him along the street.

"Don't come into my woods again," Caddy and Cody heard the man call to them. Cody turned his head around to see the man re-enter the forest.

"He's gone, Caddy," Cody informed his sister breathlessly. He bent down, placed his hands on his knees and breathed deeply. "What were you thinking?" Cody yelled at Caddy, after his breathing had returned to normal.

"I...I don't know," Caddy stuttered. "I thought it was Mr. Tennessee in the forest; I was so anxious to find him."

"He's not our responsibility, Cad," Cody told Caddy quietly. Cody could never stay angry with his sister for more than a few minutes.

"It doesn't feel that way," Caddy protested.

"Listen to me," Cody said, grabbing his sister by her shoulders. Caddy looked the other way; she was too embarrasses to face Cody. "Caddy," her bother persisted. Caddy finally met her brother's eyes. "This is not your fault," Cody told Caddy firmly. "You have nothing to do with Mr. Tennessee's disappearance." Cody let go of his sister's shoulders. "Where did you get the idea that you're responsible anyway?" Caddy just shook her head in confusion. "Let's go home. We'll look for Mr. Tennessee tomorrow; that is if he hasn't been found already."

When Caddy and Cody got home their mother and father were waiting anxiously for them. "Where have you been?" Mrs. Phillips cried, upon seeing her children. "I'm afraid we have some awful news about Mr. Tennessee."

"What is it?" Caddy asked anxiously. Images of Mr. Tennessee lying dead in a ditch filled her mind.

"He's missing from the retirement home again," Mrs. Phillips exclaimed. "They noticed him missing and..."

Cody interrupted his mother by releasing the mouthful of air that he had been holding in. "Thank goodness for that," he replied in relief.

"Excuse me?" Mrs. Phillips asked in bewilderment. "There is nothing good about a missing elderly man."

"That's not what he meant, mom," Caddy quickly said, defending her brother. "We already know that Mr. Tennessee is missing. We've been out searching for him all day." Caddy shook her head sadly. "We haven't been able to find him. What's the latest news on him and how did you find out anyway?"

"Sophia called," Mrs. Phillips explained. "Since you found him the last time he disappeared, she thought you two might know where he is now."

"I wish we did," Cody said sincerely, while casting a concerned glance at Caddy.

"You two look famished," Mr. Phillips noted. "Why don't you guys go upstairs and get cleaned up. There'll be a warm meal ready when you come down."

"Thanks," Caddy and Cody said in unison as they made their way up the stairs.

"Don't worry too much," Mrs. Phillips called up the stairs. "There are many people looking for him. Sophia promised to call if she finds out anything new."

"Thanks, mom," Caddy called down the stairs. "It's Sophia's fault he ran away in the first place," she complained quietly to her brother.

* * *

Three weeks had passed since Mr. Tennessee ran away from the retirement home. There were posters on every building and street lamp, informing people of Mr. Tennessee's disappearance and begging for their help in the search or for any relevant information.

Caddy had been having trouble sleeping for three weeks now. She wasn't able to concentrate on anything. She was also mad at her brother whom, in her opinion, was not taking the business with Mr. Tennessee's disappearance seriously. Cody claimed that he was extremely concerned about Mr. Tennessee but complained that Caddy had become obsessed with him. Caddy knew there was some truth in

Cody's criticism, but she couldn't stop her mind from traveling to thoughts of Mr. Tennessee.

Caddy got up early on Friday morning, grabbed a bowl of sugary cereal and sat on the bay window ledge with her blossoming bonsai tree. She had gotten very little sleep and she didn't feel like trying to get any rest now. All night long she had nightmares about attending Mr. Tennessee's funeral. The staff from the retirement home were there as well as Sophia. They were all dressed in the same black pants and Cody's black t-shirt that bore the evil looking mushroom man. The only differences between the mourners were the staff of the retirement home. They wore heavy silver handcuffs, which were much too big and dragged on the ground. The minister was just about to say a blessing when the coffin suddenly popped open and Mr. Tennessee sprang from his grave, full of life. Caddy had woken up at this point and wasn't able to get back to sleep.

Caddy now stared at the hemlock tree. It had grown two feet high and was adorned with lush green needles and miniature cones. Caddy had revived the tree and made it thrive in the process. She didn't like to be boastful, but her bonsai tree was much nicer than any other she had seen in books or on the Internet.

"You're up early," Mr. Phillips said as he walked into the living room with a bowl of cereal.

"Yeah, I wanted to see the sun rise," Caddy replied quickly, not wanting to go into detail for the reasons behind her early start to the day. Fortunately, Mr. Phillips said no more and turned on the television instead. Mrs. Phillips entered the room as few minutes later.

"I'm glad to see we have an enthusiastic worker," Mrs. Phillips chimed happily.

"What?" Caddy asked with a confused glance at her mother. Her thoughts quickly turned to the time Mr. Tennessee had called Cody and herself good workers.

"Aren't you up early because you promised me that you'd empty the compost heap into the garden?"

"Of course," Caddy said through a forced smile. You've become so forgetful lately, Caddy silently scolded herself.

Caddy waited until her parents went to work before changing into some old clothing and heading to the backyard. The sky was a brilliant shade of blue and the sun was already shinning brightly.

Caddy's surroundings made her feel a little bit better. She felt the warm sun taking the dreariness away from her eyes.

As soon as Caddy had entered her backyard, she let out a startled cry. There, rocking back and forth on Caddy's and Cody's old rusty swing set was a boy who looked to be around the twin's age.

"Hi, Caddy," the boy said with a big warm smile.

"Who...who are you?" Caddy stuttered in fright.

"Don't you remember me?" the boy said in a gleeful voice as he jumped off the swing and made his way over to Caddy.

"Stay...stay back," Caddy warned, stuttering once again.

The boy stopped suddenly as if he had just realized something. He playfully knocked himself on the head with his hand and laughed. "I'm sorry, Caddy," the boy apologized. "I was just so excited to show you my new...well, old self that I didn't think about how you would react to the change. I do hope I didn't scare you."

My old self? Caddy questioned the meaning of the boy's words. What does he mean by his old self? "Wait," Caddy suddenly shouted out loud in terror. "What was the last thing you said?"

The boy looked confused but finally answered, "I didn't think about how you would react to the change."

"No. After that," Caddy demanded with a pounding heart.

"Oh," the boy said in realization. "I do hope I didn't scare you."

"Come closer," Caddy demanded more forcefully. The boy stepped closer and smiled. His twinkling blue eyes met Caddy's. "No way!" Caddy shrieked in horror. "It can't be! Can it? Are you really Mr. Tennessee?"

The boy smiled and clapped his hands. "You're so smart Caddy! I knew you'd figure it out."

"But how?" Caddy asked, looking at the young Mr. Tennessee with an opened mouth. She had realized that it was Mr. Tennessee by his use of the word "do" and by his twinkling blue eyes.

"I don't know," the young Mr. Tennessee confessed. "And to tell you the truth, I really don't care."

"Everyone's looking for you. Sophia and the staff at the retirement home are worried sick."

"Well, they're not going to find me. Not the "me" that they're looking for anyway," the young Mr. Tennessee said laughing, as if it were the funniest joke in the world.

"Mr. Tennessee," Caddy began to lecture. "We have to find out what's going on. You need to get checked out by a doctor."

"Call me Herb," the young Mr. Tennessee interrupted.

"Okay, Herb," Caddy corrected herself. "We have to get you to a doctor. Something is definitely wrong here."

"Alright, Caddy," Herb responded. "I'll go see a doctor, but they'll just send us to a psychiatrist when we tell them what's happened to me."

Caddy bit her lower lip in concentration. "You're right," she admitted. Caddy stared at Herb, still amazed that her once elderly neighbor was now her own age. "Did you just wake up in your old body?" Caddy inquired, finally realizing what Herb had meant by his "old self" comment earlier.

"Yup," Herb answered casually. "That's basically what happened."

"And you have no clue how this happened?" Caddy asked again.

"Nope."

"So, what do we do now?"

A playful smile spread across Herb's face. "How about a game of football? Go get Cody and let's play!"

When Cody learned about Herb and came to the realization that it was true, he had no interest in playing football.

"This is so cool," Cody muttered as he walked around Herb and admired his new youth.

"Thanks," Herb replied, "but I won't spend my second chance at youth being ogled by the youngster next door. Let's play that game of football. This time you won't have to worry about me breaking any bones if the ball hits me."

"Will you never forgive me for that?" Cody asked in annoyance.

"Sure," Herb replied, "in sixty years."

Caddy shifted uncomfortably as Cody and Herb laughed at the joke. "Maybe you should get a physical or something," Caddy interjected. "Just to make sure that everything is okay inside of you."

"I feel fine," Herb said, slinging his arm around Caddy's shoulders. "Beside, there's no way I'm getting any more blood work done. I'll have enough of that in the future. Trust me on that one, I know!" Herb's joke sent Cody and himself into more laughter.

The football game really wasn't much of a game. Herb didn't want any rules or any point keeping. He just wanted to throw, run, and laugh. Herb's movements were fast but jerky. It was clear to see that he had not run for quite a while.

"This feels so great," Herb said, falling to the ground happily.

"Don't overdo it," Caddy advised Herb.

"Oh, you youngsters today are so cautious. In my day we lived a little!"

"A word of advice," Cody said, while playfully slapping Herb on the shoulder, "don't use the word youngster."

"Still," Caddy interjected, "I think we should go inside and get something to drink. I don't want you to get dehydrated."

Herb rolled his eyes. "You sound like my Bingo partner, Mrs. Winston. Man, was she ever old! Seriously, I think it's her ninety eighth birthday today." Despite his objections, Herb followed Caddy into the Phillips house and waited in the living room for his drink.

Caddy brought in three glasses of orange juice. They all drank in silence, thinking about the weird event that had occurred.

"The bonsai looks thirsty," Caddy commented as she disappeared into the kitchen and re-appeared with a cup of water. Herb admired the hemlock tree as Caddy sprinkled it with water. "You've really brought it back to life," Herb complimented with a secretive smile.

"Thanks," Caddy smiled. "It is beautiful, isn't it?" Caddy brushed her hand along the needles in admiration. "Oh no," she said out loud as she broke a needle in half.

"Ouch," Herb moaned as if he were in a great deal of pain.

"Herb!" Caddy cried as she turned to face him. However, in the excitement her hand hit the bonsai tree and sent it flying to the ground. The bonsai lay in a heap on the ground. The soil and the pretty yellow pebbles littered the floor. Herb let out the most painful holler Caddy and Cody had ever heard then he collapsed to the floor.

"Oh my gosh," Caddy cried out loud as she watched Herb's body grow into an adults then become old and wrinkly. It was like watching the life cycle of a human in fast forward. Caddy and Cody bent down next to Herb. He was still lying on the floor but he was no longer yelling in pain. Herb looked at Caddy with his blue eyes. There was something unfamiliar about his eyes. They were positioned in a way Caddy had never seen before. His eyes were glaring at her.

207

"Look what you've done," he scorned. "Look what you've done."

"Me?" Caddy shrieked, a little louder than intended. "How in the world is it my fault?"

Mr. Tennessee motioned for Cody to help him up. When he was standing up he glared at Caddy once again. "You destroyed my bonsai tree. You destroyed me."

"Excuse me?" Caddy asked in disbelief.

"Do you remember me saying how the bonsai tree was connected to its owner?"

"Yes," Caddy interrupted. "But you also said it was just a myth."

"I thought it was," Mr. Tennessee chocked. "Or at least I did until I was in your house on that rainy day. When I saw the bonsai thriving and I felt the same happening within me, I knew I was connected to it."

"That's impossible," Caddy answered. "How can a hemlock tree affect your health?"

"After everything that you've seen and heard can you really doubt anything?" Cody asked.

"Well, no," Caddy admitted.

"Fix it," Mr. Tennessee suddenly pleaded passionately. "Reassemble it and make it thrive once again, make me thrive again."

"It's too much to bargain with," Caddy exclaimed. "We don't know what the reversal of age is doing to your body." Caddy wrinkled her nose and looked as if she were contemplating something. "What if I fix the bonsai but you don't become young again?" she finally asked. "You'd be so disappointed."

"I'd be more disappointed if you didn't try. If you nurse my bonsai back to health and I don't regain my youth, I'll be disappointed in the supernatural. But if you don't even try, I'll be disappointed for a much more sentimental reason."

Caddy frowned. "You're putting a lot of pressure on me," she complained.

"I'm putting a lot of hope on you as well."

Caddy just opened her mouth to reply when she heard someone tapping furiously on the window. They all turned around to see Sophia standing outside the window with an expression of confusion, relief, and anger all mingled together.

"Look who we've found," Caddy shouted to Sophia. Caddy motioned with her head for Cody to answer the door. He obediently followed her silent instructions and let Sophia in.

"Oh, father," Sophia gushed as she ran to Mr. Tennessee's side and threw her arms around him. The look of relief fell from Sophia's face and was replaced with a look of anger. "You two have been hiding him from me the whole time, haven't you?" she unreasonably accused.

"Of course not," Caddy snapped back. "We just found him this morning. We were just about to call you."

"You're lying."

Well, partly, Caddy thought, but it's not like you'd believe the truth anyway. "I'm telling the truth," Caddy lied.

Sophia shook her head violently at Caddy and Cody then turned back to her father. "Are you okay?" she said in a slow voice as if he were a little child.

"I'm fine," Mr. Tennessee assured his daughter.

"You're going to the doctor for a complete physical then I'm taking you back to the retirement home and demanding better security. Oh, why did you do it, father? Why did you run away?"

"I wanted some fresh air," Mr. Tennessee said coolly.

Sophia shook her head sadly. "Poor thing," she said. "You've been through so much." Sophia began to guide Mr. Tennessee out the door. She stopped when she saw the mess that the bonsai tree had made on the floor. "What happened to that plant?" she asked in confusion.

"It fell," Caddy replied in a steady voice.

\* \* \*

Ding Dong.

Mr. Tennessee slowly got up to answer the door.

"A teenaged boy and girl just delivered this package for you," a worker at the retirement home said, handing Mr. Tennessee a large box. "They insisted that I hand deliver it to you. Nice kids they were. Are they your grandchildren?"

"No," Mr. Tennessee replied, looking curiously at the box.

"Oh," the staff member said in surprise. "In that case I hope to make friends with people like that when I'm older."

"Thank you for bringing it to me," Mr. Tennessee said.

The staff member got the hint and closed the door behind him.

Mr. Tennessee put the box on a nearby table and opened it in a hurry. He had a very good idea of what was in the box. His guess was accurate as he pulled out the bonsai tree. Mr. Tennessee examined the bonsai carefully; the hemlock was in okay shape. It was not in great shape nor was it in bad shape; it was just mediocre. Mr. Tennessee saw a yellow piece of paper attached to the pot and read it out loud with great interest.

"To Mr. Tennessee, I've fixed the bonsai tree like you have asked. I've fixed it but not cared for it as to make it thrive. The health of the bonsai is now up to you. I've written the proper care instructions on the back of this piece of paper. Do with it as you wish. I only hope that you get the results that you want. Much love, Caddy Phillips."

Herb stared at the bonsai tree then smiled widely. "I feel better already," he proclaimed out loud.

\* \* \*

Printed in the United States
111232LV00001B/207/A